CW01086327

CARNIVORE

K. Anis Ahmed grew up in Dhaka and studied at Brown, Washington and New York Universities. He has published both short fiction and a novel (in the US, Bangladesh and India). Ahmed is the publisher of *Dhaka Tribune*, a national daily, a co-director of Dhaka Lit Fest and a co-founder of the University of Liberal Arts Bangladesh. He has also served as President of PEN Bangladesh. His opeds have appeared in *The New York Times*, *Wall Street Journal*, *Guardian/Observer*, *Financial Times*, among other places.

CARNIVORE

K.
ANIS
AHMED

HarperCollins*Publishers*

HarperCollins*Publishers* Ltd
1 London Bridge Street
London SE1 9GF

www.harpercollins.co.uk

HarperCollins*Publishers*
Macken House, 39/40 Mayor Street Upper
Dublin 1, D01 C9W8, Ireland

First published by HarperCollins*Publishers* Ltd 2025
1

A catalogue record for this book is available from the British Library.

ISBN: 978-0-00-873333-9 (HB)
ISBN: 978-0-00-873334-6 (TPB)
ISBN: 978-0-00-873335-3 (PB – India)

Typeset in Sabon Lt Std by HarperCollins*Publishers* India

Printed and bound in the UK using 100%
Renewable Electricity at CPI Group (UK) Ltd

For my son Alex,
a born foodie

CHAPTER 1

I always felt that I could stand up to any man, but I had not factored in getting caught while in the nude. Boris and his boys knew where I lived and where I worked, so why they came to the gym is a bit of a mystery. Perhaps to show me how well they knew my routine. Or to take advantage of the relative quiet of a dingy muscle shop in Little Italy on a Monday morning. Whatever their reasons, they found me waiting to get dressed, pustules of water forming dew drops at the ends of my hair. I was just out of the shower when Boris and his goons invaded my row of lockers, like a Russian tank squad breaching the Suwalki Corridor.

'Looking good, Kash. Looking good.' Boris smiled with a flare of crooked and yellowing teeth. Two men who flanked him wherever he went – I imagined them standing on either side of his bed even when he was screwing $1,000-an-hour escorts – mimicked their boss's grin. The three of them sported the reddish skin and inflamed pores I had come to think of as typically Russian.

Boris as a physical opponent didn't scare me. He was a few inches taller, sure, but he was flaccid. I expected him to move at the speed of an overfed panda. But the goons were covered in tattoos as plentifully as the graffiti on the sides of

1

a Bronx garage. Men who would willingly suffer so many pricks of a pointy needle weren't types you wished to tangle with.

'You don't take my calls,' Boris said, his arms slightly open, flexed at the elbows, palms upturned in false conciliation – unfriendliness clear in his yolky eyes. It seemed a miracle that such narrow apertures could receive any light at all. I didn't think Boris saw anything; he navigated purely by smell.

I reached behind to grab a towel and held it in front of me, covering my vitals.

'You don't call, I feel hurt,' Boris said. 'I thought we were like brothers.'

The fat flunky let out a noise, somewhere between a titter and a snort. The other one, the taller, skinnier, scarier of the two, whom I'd privately nicknamed 'Snake Eyes', remained impassive.

An unknown gym member turned on a shower; the locker room was small enough that it soon filled with steam, adding to the dankness of the place, which reeked of a scent akin to an admixture of damp laundry and cat piss. A lone stranger in the shower and oblivious to my immediate peril spelled poor defense against my accusers, but *in extremis* one takes inventory of even the tiniest resource.

'My brother? I don't talk to him,' I said by way of deflecting Boris's sarcastic, faux-hurt opening.

This was not true. My brother, Hafeez, and I had grown apart before I had left home, but we had not stopped talking. Desis – and by that I mean all South Asians, and not just Indians – tend to stop talking to family only when there is a property dispute. As it happened, I had no properties back home in Bangladesh. Not that I thought of Bangladesh as home anymore, but one can never escape all traits of one's origins and, despite our ever-widening differences, an unbreakable bond with my brother was one of my legacies.

'See, that the problem. You don't know how to respect people,' Boris said, stepping closer to me. And taking my repartee in a different spirit. My locker was nestled in the corner of the room, with rows of green metal doors extending on both sides, their surfaces scratched and dinged from years of rough handling by rushed members.

'That's not true, Boris,' I said, in an attempt at pacification. 'Believe me, respect for you has nothing to do with the delays – we are actually that short. Business is that bad.'

Boris shrugged, as if to say, 'Not my problem.'

'Listen, we're putting in a new menu. Antelope burger, Boris! People will go crazy for that! Things will turn around from this summer. I'm sure of it. Look, I'm not taking one penny in profits until you're paid back in full.'

Boris was unimpressed.

I took a step back and wrapped the towel around my waist. During this procedure, I had broken eye contact with Boris only for a second but, when I looked up, he was within arm's length. They would not kill me, I knew that. Not here, not with an idiot belting out 'Livin' La Vida Loca' a few steps away in a verruca-infested shower stall. But there were many things they could do to me, short of killing me, and I didn't cherish the prospect of broken bones, or a bruised and battered face.

'That eez problem, you see,' Boris said, coming closer, the odor of his breath washing over me: an indeterminate mix of vodka and wood smoke, boiled cabbage, and rotten desires. 'I have many clients. They start deciding when to pay, then my business eez all fucked, you see?'

I did see. What I didn't see was the money. I didn't have any. The crash was killing all of us.

It was in the first shock of those hard days that I had turned to Boris – and pitched the prospects of our restaurant. Back then I enjoyed membership in a tony mid-town gym where Boris was also a regular visitor. I say 'visitor', as I saw him do little exercise, but he was diligent in his appearance. Perhaps he believed that proximity to training equipment and human exertion would translate to better health. Our timings matched and now and then I found myself sitting with him at the juice bar next door. Chit-chats led to more extensive conversations; and the scent of money has a corrupting influence. Also, like all true sociopaths, at first Boris oozed charm. A rough brand of charm, but there was an unmistakable effulgence of warmth there. And that too lulled me into accepting loans despite the obvious perils of such an unorthodox creditor.

'You see, Kash, I let you delay, word gets out. Then others think they delay, too. You see how it eez problem for me?'

The singing in the shower had stopped. I hoped that the off-key Ricky Martin would come into my row of lockers – and soon.

'I understand, Boris,' I said. 'We are going to bring in some big money. Real soon.'

'So, what I do? You tell me,' Boris said, smiling, as if a little assuaged by my signals of deference.

In fact, I was holding out on Boris because, with a character like him, you either owed him most of the loan or you paid in full. The scale of my debt, as long as it stayed well into six figures, kept me safe.

'Look, Boris, come to the restaurant,' I said. 'I'll hook you up. A special gift! Trust me, you'll like it.'

'Special gift, eh?'

'Yes, I promise. Come tomorrow. Kang'll make you wild grouse with shallots in robust red wine reduction. And I'll give you a gift that will tell you how serious I am, and how much I respect you. A surprise.'

I could tell from the noise of a bench moving that Gym Ricky was out of the shower and changing, but in a different row of lockers.

Boris took a half-step forward, and with a swiftness and precision of movement I did not expect, reached through a parting in my towel to take hold of my balls.

'Eh, you give me plenty surprise already,' he said, tightening his grip around the gentle orbs of my very existence. I remained as still as I possibly could. His palm cupped my testicles and the thin-skin vessels and cords attaching them to my pelvis. If he increased pressure by even a millimeter, I'd either squeal or faint. I didn't dare disturb the equilibrium of the situation even by a curly pube.

I should have known better; old killers can possess cell-memories of fast and lethal movements that are never to be underestimated.

'Now, I give surprise,' Boris said mincingly. 'Next time we don't visit you. My boys, they visit your girlfriend. The blonde.'

Helen's face floated into view; and I remembered the unexpected slant of her eyes like you see in some Finnish people, and the implicit trust in which her gaze seemed to hold me: the calculus of my priorities changed rapidly, as furious as the flurrying number displays on a power-ball machine.

'You make surprise good, eh?'

'Yes, it will be good, I can assure you it will,' I said tensely, when he released me a second later.

There was no more smile on Boris's face, or in his eyes. 'Eez good, you make sure,' he said as he walked back a few steps. He stopped right behind his goons, who did not turn to follow their master immediately. Gruff stayed in place, but Snake Eyes came forward. There was no point fighting; any injury I caused him would be paid back with interest another day, in another venue. I put up my hands to cover my face. Snake Eyes was quick, and the punches went hard into my ribs.

I dropped onto the bench after they'd left. The trickle down my back was no longer only ribbons of water from the shower but sweat beads of pain. What the fuck had I got myself into? Should I ask Helen to leave . . . was it too soon, or too late, to do so?

A sharp rap at the end of the row made me look up. A cheerful face peeked around the last locker. The guy looked surprisingly like a shorter and pudgier version of Ricky Martin.

'You alright man?'

I was impressed that he even came around to enquire. I lifted my left arm to wave an 'it's all cool' message, and felt a fresh tingle of pain shoot down my left side. There was no blood. And no one likes to get involved. In fact, that was the first and most cardinal rule of city life: do not get involved. My fellow gym member proved himself to be an upstanding citizen by that measure and slipped away with a loud: 'Right on bro. Stay righteous!'

We launched The Hide in the late summer of 2008. Laugh all you want. But alpha-nerds with PhDs in stochastic mathematics or God-knows-what had no clue either that markets would tank. The Dow was set to go to 30,000. Maybe 50,000! This time, it would be different. Everyone would be a millionaire. We believed it. And while we waited for that destiny to materialize, we bought McMansions in crowded new subdivisions. Those who could not afford McMansions bought gigantic TVs. Mercedes and BMW came out with ever more affordable vehicles to ensure every aspirational – meaning greedy or vain – idiot could own the badge. Yes, I include myself among that multitude of benighted marks. If you could not afford Loro Piana or Kiton suits, then you went for Bottega Veneta or Giorgio Armani; if even those brands were out of reach, you could purchase their underwear, but nothing and no one went unbranded. The future was glorious, unassailable. Soon, humans wouldn't deign to do anything that didn't have meaning: scientific experiments or engineering breakthroughs, great art, or philosophical discourse. At a mundane level they'd stoop only to tasks requiring creativity, like flower arranging or hairstyling. The vast array of essential chores, from investing and matchmaking to air traffic control and drip irrigation, would be guided by supercomputers crunching zillions of permutations per second. The tedious necessities of life, like construction and cleaning, the manufacture of widgets and fungibles, the removal of stains and garbage, would be done by robots or by dark-skinned people escaping from really, truly miserable places. They'd be glad to do it.

The crash consigned that utopia to science fiction or to the play-labs of billionaires. The plenitude that had spawned so many dreams – in the case of my partner Adair and me, in the form of a wild game restaurant – vanished with a suddenness from which we were still reeling. By Christmas 2008 we were doing fewer covers than the number of communions passed by the palsied priest in the deserted church around the corner. We fell behind on payments to suppliers. We fell behind on rent. Kang, the chef, we kept on with promises of equity. Besides, where the fuck would he go? No one was hiring.

Before the crash, everyone talked about 'commodities' or 'fractional trading' as if they had a clue what those words meant. Big data and networked systems were on everyone's lips. Folks who weren't even in the market believed that the new masters of algorithm could keep stretching the fundamental value of things to infinity.

Lesson: Fundamental values are called that because they have a limit.

Little did we know, even in late summer of 2008, that within weeks the *geist* would desert the fuck out of the *zeit*. Men who were once the masters of the we-have-no-shame laugh turned into broken relics overnight. In the first days of the calamity, I heard a few boasters talk about being too-big-to-be-fucked-with. They talked about TARP. Fucking TARP; when bankers got into deep trouble entirely of their own making, the government whipped out hundreds of billions for Troubled Asset Relief Program. My assets were in trouble too; where the fuck was *my* relief?

In time though, the mood shifted; I heard the men murmur somberly about the Feds and investigations. They stopped ordering main dishes. Only appetizers. Some just ordered drinks and dawdled too long over the free nuts. When they left, they did so with hunched shoulders, etching silhouettes of defeat in the doorway. There was no chasing down certain tabs. He's gone to Florida, don't you know? Or so-and-so's waiting to get indicted. The truly horrifying was whispered under their breaths: he's working at Gap.

From weekends of hundred-plus covers, and tables that turned two or three times an evening, we fell to double-digit counts, ever cheaper tickets and, finally, the indignity of the discounted prix fixe lunch. By now, late spring of 2010, our revenue crunch had become an existential question. And not just in a metaphoric sense; the pummeling I received in the gym heralded a phase of physical danger that was new for me.

I'd taken the first bundle of cash from Boris – my creditor, my tormentor, my nemesis – right before Christmas 2008: sixty thousand dollars. There was no way for me to get over the vacation with all the payments – staff, vendors, and instalments, utility – without a rescue fund. Back then I thought that it'd be all we needed. A little something to see us through the rough patch of winter. Soon, we asked for and received a new infusion of cash: sixty thousand by end of summer 2009, and even more by the fall.

'This is the last time I fund you, Kash,' Boris had told me. 'After this, I only want returns.'

Every time I failed to pay a monthly instalment; Boris slapped a fat fine on me. So, despite fairly regular payment of the interest and bits of the capital, we were north of

$300,000 in debt. To be precise: $315,500 – but it was a ticking meter.

I became unable to cross a street without checking both sides. I considered carrying a gun. I had nightmares involving book-keeping and getting trapped inside my little office while it slowly filled up with dirty drain water. What fueled my anxieties wasn't just the threats posed by Boris. My father was forever chased by creditors. I had vowed to avoid any fate resembling his. He had, for all we know, met his gruesome end lacerated by a hundred knife-cuts by irate lenders in a cheap motel. The case was never solved; he was too unimportant for the police to bother with. My fears were thus spun as much by personal ghosts as by practical predicaments. And I no longer dared stand within two yards of the platform edge on the subway. All I ever thought of now was how to get out from under this debt. And to feel – once again – like a free man in this land of the free.

CHAPTER 2

It was two days after the beating. I felt submerged in deep pain; it literally hurt to get up in the morning. That first minute of movement was the worst.

As the day wore on, especially when I was sufficiently distracted by other concerns, I got by well enough. But all it took was a cough or a sneeze and the full force of the injury – and the insult – would return. Fucking Boris! I wanted to hurt him. Hurt him bad. But first I had to avoid any repeat of the mauling I received two days earlier. Or indeed, anything worse.

The effort to keep my wounds – in all senses – hidden from Helen only added to my strains. Still, I could not resist the impulse to hide this episode and its marks from her.

I turned onto my good side and observed her. She was asleep with her mouth slightly parted, looking as innocent and vulnerable as anyone in that state. Why was I keeping my latest troubles a secret from her? Was it embarrassment over my financial troubles, or shame at becoming Boris's bitch?

A loud screech on the street followed by the rapid-fire exchange of slurs broke into the calm coolness of our little apartment. Good morning, New York! It was my cue to leave bed. Rising early was never my forte. Besides, as the one who usually closed the shop, it was expected that I sleep in a bit. But since the beating I was trying to shower and dress before Helen, to reduce her chances of glimpsing the blue bruise on my ribs, as amorphous in shape and as diffuse in its shades of violet as a modernist painting.

By the time I sat down at the little bistro table that served as our dining – and indeed all-purpose – table with the day's first dose of caffeine, Helen came out, eyes puffy and hair ruffled. Her favorite white sleeping shirt hung loose on her slim frame. Her blonde curls fell in lush but ruffled plenitude on her shoulders. I was always struck by her beauty, even when she was at her most natural, least made-up, and unaffected.

'You're dressed already?'

'It's bill day,' I said dully.

'But you're going in now, this early?'

It was only 9 a.m., and we didn't usually open shop until 10 a.m. 'Yeah, I really need to look through stuff. It's tight this month.'

I hated letting slip that ugly truth first thing in the morning. Helen stood with arms crossed over her chest, and one foot planted on the other. I could tell she still felt the morning cold from waking up. I wanted to give her a hug but stayed in place.

If the debt, or rather its repeated default, made me feel unworthy, the beating left me feeling downright dirty.

'Anyway, I gotta go,' I said. I rose abruptly without finishing my coffee but was stopped short by a sharp pain shooting down my bad side.

'What happened?' Helen said as she rushed over to me. 'Did you pull a muscle?'

'I'm fine,' I said, stretching my arms outward to preempt any touching.

Helen looked taken aback.

'Babe,' I said limply with no further explanation for my odd behavior.

'What's going on with you?' Helen asked, her voice as full of concern as it was of puzzlement.

'Nothing, nothing,' I lied. 'It's just the pressure of it all, I guess.'

Helen and I were two nobodies, who had connected over our desire to belong. People who were adrift, people like us, could still find a berth in New York, as pirate ships did in rogue ports. Our shared sense of being not just outsiders, but unwanted, felt like the pull of destiny. But my odd secretiveness in this time of mounting pressure was taking a toll on our relationship. I felt that I was trying to preserve an idea of who I wanted to be to Helen. And my early training as a man, and especially one in any relation to a woman, was so flawed that it had left me fundamentally fucked up. To be raised in a repressive Muslim culture, with overlays of Victorian-era puritanism, was not auspicious grounds for training in a romantic career. The more I cared for someone, the less I felt I could tell them what I truly felt or wanted. Especially if it revealed any flaws or weakness. I wanted to be infallible in their eyes. I wanted their unmitigated approval.

'You have to tell me,' Helen said. 'Whatever it is, you know you can tell me?'

But how could I? My failings had escalated our financial crisis into existential jeopardy. I was already carrying the marks, and I knew that I had exposed Helen to physical harm. I could not see how I could admit to that. I felt too ashamed. I needed to fix things first, so there would be no risk to Helen.

'Oh, what's there to say?' I said, completing my rise to full height. 'You know everything. It's just exhausting. We are doing everything right now. Still, it's never enough. We can never catch up.'

'I know, I know,' Helen said. She came closer and touched my face. Her fingers felt cool against my warm skin. Even after a night of sleep, she exuded a fresh smell, like a whiff of pine and juniper in late autumn. And momentarily transported me to a sense of safety, of well-being.

'I have to go,' I said. In a voice more of resignation than of fight.

'It's going to be okay,' Helen said. 'It's always okay.'

'How do you *know*?' I could not help a tinge of irritation in my voice.

I wanted to believe her, but the hope of a more plentiful future was now badly, pardon the pun, bruised for me.

'Because I grew up with this. Constant shortage of money. Creditors banging on our door. Collectors towing away our car. Stores refusing credit. Stitching shit together to wear. Repairing things all the time, never replacing. And, yet we survived. Even had fun.'

I was not the only one to come from rough beginnings. Continents apart, we had both been raised with many of the same stresses, similar privations. I shook my head. Even through the hardship of her upbringing, I didn't think she – or her parents, meaning her listless mom and ever-troubled but always-there stepfather – ever faced the level of threat that Boris now posed for us.

'Besides, remember, what do I always say?' She was smiling with such relaxed confidence.

'Nothing ever happens,' I said, chuckling a little.

'That's right, nothing ever happens – except birth and death.'

That was one of her mantras. No matter what happens, people get by, they adjust, they evolve, they survive and even thrive within their new parameters. As long as you didn't suffer any permanent impairment or imprisonment, everything else was chimera. It was an odd bit of Hillbilly Zen that would be easy to dismiss or make fun of, but she lived by it and in doing so had both acquired and now exuded a calm that was reassuring. I wished I could feel that sense of certainty in my bones as cleanly and constantly as she did.

The window was open, and a sudden gust of wind made the curtains billow like a flag of victorious jubilation. Helen smiled at me. She leaned in to kiss me softly on the lips. Despite all my pain, all my fear, I also suddenly felt – or remembered that I was – lucky.

'Yes, it'll be fine,' I said, as I pulled away after the kiss.

'Have a good day,' Helen said, as if radiating a beam of light. I stepped into the dark corridor, and her words rang in my ears again: nothing ever happens, except birth and death.

Bill days are never fun, and my one consolation on these grim mornings was to sit with our chef, Kang. When we first met, Kang ran the kitchen of a Korean BBQ, tucked into an ungentrified micro-corner of the Meat Packing District. The joint was too small and too modest to rub shoulders with its well-heeled cousins in Korea Town. I had discovered this hole-in-the-wall by chance. Despite the humble appearance of the place, the quality of grilled meats was exceedingly high and the light-touch cooking suggested hints of mastery. I became a regular. Recognizing my appreciation, Kang started treating me to items that were off the menu: duck tongues dipped in maple-sweetened *ssamjang* and sautéed penis fish in vinegared *gochujang*.

I took Adair to check out the place. Kang trotted out novelties ranging from stewed cow udders to curried goat brains. Adair too could tell that Kang was the real deal. Dressed in a black shirt that looked less like a chef's uniform and more like a fighter's *dobok*, Kang looked upon us with his characteristic solemnity as we fulminated with praise.

'Fuck Heston Blumenthal.'

'Fuck Gordon Ramsay.'

'We can do this, buddy. We're gonna do this!'

With such exclamations of hubris, our triumvirate took form. Adair hunted for investors. Kang devised the menu. I scoured for and secured the location – and recruited the staff. Adair didn't possess a lot of money, but he seemed always to hang about people who did. While I'd met him during my stint at a downtown bar, Adair struck me as a true New Yorker with roots going back to the early days of uptown expansion. He was comfortable in such a rarefied milieu. He did boast a pedigree of some charm; an ancestor of his was reportedly a big shot in the House of Morgan. Not in the time of 'J. P.', but in the age of Junius. Adair could actually say 'J. P.' without sounding absurd.

Whatever the mystery of Adair's access to the fragrant pinnacles of New York society, within a short time we rounded up a half-dozen takers – at $150k per head. It was a time when the moneyed were keen to purchase a patina of authenticity or exoticism, something to confer a whiff of creative glamour on themselves, by investing in ideas that were off the beaten path, preferably arcane.

I found luck soon with a spot by the West Side Highway, crammed with garages and warehouses. And the early raise allowed us to pay the deposits and advance rent. Start the work of dressing up the place. And the diesel-charged location abutting an auto-repair shop became home to The Hide.

How thrilling it was to be at the beginning of things! And how far I felt from that now.

I had asked Adair to meet me after the beating I took in the gym. He promised to come down for a 'working lunch'. God forbid he should simply come in for work. Of course, it was agreed that I'd be the one who handled the grit, the day-to-day. And that was why I, to begin with, owned 55 percent of the business against Adair's 45 percent. I also received a small salary, but none of that felt like sufficient recompense for the physical assault.

I was in a bitter mood. Bitter from the blows to our business, and to my body. And bill days did little to lift the cloud. I could tarry the utilities, up to maybe two notices, but eventually they had to be paid. Most vendors had us down to one week's credit. The fish supplier, a sly Cantonese man whose fluency in English fluctuated conveniently to his advantage, was already cash-on-delivery only. I could delay paying some repairmen on their overdue bills perhaps, and pray that our moody refrigerator or clunky stove would not throw another tantrum.

It was also the day to pay our most important supplier: Hagi, the meat man. I liked Hagi. I didn't want to muck him around. I asked him, as anyone who knew anything about football invariably would, if Hagi was related to Gheorghe Hagi – the great Romanian footballer. 'No man,' he smiled. 'No relation.' I didn't quite buy his denial. As if to tease me, he'd sometimes turn up wearing an old Romanian team shirt with CCCP emblazoned on the chest.

Before I dealt with the outsiders, I had my daily entente with Kang. Kang was not only a champion of meat but an ideological opponent of vegetarianism and their wingnuts, the fruitarians. This kind of conviction, along with his supreme skills as a cook, made him the anchor of The Hide. Hearing him recite the Daily Specials served as a little tonic for me; it tethered me to our mission. There was always some complaint: a Guatemalan sous chef whose *abuela* had died and needed sudden leave, or a delay in the delivery of a magnificent wild boar that Hagi had promised. Oh, how I longed for the days when those were the extent of our troubles! That I had heavier things on my mind must have shown.

'What happened? Girlfriend blow you off this weekend?' Kang asked, as he sauntered into my chamber.

'Girlfriend's fine, Kang. Girlfriend's all right,' I replied after a long pause.

The door to my chamber opened and one of the new staff, Julie, a fresh-faced Midwestern waitress, popped in with two steaming macchiatos. This was part of our daily routine;

Kang and I always shared this mid-morning pick-me-up, which the staff knew to bring in on time. I thanked Julie for the coffee and turned to Kang.

'Bill day,' I said.

'Yeah,' he said, 'and you got no money?'

I ignored the obvious.

'You spend too much,' Kang said. 'Much spend, much worry.'

'Where do you suggest I cut? Your salary?'

'You cut my salary when you actually pay it.'

He had a point. With the equity we had conspired to vest in him, he was effectively a partner. I had shed 3 points and Adair 2 points to bring Kang in for 5 percent, leaving my original partner and myself, respectively, with 43 and 52 percent each. The equity was meant to signal our commitment to Kang, and he returned it in kind.

But now, Kang was telling me, 'You spend too much on laundry.' He was all business. 'Spend too much on cheese.'

'You don't want cheese?' I asked with exhausted meekness.

'Basque charge too much. I get from other people.'

Our cheese supplier was a mustachioed hombre from the Basque region of Spain, and a personal bête noire of Kang's.

'But the Valadon!' I cried out. The Basque sold us a Valadon that came, he claimed, from his hometown. It smelled only slightly pleasanter than a recently exhumed human body, but the way it played on the palate, a warm and salty start dissolving into a sweet strain dappled with sharp jabs of tangerine and mulled wine – it was a rare foodie weakness of mine.

Of course, I could no longer afford such indulgences –

neither personally, nor in business. Kang was right. But he wanted to make sure I understood that.

'You stupid like white people. Think stinky make good cheese,' Kang said, waving a fat and variously damaged – bruised, lacerated, scalded – index finger before me. 'You let me choose suppliers, I bring down cost like that.' I'd never heard anyone snap a finger so loudly.

I looked at my watch. Adair was late, as usual.

'Fine. You decide.'

Kang's broad face widened further with a slowly spreading grin. It wasn't easy for a smile to break on that rough, leathery face. It had to fight against tissues and strictures that had turned taut from years of restraint.

'I sort out.'

The phone rang.

'Man, you won't believe where I was last night.' It was Adair.

I knew what that meant. Parties, after-parties. Drinks and light drugs. Adair wasn't exactly louche, but there was a streak of hedonism in him. Usually, I found his fucking around amusing, and they were always a source of new stories, but I was in a different mood today.

'You won't believe where I am right now,' I replied, with an undisguised bitterness in my voice.

'C'mon man, don't be mad. I'll get down there, I promise. But I've got to shake off this hangover first. I won't be any good for a meeting.'

'Don't flatter yourself,' I said. 'You're not much better sober.'

Adair laughed. But my sarcasm lacked the usual levity.

'So, how long do I have to wait for you?'

'This afternoon, I promise,' Adair replied.

I knew that when Adair said afternoon, it could mean anytime between noon and 6 p.m.

'Fine,' I said with a deadness in my voice.

'All right, chief, I'll shake this off, head down your way,' Adair said, in a more subdued tone.

'We need more fucking business!' I blurted out.

'I know that.'

'Do you?' I shouted into my phone. 'You live in fucking la-la land!'

'Hey, take it easy, buddy,' Adair said.

'I nearly got killed the other day!'

Kang tilted his head; this yet-unreported development interested him, too.

'What do you mean? Something happen in the kitchen?'

'No, asshole. Something happened in the gym. Boris and his goons nearly tore my balls off.'

'They roughed you up?'

'Damn right they did.'

'I told you we shouldn't have taken money from them,' Adair said.

'Fuck you. Where else was this money coming from? J. P. Morgan was chasing you around to give you a loan? Your family was going to give us a fucking gift?'

'Leave my family out of it.'

'Fuck you and your family,' I said, and slammed the phone down. It was still on of course. These new touch screens simply weren't as satisfying as old analogue phones for a big slap-down. I picked up the phone to disconnect the call and found that Adair had beaten me to it.

Kang looked at me silently with his deep gaze. I couldn't

work out what he would find more troubling: my sordid encounter with Boris and his boys, or my angry exchange with my partner.

He didn't let on; he sat there quietly and continued drinking his coffee. I don't know how anyone could sip on a macchiato for that long.

CHAPTER 3

In the hierarchy of food, nothing comes close to the supremacy of meat. To me, this is a self-evident truth. The fierceness with which its opponents try to proscribe its consumption is further proof of its unique, vital, primeval attraction. No one is campaigning to stop the eggplant. No one minds our species' over-reliance on grains. No one berates voracious eaters of fruits. Indeed, the inane and recidivist cult known as vegans, who wish to negate all the arduous gains of civilization and revert to the scavenging origins of our species, are the new self-styled legislators of morality when it comes to food. I see no virtue in returning to tree-worship with ash-painted faces. I was raised in a culture where the ritual killing of beasts is a sacred duty.

I was only eleven, I think, when I experienced my first slaughter. What I remember most vividly, after all these years, is the glint in my grandfather's eyes, the broad blade of his butcher's knife and the tremendous dust-swirling tussle between man and beast. That year it was a large, black ox, which my grandfather had purchased from the Gabtoli Bazar. Back then, in the mid-Eighties, Gabtoli was virtually the outskirts of Dhaka; scruffy, jerry-built, and spiky with exposed rebars of new construction. But the bazar was among the biggest and best for the annual cattle markets. At night, aglow with their kerosene-fueled hurricane lamps, the bazar felt like a scene out of *One Thousand and One Nights*.

Of the two Eids, everyone favored the Eid-ul-Fitr – which marks the end of the month of fasting. Eid-ul-Azha, on the other hand, focused as it is on animal sacrifice, was a great embarrassment for most polished urbanites. The spectacle of thousands of dying beasts, thrashing on driveways with slashed throats, made a mockery of the modernity that the new middle class, like my family, tenuously clung to. Those of ordinary means, however, cherished the holiday. So did children like me, who are often less appalled by gruesome things than one would imagine in this over-protective era. My grandfather, surprisingly for someone who wasn't terribly religious, reveled in this ritual. Like many Bengalis, he was as firm in his faith as he was relaxed in his practice. But come the time of Qurbani – the sacrificial slaughter – and he was all business.

I went with my grandfather to the bazar and helped him choose the hapless animal. I remember that crooked sellers would knock off a couple of teeth to present their fare as younger – and thus more tender-fleshed – than they were. But there was no fooling my grandfather or his devoted valet, Rahmat. The cow or ox of a suitable age, once chosen, would be brought home, and put on a special diet to fatten it up. Back then, like most houses in the Bangladeshi capital, our back lawn was half a farm, and the beast was tucked away under a tin shed stocked with straw.

If the Abrahamic ritual were to be performed correctly, one ought to cull a head from one's own herd. Harboring one's sacrificial offer even for a week at home was deemed a suitable alternative for city-dwellers. My grandfather brought a noticeable assiduity to his care for the animal, motivated by a mysterious force, not primarily faith, which to this day is not entirely clear to me. He would go to the shed at least twice a day to make sure the animal was being fed properly. Depending on the season, he would even put a net around the enclosure to protect the cow from mosquitoes.

On Eid morning, my father took refuge inside the house. He kept a distance from the proceedings, ostensibly because they were too primitive. As a modern citizen of newly liberated Bangladesh, a nominal Muslim tethered more firmly to rationalistic ideas of life and the world, he felt it beneath his dignity. As I grew older though, I began to suspect other motives. I thought he felt too ashamed to be part of a ritual to which he had nothing to contribute, neither money nor mumbled prayers. However, when the sacrificial meat was presented as a meal, my father would sheepishly emerge from his hideout and partake of the offerings with gusto.

My grandfather, with me dutifully in tow, headed to the backyard. Rahmat coaxed the creature out of its bunker and walked it to the strip of green by the boundary of the house, next to an open drain. Being docile by nature, the ox came along without any resistance. But no sooner had the men started roping its feet, than an instinct higher than any cerebral intelligence took over. The beast flared its nostrils and let out an eerie wail. The front and rear legs were tied separately. Once the animal lost its mobility, it could be flipped on its side. But the ox kicked up such a fuss that four men could not get the rope around its ankles with a proper turn. Instead, they got it into a great jumble. 'Don't strangle it!' shouted my grandfather, his eyes glowering from the deep wells of his eye sockets.

Twice the men flipped the ox, and twice it struggled back to a half-risen position with only the immense strength of its gut. When it was finally pinned down on its side, wheezing in panicked protest, two men held down its rear legs, and two the front. The houseboy, only a little older than me, who had by now joined the fray, helped twist the ox's head to one side. I marveled at the strength of his ropy muscles.

My grandfather approached the beast and then turned back to look at me, and said, 'Come.' His white hair, shorn to stubble, and his high cheekbones cast his usually kindly mien into a mask of unexpected severity. There was such a force of intent in his voice that my legs pulled me forward. My grandfather motioned for me to crouch beside him. We were facing the ox's twisted head. One panic-stricken black orb cast a great accusation at us from the outer corner of the beast's eye. Undaunted, my grandfather positioned the knife against the ox's throat and then said to me, 'Put your hand over mine.' I did as he said. My small, smooth hands tightly clasped his veined, freckled fist. As he uttered the customary prayers and pushed down, a hot jet of blood splattered against us, and I could feel the trachea crunch under the pressure of the blade. The ox shuddered with great force and nearly escaped the clutch of its trappers. Custom ordained that the slaughter be accomplished with one swift motion forward, one draw pulling back, and then a final half-thrust. In the hands of amateurs, the precision of the strokes was not always sufficient to sever the thorax, but my grandfather did the job flawlessly.

We stepped back, watching the muscles spasm even after the ox's gaze fixed into a gray vacuity. The moist, black nostrils of the beast quivered with the pulse of some prehistoric pain. Crows began gathering overhead almost right away. Flies landed on the ox's head and open wounds. The butcher's assistants took over then, hacking away the limbs, skinning the torso and other parts, and cleaning out the gut. It was remarkable how quickly they could dismember a whole animal into constituent parts. Rahmat sat close by, a look of satisfaction fixed on his face, chopping the big hunks of meat into smaller pieces, and flinging them into a large red plastic tub.

Boys from a nearby madrasa came by soon enough to collect the hide. Some of the boys were not much older than me. Even then, I knew that selling donated hides would earn most of the madrasas their highest revenue of the year.

When we walked back inside, my mother caught a glimpse of us and shrieked, thinking that I had been wounded. A second later, when she realized what had happened, it didn't lessen her shock. Her face, usually calm and soothing, contorted in a rapid succession of emotions: horror, repugnance, reproach.

She was too polite in general and too respectful of her father to accost him directly. In this case, she was perhaps simply stunned speechless. My grandfather could read her thoughts and said: 'There are things his father won't teach him.'

That was all the explanation my mother could hope to get. Not because my grandfather was too chauvinistic to make apologies to someone younger and, in this case, to a daughter, but because he could not see what the consternation was about.

My mother didn't touch the meat at all that year. That was her form of protest, and no one said anything about it. It was served in the usual sequence and enjoyed by everyone with relish. Lunch on the first day consisted of meat curry in a blazing red soup of hot chilies. At night came blackened beef, cooked with ginger and cloves. A separate presentation of the squishy muscles from the neck followed the next day. My father tried to show solidarity with my mother by skipping the first day's servings, but by the time the real delicacies came out – spicy brain curry, and braised tripe – he could no longer hold back. I had grown up eating meat, but never really noticed it before then. Something clicked inside me, and I realized that I liked the texture and the flavor of meat more than the taste of any other food. Every morsel filled me with a new frisson of delight. Without knowing it, my grandfather had sown in me the seeds of my eventual mission, my métier.

CHAPTER 4

Adair and I had of course made up since the little dust-up a couple of days before, and were putting our heads together for some crazy, breakthrough idea.

'So, yeah, this kid, his uncle is rich. I mean private-jet rich,' Adair said.

We were sitting at the bar. It was the off-hours between lunch and dinner. I had let a second macchiato go cold, whereas Adair had poured himself some premium cognac.

'Need to shake off last night's haze, y'know,' he said.

I thought it was charming that he felt the need to give me an excuse. And that he believed that fine liqueur was the best remedy for a hangover. But I let any repartees on that classic slide; my mind was riveted on this new prospect he was touting.

'And he will hire us – instead of asking a Michelin-starred fucker?'

'He will, 'cause he's in a hurry. And he needs something special.'

'What's that?'

'The guy wants peacock. He wants a whole peacock, done up in grand Chinese style, for a visiting delegation of Chinese investors.'

'Then why won't he ask a Chinese restaurant?'

'Oh, you know how the Chinese are.'

'How are they?'

'They're so cagey. The Chinese won't do anything off-menu for a non-Chinese client.'

'I thought the Chinese would do anything for a price.'

'Yeah, maybe, but even the Chinese won't take this on with just a week's notice.'

Whatever the cause, I wasn't going to question it too much. The client was Viktor Karakozov. A Kazakh billionaire. He would be renting out The Hide, even though it'd only be a party of six. It was a small mercy that we would get to use our own kitchen and space. Adair's great gift in life was to befriend men and women of perennial luck and golden smiles, and within a week of my increasingly abject importuning, here he was with an uncommon pitch.

'And you've met this guy?' I asked Adair.

'No, this is all through his nephew,' Adair said.

The nephew, Yusep, was one of Adair's latest projects. Like so many tall, good-looking men in New York, Adair had dabbled in acting, but unlike many of them he quickly figured out that an actor's life was a shitty one, dependent entirely on the whims of others. So, he took his training and found a way to monetize it more quickly and profitably: as a public-speaking coach. And he had found a niche in coaching foreigners with a hankering for some cultural cachet. He'd coach rich Arab men on how to date white American women. It was apparently a thing. A new strain of Arab was no longer content simply to throw money at women – they craved acceptance. He took uber-rich families from Nigeria and Kenya on weekend tours of historic America: from Ben Franklin's sedan chair to the slave quarters at Monticello – the bitter symbols of America's slaving past resonated with this crowd. He had advised a Chinese real-estate tycoon and art tyro on new multimedia and installation buys. He compiled playlists for sub-billionaires who still craved to be 'with it' in music. He was a maven of the new gig economy before that moniker had even caught on with the public.

The pendant lights at the bar caught Adair from one side and threw his articulated bone structure into stark relief. I could see why foreigners would find him convincing – forgetting that I too was a foreigner.

So, a client like Yusep was no surprise. The boy's over-protective mother had prevented him from going to university in the West. But he was to join the consulate of his country in DC at the end of the summer, and his uncle – Viktor – was paying for him to be brought up to speed.

Ever since the mockumentary assault of Borat, the Kazakhs were extra-sensitive about how Westerners perceived them.

'Buddy, this peacock dinner is just the start,' Adair reminded me. 'This is going to open new doors for us, not just doors; it'll open vistas we haven't even dreamed of.'

Adair was in his element. I enjoyed his enthusiasm, even when it was expressed in such an absurdly fulsome manner.

'Yusep is a godsend for us,' Adair continued. 'We have to do this peacock dinner and make it good.'

A week was a tall order for a peacock. But the challenge quickened my blood. My mind was whirring about how we could source this coveted fowl. I waved at Patti, our head waitress, and asked her to bring over a bottle of my favorite Armagnac, a Laressingle VSOP. This time, I would join Adair.

'What are you boys celebrating?' Patti asked. She placed a pair of brandy snifters on the table, giving us quizzical looks.

'Breakthrough, Patti! Big, big break.'

Patti uncorked the bottle, still shaking her head skeptically, but an indulgent smile hung from the corners of her broad mouth. Patti cut an impressive figure in her black shirt and curly hair braided into spikes that stood up like porcupine quills. She exuded an aura of solidity, as if a pillar of the New York subway had come loose and decided to go sauntering about town. Patti was herself an ex-con and doubled up as a mentor to the bevy of ex-cons who manned our kitchen.

I thanked the lucky day when I agreed to hire them at the behest of a nonprofit which tried to mainstream former female inmates back into society. Most of the ex-cons in our kitchen were Guatemalan and Honduran women, whose crimes ranged from selling weed and meth to prostitution and solicitation, or some form of assault which, in most cases, was a long time coming against an abusive partner or boss. It took someone like Patti to keep them from breaking into inter-ethnic spats or other shenanigans, but they proved to be more punctual and hard-working than your typical kitchen staff.

If illegal immigrants, who over-populated the lower rungs of restaurant kitchens, were desperate, former cons were more so by degrees. The risk of being deported was a strong motivator. But fear of getting thrown back in jail was stronger.

No sooner had we finished toasting than the main door opened. In walked Snake Eyes and Gruff.

'Motherfuckers,' I murmured below my breath.

Adair met my eyes, and a simple nod from me confirmed his guess. This was the new protocol. Boris wasn't fucking around. Boris had already sent his boys to get the surprise gift I had promised: a cherished TAG Heuer, my most valuable possession. What made it special to me, and painful to part with, wasn't just its cost. It was a genuine vintage; from the same year as the one worn by Steve McQueen in *The Great Escape*. Boris might sell it for the cash or hold it as a kind of 'scalp', but he would never appreciate its value as an artifact.

And now the two assholes were back to check up on the instalment that was due earlier this month. They walked up to our table. Snake Eyes, tall, lean, with cold, impassive eyes, sported hair that was slicked back, as tight and implacable as his mood. Gruff, who appeared to be the junior partner in this pairing, always looked saggy by comparison, but no less dangerous.

'Have a seat, guys,' I said, trying to strike a natural tone.

The two of them stood before us wordlessly. Snake Eyes' hateful slits focused on me, while Gruff sized up Adair. I turned my head for a second and caught Patti standing behind the bar, arms folded, alert to the drama playing out. Her shoulders, ample as the humps of a roasted hog, gave me strange comfort.

'You got the money?' Snake Eyes asked.

As it happened, I did have a packet ready for them, tucked into my desk drawer. I touched Adair's arm and said, 'Give me a second. I'll be right back.'

Adair sat there, subdued like a boy called to the principal's office. Adair was, to be fair, no pussy. I knew that from our first encounter. It was a late summer's day when I was still new to Brown's – a whiskey bar where I found my first Manhattan job. An early hour drunk, an obvious churl with rolled-up sleeves and bundled rage, started harassing me about my name.

'Khashh,' he said, mangling the noun as if it were a wad of chewing tobacco tucked inside his mouth: Ka-ka-ka-khash. And then asked me for my last name.

'Mirza? What the fuck kind a name is that? You Arab?'

It wasn't the first time I had come across a drunk who wished to avenge 9/11 by picking on an undermanned stand-in. But before I could respond to this asshole, Adair, who was sitting at one end of the bar, slid up to the guy and asked, 'What's your name, pal?'

The guy gave Adair a cold and disdainful look. Adair stood up to the full length of his six foot three figure. Although he was dressed like a dandy, in striped white pants and a white Panama hat, there is something about height, and confidence, that can intimidate people.

'I know the owner,' Adair said. 'His parents fled the Nazis. He doesn't like racists or assholes. He'd ban you for life. You want me to talk to him?'

The guy ignored Adair but also didn't speak to me anymore. Adair gave me a wink and sat down next to the brute. I made Adair a cool, dry martini – on the house.

The jerk gulped down his drink and left. Once he was gone, I asked Adair, 'So, you're a friend of Brown?'

'Fuck no,' Adair said.

We both laughed, and I poured myself a shot of vodka and clinked glasses with him. I had not noticed Adair before, but he became a regular after that day.

A bar-room churl is one thing. Goons from the Russian

mob something else. And life isn't a movie. If it were, say, a Clint Eastwood movie, then this would be the moment I emerged from my den with a shotgun. Instead, I trotted up with much of our week's take, tucked into an envelope. And found the two thugs still standing in the same manner and Adair stuck to his chair, making no eye-contact with our tormentors.

I remained standing. I noticed that Patti too had repositioned herself to our side – that is the customer side – of the bar. I knew Patti's case history. She was often called to tend to her younger sister after a beating, and on two occasions to rush her to Emergency. One time, when she had gone unannounced to drop off some rhubarb pie made by their mother, she could hear the screams from the pathway. The front door was unlocked and, when she ran inside, the sister was cowering on the kitchen floor and her three-year-old nephew crying with a spittle-filled mouth opened wide. Patti says what happened next was a blur. But it was well reported in local papers, and I had read that she had in a split second of reaction bashed the brother-in-law's head against the counter-top. Her intent was not to kill or punish, but simply to stop the beating. But the man died on the spot. As she, reportedly, told the cops later, 'I tried to stop the bleeding. But couldn't put the brain back in.'

A near-empty bottle of vodka rested within her arm's reach – and I could not recall if it had been there all along. But knowing what she was capable of gave me a certain amount of confidence.

Adair, clearly at a loss, remained quiet.

I handed the envelope to Snake Eyes.

'Feels thin,' Snake Eyes said, slapping it against his palm.

'It's the full amount,' I said, a little deflated that a solid payment after a few missed dates wasn't received with more encouragement.

'Boris say this not enough. Need back amounts,' Snake Eyes said humorlessly.

My mouth was dry. 'Look, this is the full amount. If you give me time, I can get the rest. He will get his full amount.'

They didn't seem convinced. Nor satisfied. Snake Eyes kept tapping the envelope against his open palm. He exchanged a quick glance with his reticent partner.

'C'mon, we are back to making full payments! Have a drink, make a toast!'

Snake Eyes looked at me coldly, while Gruff plunged his hands deeper into his pockets. I picked up the bottle of Armagnac, in a gesture of making an offering. I held it aloft, wondering fleetingly if I'd need to switch over to a weapons grip.

I noticed their clenched jaws. Snake Eyes had a decision to make. He could accept the envelope or throw it back in my face. Even as I awaited his dreaded verdict, I could not momentarily help but wonder who was guarding Boris while these knuckle-draggers were out making collections. Or, perhaps, I'm the only one for whom he sent out his best boys. A thought that filled me with a weird twinge of pride.

'I tell Boris,' Snake Eyes said finally.

Refusal to take the money would have been really bad news. This felt like a draw by comparison. I kept a straight face, even though a big grin was breaking inside me.

'He not be happy,' Gruff said, breaking his customary silence.

'I will make him happy. You guys tell him that. I will make

him happy, real soon. This is my partner, Adair,' I said. 'He's got great ideas. We are doing new business. You tell him that.'

Lesson: In the face of serious trouble, always double down.

Adair gave me a startled look when I uttered his name. He was not much in the mood to talk after the goons left. This was a bit of a pisser; we were meeting so I could learn more about Viktor. But there was no point trying to get a narrative out of Adair when he wasn't game and, frankly, shitting it a bit.

Once Adair left, I moved over to the bar where Patti was drying glasses and tucking them into the rack.

'So, a peacock in six days?' Patti eyed me with skepticism.

'We can do it. Kang will know what to do. We just need the bird.'

'Right. Shall I go ask Balducci's?'

'Don't worry, I'll find a way,' I said, ignoring her little jab.

'You know what you into, man?' Patti asked me, pausing at her task. She held me with her cool hazel eyes. Patti wasn't fully American. Her father was from Zimbabwe and she had spent many summers in Harare, at least until Mugabe went 'full loco', in her words. Even partial attachment to the Third World meant there was a kind of skepticism in her to which I could relate. Perhaps that doubting quality is common to all black folks in America, but I attributed it to her Third World origins. One effect of this questioning nature was a seeming aloofness; her real self resided so far behind her gaze, there was no telling what she was thinking.

'They could seriously fuck you over,' said Patti, since I had not responded.

Suddenly I felt exhausted; the back of my shirt was soaked through, and I could smell the stale, sour reek of fear on myself. I tapped my glass to indicate a refill. I had left the bottle of Armagnac on the table, so Patti just splashed some vodka into my snifter.

She pulled down a glass from the rack and poured herself a shot.

'Bad enough to bruise, but probably not much more,' I said at last.

Patti's lips curled up in a smile. I could tell she was trying hard to control her pessimism. She knew the rough side of life more intimately than I did or harbored any wish to know. She finished her shot in a gulp and looked at me again, dead serious.

'You know what I've seen?' Patti said. 'Everyone . . . perps, victims, even cops . . . everyone, they think nothing will go that far . . . until it does.'

CHAPTER 5

'Kash! Kash, you up?'

'I'm up now,' I said, mumbling into my phone, which against all good counsel I always kept tucked under my pillow. Not even on the bedside table.

'C'mon, man, we need you up here. You gotta hurry.'

'What? Where? What?' I mumbled, disoriented.

'The farm, man, the fucking peacock farm. Where do you think?' The urgency in Adair's voice was unmistakable, and unwelcome.

'Isn't Kang with you? What the fuck do you need me there for?' I tried to compress my irritation into a hushed tone, so as not to wake Helen.

'It's an emergency. I'll explain but get your ass into a car ASAP.'

A car? For Christ's sake, I would have to find a car, too?

In a week of sixteen-hour days, even Sundays sacrificed to brunch crowds and the clearing of bills, laundry and other engine-room chores of life, Saturday mornings were my one inviolate sanctuary. And this particular Saturday, I had hoped, would be spent pleasurably with Helen.

Things hadn't been easy for her either for some time. Her ambition was to work in some branch of design. But her family was perennially short of money and unable to send her to college. She worked briefly as a fashion model while grabbing design courses at Cooper Union. She had the looks but not the tolerance for the indignities that one had to sustain merely to operate, let alone flourish, as a model. In time, she found herself a footing in the underground design ecosystem of New York. She had worked for a music label, designing covers for CDs, during the final years of that lost artifact. She had also done work for magazines in the music world, organized photo shoots for emerging indie bands and hustled sundry gigs of a related nature. But the post-crash world had been brutal. People who should be hiring her were themselves looking for jobs.

It was at this juncture that Helen became more involved with The Hide. She was adept at graphics – specials, notices, little flyers – that we needed almost every day. And she started coming in too, at peak hours, to help diners get seated, or soothed in case of delays. She was a natural and became our de facto maître d'. It helped too that she was a genuine enthusiast of wild game. She was, as it happened, the only one among all of us who had grown up with any experience of hunting. Mainly birds, she said, bobwhite quail and ruffled grouse, ducks and pheasants too. On ground, turkey and hare for food. And skunks and weasels for pure sport. I felt we should have asked her to source the peacock; instead, I had sent Laurel and Hardy up there and was now faced with the fallout.

I could not guess what was so hard about transporting a bird – especially once slaughtered and ice-boxed – and Adair would not say over the phone. I called up Samad, an old pal from my early days in Queens. If anyone could, he'd be able to find me a car in a jiffy. He worked for a liveried limousine service. But even Samad could not be reached on a Saturday morning. Fuck.

Helen was still sleeping, enveloped by the duvet, her golden hair splayed over the white pillow. I was dressed and trying to think of the nearest car rental when my phone beeped. It was a text from Adair: GO TO CHRIS'S. TAKE HIS CAR.

I taped a note on the bathroom mirror for Helen and took a deep breath. Chris lived way over in the East Village. I liked the city in the early hours on a weekend; in the quiet I felt as if the city belonged to me. I picked up a coffee and a croissant from Grey Dog's Coffee on our street and headed across. With no traffic, you could see the streets clear through to a rise in the island's rocky contours, where the road dipped suddenly into unseen possibilities.

When I got there, I found Chris, one of Adair's innumerable and ever resourceful but vaguely derelict friends, sitting on his stoop. He was a tall fellow with Jesus hair and hipster scruff on his face.

'Don't fuck up the car, man,' Chris said, holding out the keys.

'Where is it?' I asked, skipping any niceties to match his matter-of-factness.

He indicated a spot down the road. 'The green one, after the fire hydrant.'

'Anything I should know about it?'

'It needs gas, a whole lotta gas,' Chris said, turning, I assumed, to go back to bed.

It was a 1970s-era Duster. Trust Adair to know a guy who owned a relic. It was a beauty, though. I tested the lights and indicators and stepped on the tight pedals of the old workhorse.

I knew few drills as unfailingly liberating as speeding down an American highway. After my time at Brown's, I moved onto a whiskey company, and had driven quite a bit for them up and down the Eastern Seaboard. The road kept rolling out before me like a magic carpet. The mesmeric voice of Stevie Nicks gave way to Ann Wilson letting rip one of her killer octave-busting phrases. I felt a sense of lightness.

As far as I knew, the president or the Pentagon had never bestowed any kind of medal of valor on an American rock star. Yet where the American air force had failed to bomb native populations into submission – at a cost of billions and billions – American rock music had succeeded without effort. One by one, more favorites from the golden past came on Chris's selection – Jefferson Airplane and Janis Joplin, Dire Straits and America – and I felt momentarily transported to a cocoon of safety and freedom.

As I exited the city limits though, the phone rang and broke my trance. It was Helen.

'Hey honey, what happened?'

'It's Adair. Something's up.'

'Isn't Kang with him?'

'Yeah, but they're in some sort of fix. Up at the farm.'

'Oh, right. They went to get the peacock. So, what do they need you for?'

'I don't know. Adair didn't say but wanted me to come up urgently.'

'Maybe he's being held hostage by a hillbilly,' Helen said, but I could sense bitterness beneath the witticism.

'That's very possible,' I said with a chuckle.

'You know I skipped an invitation to go see my little niece at her school play this weekend?'

'I know, I know. I'm so sorry, hon. I promise I'll make it up to you.'

'Don't say that. Just say, "Sorry, I fucked up."'

I knew I had fucked up. I also knew that I should not make promises when I was being chided for breaking one. But it was a reflex I could barely control.

'Please don't be mad. I'm so sorry. I really am, but you know how critical this time is for us.'

I could see her standing in our little kitchen in the long blue shirt she used in lieu of a dressing gown. She would be holding a red Cardinals mug in one hand, while the coffeemaker percolated in the background.

'I'm sorry, really. I was so looking forward to spending today with you.'

'Go spend it in the mountains. Or wherever they're holding your boys hostage.'

'They can keep Adair,' I said. 'I just need Kang and the peacock.'

This made Helen laugh, but I knew I'd have to do some serious making up to her when I got back.

Once I entered Westchester, the roads became more narrow and sinewy. I was struck by how tall the trees were in this country. The leaves broad and thick. The land and the trees geologically ancient. Back in Bangladesh, only the rivers boasted majestic immensity; everything else – the people, the trees, the goats – felt stunted. I came across a river with spirited curves. After about two hours on undulating roads, I entered a dirt path to the farm. Presently I alighted on a weather-beaten sign dangling lopsidedly over a wooden gate. A gray van in the driveway, given its mint condition, I took to be Adair and Kang's rental. I stepped out, pocketing the keys, and was struck by a view of what I guessed must be a ridge of the Appalachians. Bluish mountain peaks shot into a low, slow procession of gray clouds.

I walked towards the small house. A corner of the roof sagged, like the jowls of an old dog. I cast about for signs of my associates, or anyone. A small boy peeked from one corner of the house and disappeared before I could say anything. I followed the little runaway's footsteps and, as soon as I turned the corner, I found Adair loping toward me.

He threw me an uncharacteristically big hug and said, 'The Great North, my friend.'

'No, it isn't,' I said. 'It's not even upstate. It's barely out of town.'

'Where I come from, anything north of Westchester is upstate,' Adair said. And he waved at the vista and at the mountains with inordinate pride, as if they were the result of his conjuring.

'Smell the air, man, smell the air,' he continued, as two more figures approached us.

I smelled the air, and it reeked of rotten leaves and sodden earth, dung heaps and woodsmoke, universal essences of all working farms. Kang was sullen as ever and greeted me with a barely perceptible nod. Our host stopped a few feet away.

'That's Jessie,' Adair said, by way of an introduction. 'Jessie, this is Kash.'

Jessie looked like Chris's twin; tall and scruffy haired, but the beard was a longer, unwashed mess. Jessie grunted, turned, and led the way. We trailed across a stretch of overgrown grass to a broader open area with more sheds, mostly abandoned, littered with relics of farm equipment, and all of it anchored by the remains of a stone-walled water well. Jessie led us to the last of the enclaves, a wire-fenced area of about a third of an acre. A line of trees along the right cast long shadows across the penned area.

'Poplars?' I asked Jessie, in an attempt to establish a rapport.

What he said in response sounded like 'cuttinwood'. His singular enunciation left me uncertain if he was offering a more specific name for the tree or suggesting a course of action for them.

'So, where's the bird?' I asked, anxious to get the introduction over with so we could proceed to the actual business.

'Thar,' Jessie said, pointing at a full-sized peacock in the shade of the poplars.

I looked at Jessie and then at Adair and, with nothing forthcoming from this unlikely pair, asked, 'So what seems to be the problem?'

'You can't take it alive,' Jessie said.

This was a fair point. Transportation of live fowl into the city wasn't permitted, not in the backs of passenger cars.

'I know. It needs to be killed, quartered and skinned before we can put it in the cooler,' I said.

'Right,' said Adair.

'So, what seems to be the problem?' I asked again.

'None of us can do the slaughter,' Adair said, very matter of fact.

'I raise 'em and sell 'em. I don't kill 'em,' Jessie said.

Fuck me! Did we find ourselves the one Zen farmer in the region? And what did he mean by 'em' – all animals, or only peacocks?

It didn't matter, as it was clear that he wasn't going to do the job.

'You didn't know this before you came up here?' I asked Adair.

'I hadn't thought to ask,' Adair replied flatly. Fair enough; one expected a farm, however slovenly, to do the dirty work.

I turned to Kang. He stared at his toes. Kang had grown up in a fishing village until his father died. And then his mother moved with him to a slum in Busan. Given his hardy background, he knew I expected more of him. But it was Adair who supplied the excuse. 'He's never done it either. He's afraid of mucking it up. We don't want the flesh or the feathers to get bruised.'

'So, you figured, hey we need a slaughter, let's call up the Muslim?'

'Don't be ridiculous. That's not why. But you've killed so many cows. And chickens. You told me.'

It wasn't just the cows at Eid. After being initiated into the holy ritual, I developed a fascination with butchering. I didn't understand most people's repugnance or horror of this necessary act. To eat meat but eschew the slaughter seemed hypocritical. When I was growing up, chickens were bought live at the wet market and slaughtered at home. With the patient guidance of Rahmat, I had developed a skill for it by early adolescence.

Lesson: Casual boasts will always come back to bite you in the ass.

At least, for once, the crisis wasn't about money.

'You have a knife?' I asked Jessie, as I began to roll up the sleeves of my blue denim Gap shirt. Jessie hollered something in his vernacular and the boy, neither named nor introduced, ran into the shed and came back with a long butcher's knife. The blade had a spot of rust on it. The corroded wooden butt confirmed the instrument's vintage nature. But I touched the sharp end lightly and found it to be true enough for our purpose.

'You need to catch it,' I said to Jessie.

He grunted in assent and the boy, a sprightly, dirty blond who seemed to occupy an enchanted space between our own species and that of others, followed the older man into the pen. We approached the bird, which stood still until we got close. It took a few tentative steps and then it emitted a choked squeal of protest.

I didn't fancy this turning into a farcical chase. I needed to return to Helen. And we needed the damned peacock and my sorry crew back in town as fast as possible.

'You got some feed or something?' I asked.

Jessie fished out a Ziploc bag full of pellets and handed it to the boy, whose solitary approach seemed to be less disturbing to the prey. 'Tch, tch, choo,' the boy intoned as he tossed out the bait at measured distances.

Father and son, assuming that's what they were, worked with practiced rhythm. I held my place and could sense Adair and Kang inching into the pen. The event of a slaughter, for all its horror, possesses a dense attraction that few can resist. The boy led the bird to a large bowl half-filled with water. Once the bird bent to take a sip, Jessie nabbed it by the base of its wings from behind and at the same time pushed down on its back. The bird could not spring its wings or run away. It could only let out a piercing scream, lacerating the air with its elemental terror.

I glanced up at the distance for a second; the mountains seemed placid and eternal. I motioned for Jessie to lay the prey on its side. Adair and Kang were crowding us now. The boy tied up the bird's legs with a cord of rope pulled out of his pocket. To make the sacrifice quick and clean was the kindest act. I twisted its neck to stretch the skin, placed the knife edge on the throat, and with one motion forward, one pull back, and a final half-thrust severed its throat.

The bird's bleak, blaring cry turned into a horrific, gagged gurgle before it fell silent. It'd take a few minutes to drain the blood, and I asked Jessie to wait until then. Kang would take over the carcass.

I stood and stretched. Adair's stare guided my eyes to the front of my shirt, and I noticed that it was finely sprayed with molecules of blood. The hem of my pants, too. I could not recall if it was lemon zest that was most effective at removing bloodstains. Helen would know.

'You could have told me to bring an extra shirt,' I told Adair. He stared at me blankly as if I were speaking in tongues. 'Good luck bringing it back,' I said, patting Adair on the shoulder as I headed for the gates of the pen.

'You taking off?' Adair asked, recovering from his rare spell of stupor.

'You've buggered my Saturday already. I've got a whole lotta making up to do.'

Adair put up a hand, as if to say, mea culpa . . . and also, good luck!

* * *

The sun was high in the sky when I began the drive back. But something had shifted inside me after the performance of this bizarre little task. The world looked small from the high corners of the mountains. I felt good about the kill. I recalled that even a personage of the chef-ing world such as Anthony Bourdain had never seen a real slaughter until he was well established in his career and visiting some farm in Spain. That captured in a nutshell the trouble with modern cookery and its fundamentally effete nature.

Modern cookery, thanks to public displays and the transmission of knowhow via ubiquitous cooking shows, had come to acquire the charm and depth of old-school parlor tricks. The same fucking high ceilings and dimmed or dramatic lighting to set the mood. Finely calibrated casualness in the staff, and the obligatory recitation of obscure ingredients, which sealed either the authenticity or the novelty of the dish. Huge plates with small portions were presented with a dab of color in the corner, like the finishing stroke on a Zen painting. This charade was dreary in its repetitiveness and lacked vitality.

What we were doing was more honest, and full of a reviving energy. It was a pity the collapse in finance had deprived us of a true test of our concept. But I believed we could turn this around. People would come to us, as was always the goal. We would not be mere attendants to the wealthy; they, too, would have to ask us for the favor of a booking. We wanted to be the kind of a place where the high and the mighty felt they needed to pull their strings to get a seat on the night of their choice.

The landscape shrank as I began my descent, but my confidence felt renewed and robust. And so did the dream that had driven me this far. All those years ago, when I was still working at my brother's shop, and as the hopes of making it big through trading faded, it had become clear to me: I had to get the fuck out of a place like Dhaka. I needed to be out in the big world, on the greatest of stages: New York.

CHAPTER 6

We served the peacock deconstructed so that it could be spread across courses and with different treatments. The appetizer consisted of dumplings made of peacock liver and sherry-scented rutabaga. First course: bones, feet and gizzards crumbled and tossed in a red-hot skillet. Main course: slices of peacock breast slow-cooked in kaffir lime and diced cilantro roots, and all of it lit with fiery specks of *bhut jolokia*. Net effect: the Chinese were impressed, and that meant Viktor was happy.

Our guest of honor was surprisingly congenial. He was a man of medium height, mild demeanor – a slightly older and more heavily sun-battered version of the actor Aaron Eckhart or take your pick of a square-jawed dirty-blond Hollywood hero – and dressed demurely in a dark but finely tailored suit.

The day after the dinner, I took two days off – 'You guys owe me,' I said to Adair and Kang – and whisked Helen off to a canvas-tented luxury campsite on Lake George. We felt protected by the proud peaks of the Adirondack Mountains, and the air was thick with the scent of bursting green fresh foliage. We spent the first day and night inside our tent, catching up on sleep – and making love. We had not been intimate with such feral energy in a long time. Perhaps it was the success of the recent dinner, and the erotic charge of open nature in springtime. At three in the morning on our first night we were famished and raided the camp's pantry. All we found was a giant platter loaded with cheese – sharp Cheddar, meaty Gouda and salty Manchego – which we gorged on with unbridled delight.

I felt as if I was discovering Helen's beauty for the first time. When she got up to fetch the unfinished Malbec off the dining table, I stared at the movement of her body with a sense of wonder. I liked the narrowness of her waist, the toned ripples of her muscles. The improbability of our affinity struck me in a way that it didn't seem to affect her. I suspected that in some ways she was more lost than I was. I had found a calling with restauranting – and in particular with my evangelism of meat, my fetish for wild game. And with some satisfaction, I was pleased to discover that Helen increasingly shared this passion with me. She would sit with Kang and hear details of new recipes. Paid attention when Patti coached the girls on how to serve a particular dish. And came up with ideas of her own on how else we might be able to entice high-end clients: why don't we partner up with some super-luxe glamping company and do whole roast boars? The rich would like that; something to harken back to our fireside origins. Authenticity is all that everyone wants now.

How could I be so lucky? The dips and shadows of her lithe form in the dimness of the room felt as eternal and mysterious as the hills and cloughs surrounding us.

Whatever points I had lost with Helen during the peacock

escapade were fully restored. We came back to the city full of gumption for our new line of business: private dinners. Within a week of the peacock, we received a couple of referrals from Viktor. A friend of his, a Balkan prince, wanted to serve horsemeat burgers for a picnic in Long Island. And a Brazilian tycoon wanted an array of rare seafood – fermented fish viscera and monkfish liver, lampreys and geoducks – to serve on a little cruise around the island for a bunch of guests from back home. These one-off gigs fetched far bigger sums than most weeks at The Hide.

Besides, sourcing such a variety of God's creations was proving to be a real challenge. I was making connections in the Brooklyn and Queens underground black markets in bush meat – I had better luck with the Africans than with the Chinese, who were very wary of strangers – but even they could not bring things in as fast as I needed them. I considered teaming up with an importer, like Askari in my own community. He had started out importing shrimp from Bangladesh, but then he expanded his sources from Ecuador to Vietnam. In time, he widened his range as well to almost everything that needed shipping in refrigerated conditions: cut flowers, Desi veggies, freshwater fish and seasonal fruits. And by now his operations had extended across Africa too. Other Desis were jealous of his success and would titter, 'Who knows what comes in on his frozen containers?'

That sounded like just the person I needed. Who would be willing to take risks – for a price.

When I shared news of this new sourcing channel with Adair, though, he responded with a whole new line of thought.

'That's great, buddy,' he said. 'But you know what I am thinking?'

'What?'

'Look at how much we are making off these dinners. How many will we need to get the full amount for Boris?'

'I don't know, maybe twenty or thirty?'

'Yeah, and how many do you think we do a month?'

'At our current rate, we'd be lucky to get two or three a month. That is ones that are big ticket enough.'

I could see that the math wasn't adding up: at our current rates we'd need many more months than we had to gather the full amount.

'We can't get more dinners, sooner?'

Even as I asked this, I knew I was asking too much of Adair. We were in my cramped office, hunched over soups from Shopsin's. I was slurping down my African Jungle Soup, while Adair lingered over a Wild Rice in Tomato broth.

For him a work meeting had to involve lunch or drinks, or at least super-gourmet coffee. But we were tightening our belts, for real, and I was in no mood to offer anything more than takeout from our neighborhood soup shop.

Adair, however, seemed buoyant enough, despite the humble nature of our fare. It was good to see him like this. I was laying a bigger burden on him now with requests for more private dinners. For the kind of meals we meant to sell, and the bills we hoped to charge, more frequent dinner was a big ask, even for someone like Adair. He was connected. Both thanks to his own charms and verve and his indefatigable energy for people, for strangers. But also, thanks to his family. There was Aunt Marge, the lady who had raised him and with whom, oddly, he still lived. She had taken charge of Adair when his parents died close together, one in a fatal car crash and the other from accelerated sclerosis. Treatment in the late Seventies was nothing compared to these days. But, despite the twin tragedy of his parents passing, Adair was raised like a prince. Private school and the best of many different types of camps and coaching. And, of course, connections. Some of his introductions were still thanks to his Aunt Marge. And I kept hoping that his grande dame would be able to conjure more leads for Adair to chase.

'We can't be just running down the rich. We need something big. A one-shot solution.'

'Like what?'

Adair's face broke into a broad smile, and he said, 'There is only one game in town for such a big windfall: the Miner's Club.'

'Is that even real?'

'Oh yes, it is!'

I had dismissed it as an urban myth. A clutch of globe-trotting billionaires who convened, once a month, always in a new place, hosted by one of them, to lay out the most lavish, exotic, indeed unprecedented meal for their friends. The cost of a single night ranged into the high six figures. The caterers stood to make more than they could in months of toil in restaurant kitchens or at any other foodie gig.

'How would we even get to them?'

'That, my friend,' Adair said, smiling again, a bit coyly, 'you leave to me.'

Barely a week after our return from Lake George, Adair had managed to secure a meeting for us with Viktor's nephew,

Yusep. Yusep was, like his uncle, a man of medium height and build, but with darker hair and dark brows. He looked dapper in a blue blazer, and in keeping with his constrained character, had asked for black tea.

'We're going to get one shot to pitch Viktor,' Adair said. 'No missed beats, no false notes; it's gotta be perfect from the word go.'

'I've seen him throw people out after just a minute,' Yusep said.

'He's kept you around a good while,' I said.

Yusep laughed and Adair emitted a nervous titter. Dealing with big men meant having to deal with their minions. To be attuned to transactions of uneven power was a Third World specialty. It was essential to show deference to the big man himself, but showing an excess of compliance to the underlings lowered one's worth in their eyes. No white man could be expected to appreciate that, unless they had spent at least half a lifetime as a *gweilo* in the service of the boss of a Cantonese triad.

Yusep straightened up in his seat, resuming an expression of earnestness. This young man was our entrée to the Miner's Club. The ace up Adair's sleeve. He didn't tell me until he was sure that Yusep could and would pitch us to his uncle, Viktor, one of the members of the super-secretive and famed Miner's Club. People always speculated, but there were no confirmed lists. When the super-rich choose to keep something secret, including how they became so rich, they mostly manage to do so.

The Miner's Club, he told us, started out as a half-joking bet between a Chinese coal billionaire and his Indian counterpart: they got into a spat over whose culture boasted finer cuisine – which, by their definition, would make it the finest cuisine in the world. Since the Indian would host the first dinner, the Chinese man got to ask a third billionaire, a common friend, a Frenchman who, like Viktor, dealt in the niche area of rare earth minerals, to play arbiter. The Indian billionaire rented a stunning palace in the city of palaces, Jaipur, and recreated an evening fit for a Mughal emperor, with 10,000 lamps, dancing girls, and a banquet as long as the Maharajas' Express.

What splendor, what perversion!

Not to be outdone, the Chinese billionaire rented the Ancient Temple in the Forbidden City and served a 101-course meal, expounding every flavor and delicacy from the multimillennia history of his Chinese cuisine. It was the Indian's turn to pick a judge and he invited a Mexican gold baron, along with the Frenchman. Once the second dinner was over, though, the judges refused to name either Chinese or Indian cuisines as the 'best', and demanded the right to host their own dinners. And thus, the Miner's Club, though not yet called by that name, was born.

The Mexican gold baron rented out the Palace of Palenque and recreated a royal Mayan dinner. He invited a Motswana copper tycoon, who asked an English oilman. It was the Englishman who invited Viktor, making him the last of the 'founding' members. Other billionaires, but only from the mining industry, were allowed to audition, but no one else had met the mark for entry yet. It wasn't enough to have money; one needed imagination to impress this crowd.

The Motswana, for example, brought Argentine celebrity chef Francis Mallmann to his Berlin home to dazzle his friends with a dinner of 'seven fires'. The Frenchman responded by flying all members of the Miner's Club to the tiny village of Laguiole in southern France for an exclusive evening with the master of masters, Michel Bras. The Englishman took the crew to the Faroe Islands for a meal of exquisite Arctic delights.

The Englishman was the one who, living up to the reputation of his countrymen, did the one thing that the club needed to become a real club – set down some rules:

1. One had to be a member of the mining industry to host a dinner.
2. Only members with hosting rights could rate a meal.
3. Only three ratings were allowed: unprecedented; exquisite; and, unrated. (It was understood that any meal that was 'unrated' was a slap in the face of the host.)
4. Any member with two consecutive 'unrated' meals would lose his membership.
5. Any first-time host had to be nominated by two existing members, provided no other existing member cast a veto.
6. Any new member could become permanent if their very first dinner was 'unprecedented'.
7. Any member who hosted at least one 'unprecedented' dinner could never be expelled, even if they only hosted unrated events thereafter.

No one had hosted an unprecedented dinner so far. How would you? What is there that one can serve that people have not had before? And especially when it involved people who could afford anything on earth. And Viktor, to his distress, was the first to have received an 'unrated' designation with his opening foray. For his first attempt, Viktor had chosen to stay true to his Central Asian roots – despite being a white Russian by ethnicity – and he had flown everyone to Kazakhstan to treat them to a full-on display of *kokpar*, a form of polo played by rugged herdsmen racing to place a goat carcass behind the enemy goal line. This spectacle was to be followed by a serving of seventeen kinds of kebabs drawn from the Turkic and Mughal court traditions, to Levantine and nomadic specialties. All this seemed exotic enough in conception but was folksy in reality – an air-conditioned yurt didn't help – and then a sudden sandstorm erupted that not only cut short the horse game but caused the Frenchman to have an asthmatic fit.

One more unrated event and Viktor would be out.

He knew that Westerners looked down on people like him; assuming some crookedness or chicanery to be the real source of his wealth. To be ejected from the Miner's Club would only confirm that suspicion. See, they don't have ideas or creativity. They can't compete on level playing fields. They can only amass loot based on old networks and political patronage. At the end of Viktor's first dinner, the Frenchman had asked, 'You know poor Loiseau, who killed himself fearing a Michelin downgrade?'

'Never went,' Viktor confessed.

'Your chef should follow Loiseau. There is honor in that path.'

Everyone laughed. Viktor laughed too. But the insult was unmistakable and stayed with him, a corrosive reminder of the prestige imbalance with his First World counterparts. Viktor was no oligarch; he had not 'stolen' mines by teaming up with the right people at the right moment or by serving as a front for them. But with the Frenchman it was more specific and personal. They were in the same neck of the woods – rare earth minerals – and the Frenchman had suffered some setbacks in recent years with his plant in Vietnam. Viktor rightly assumed that the jibe about his dinner was meant to say: you upstart can make all the money you want, but you'll never reach the heights of our cultural refinement.

This single anecdote had clarified Viktor for me. Beneath his placid demeanor lurked an assassin. What he wanted wasn't just an outstanding meal; he wanted revenge.

Later, when I shared the latest information about Viktor with Helen, her first response was, 'You should let me do the pitch.'

'Why?'

'Because I am a blonde. I am pretty and I am better at talking to all sorts of people, including the rich.'

Those were valid points, but somehow her bluntness triggered some ancient trauma inside me, and I felt a sudden revulsion at the thought of having to charm a billionaire by fronting my beautiful girlfriend. And with unexpected vehemence I blurted out, 'NO!'

Helen looked at me with surprise. She had said it in a tone partly of jest. It didn't warrant such a passionate objection.

'What do you mean "no"?'

'I don't think it's a good idea,' I said dully.

We were standing in the living room. Helen put down the laundry she was folding to turn in my direction. I could see a flash of color rising on her cheeks. I knew I was wading into a territory of trouble.

'Not a good idea, because?'

'Getting this gig is my job. The debt is my problem; I have to find the solution too. I don't want to put the burden of this responsibility on you.'

It seemed like a cleverer tack for me to take, but that was not how Helen took it. 'Is that your way of saying you don't want to risk me fucking it up?'

Helen was now facing me, arms clasped across her chest with reproachful tightness. Even as I stood there feeling foolish and annoyed, in the middle of a needless spat, I was struck by how absolutely, ravishingly, unreasonably gorgeous she was. She looked arresting even in this mood of gloaming resentment, her eyes an opalescent pair of wonder, the lips pursed tightly in red remonstrance.

'You are twisting my words,' I said feebly.

'You are twisting our relationship,' replied Helen. 'Listen, Kash, don't ever tell me this is just yours. It stopped being just yours from the time we moved in together. From the time you took on the big loans from Boris. From the time I started pitching in – without wages. While we haven't done the paperwork, I feel I have equity here.'

'Fair enough,' I said, head bowed in surrender.

'And one more thing,' Helen said.

'Yes?' I looked up.

'You don't get to decide where I can go or not go. Whom I am fit to see or not see.'

I signaled my acceptance in silence with a softening of my look. I felt I should give her a hug, but ancient forces left me immobilized. I was, I knew, ill-educated for a relationship with any woman, let alone one who seemed as self-possessed as Helen. And yet Helen had chosen me. She was still with me. I needed to keep learning, keep evolving. I needed to catch up on all the pages I had missed in the book of love during my formative years and, just as crucially perhaps, unlearn the lessons – brutal or twisted – that life had seen fit to bestow on me.

CHAPTER 7

I was raised in a culture where the sexes were kept apart like soldiers in opposing trenches. Unlike the soldiers, however, the privates on both sides here were keen to get to the other side. But the generals and their minions on both sides deployed regimes of discipline that'd make the custodians of the Maginot Line proud. Aunts, servants, siblings – there was no dearth of willing spies to report on any breach of the defenses. House-guards and drivers served as the retractable turrets of this elaborate apparatus of separation. Still, like the fabled defensive line, this one too eventually failed.

There were intrepid souls who found ways to form and sustain relationships – even if they amounted to little more than eye contact across rooftops or furtive phone calls – without getting discovered. But the ratio of effort to reward struck me as unattractively meager. Besides, going to an all-boys' school meant I had even less access to girls. For most boys in my straits, the only girls of one's age we came across were cousins or housemaids. I was not lucky in the department of cousins: they were older, lived far away or unattractive. And all the maids my mother had ever hired were elderly women with betel-stained teeth. Back then, in the Eighties, Bangladesh was still so poor that even families like ours, whose place in the middle-class ranks felt perennially under threat, could afford at least one servant. Like with the wealthy in the First World, our world had infinite rungs of poverty, and everyone could always find someone a few steps below them to do their menial jobs for them.

The problem with having only one maid at a time was of course that you were left with none when they suddenly left. And that's where we found ourselves the summer of my fifteenth year. After a few weeks, though, no one could bear the situation. My brother, Hafeez, and I could manage the dusting and sweeping. But we hated laundry and proved pitiful at ironing. My father's quick temper kept flaring up even more often. He took little interest in domestic management but felt free to rail at its inadequacies at the slightest diminishment of his own comfort. Then one evening, to the surprise of us all, my father came home from work with a girl in tow. Her brother worked as a teaboy at his office. On bringing her into the house, he handed her to my mother, saying: 'Here, take her. Now I can have properly ironed shirts.'

The girl, Rubina, was barely two years my elder. She brimmed with a natural excess of affection and boasted a lissome figure. Unlike her many predecessors, she was not a demure or depressed personality. She wasn't content simply to perform her tasks, but called on all of us in different ways for active engagement. She would volunteer to oil my mother's hair and insist she rest if she looked tired. She knew exactly how my father wanted his omelet, a morning staple, and polished my finicky brother's shoes to shiny perfection. She excelled at the housework; swift and punctilious. She spent her one day off visiting her brother, and sometimes went to see him in the week, too. Apart from those well-earned breaks, she was ever-present and assiduous.

Rubina earned everyone's praise in no time. Even my sullenly aloof father and my prematurely dour brother sang her praises. My mother, always exasperated by the perfidy of house-helps, could find no fault. I alone took a different kind of notice of the girl, or so I thought.

The first time she caught me staring at her, while dusting the living room, I was half-reclined on a sofa with a magazine open on my lap.

'What are you looking at?' Rubina had asked, a twinkle in her eyes.

I was mortified. I returned my gaze hurriedly to the magazine and became more deliberate and surreptitious in eyeing Rubina: her shape, her movements. I liked how her braided hair swayed when she walked. Her skin was the color of bright ocher – dark yet exuding a rude radiance of sexuality. Her smile felt luminous to me. I stopped seeing her as a 'servant' – while remaining acutely aware of that status and the unbridgeable gap it created for us. Still, when she peeked into my room in the afternoons and asked if I wanted a cup of tea, I felt a strange stirring. She'd ask what I was reading, and I would say that it was a story, as it often was. She'd then ask me to tell her the story, placing herself on the little rug by my bed. She had a way of sitting with both legs tucked to one side of her and leaning on one arm. To see her like this and at such an intimate distance was enough to set aflame all my adolescent urges.

Thankfully, I had my own room by then. This relative privacy afforded enough opportunity for new provocations to ensue. One day, Rubina asked me if I liked a new blouse she had bought – and displayed it for inspection without the adornment of a sari. To see her body, a slim, taut frame with her firm breasts cupped tightly inside her new blouse, filled me with an inexorable sense of desire. When she put *mehendi* on her hands for the Bengali New Year, I studied the decoration closely and for too long. Her fingers were long and delicate. But I found the fragrance that she wore to be too strong. With the sentimentality of youth, I decided pretty girls in cheap perfume were an anathema – and one day I presented her with a bottle of French perfume.

'But don't tell anyone I gave you this,' I said.

Little did I know the potency of gifts. Or that of a secret. The gift earned me a kiss that lingered long enough to inspire other gifts. And that led to more expressions of appreciation on her part, though even the sense of gratitude was probably higher inside me. What followed was a summer of enchantment, intensified by furtiveness. Our intimacies were a matter of me pushing for ever more license and her alternating between enticement and restriction. 'No, no, not so far' – if I reached into her blouse and touched her nipple. 'Not yet, not now' – if I reached up under her sari and strayed too close to her pelvis. I was drunk on the heady first taste of physical intimacy. And terrified of being discovered. We knew there was no future in our relationship, but this much, right here and right now, this is enough, I told myself. Whether she stroked my hair or took extra care in tidying up my room, I was enraptured with the attentions she bestowed on me.

By the end of the summer, when I had finally been granted permission to touch her everywhere, and she too had gotten to know me similarly, I was sure that she'd soon become my first. She came to my room in the dead of night. Not every night, but when she visited, we threw a sheet on the little rug on the other side of my bed. In a darkened room, even if anyone opened the door – who'd do that at 3 a.m.? – I'd still have enough time to slip back under my sheets and she would stay curled and hidden on the floor. She had jerked me off more than once. And she had allowed me to insert my fingers into the warm moistness between her legs a couple of times. Oh, the thrill of those first touches! They're still so fresh in my mind. I wasn't allowed to look at her – and what would I see in the dark? – so, I groped under her clothes, trying to memorize the map of her mystery by its folds and ridges, its hairy surrounds and slippery depth.

Given our social strictures, I knew that this was not a relationship that could grow or last. Still, I believed myself to be in love – elemental, physical love. I was sure that any night now she would allow me to plunge into the ultimate knowledge.

Then, one morning at the end of that summer, she eloped with my father.

We realized when she didn't turn up for work one morning after my father had left for the office as usual. As she was normally so reliable, it was surprising.

'Better check if anything is stolen,' opined my brother Hafeez, who was already hardening into a typical householder.

Nothing of value was missing. But as we began to inventory our belongings, we noticed that half my father's wardrobe was empty, and two suitcases were gone. It wasn't like him to go off on a trip without telling us. By the next day 'well-wishers' came bearing the news with barely suppressed glee: my father had rented a small two-room house on the edge of the city. The rumors in the weeks and then months to come grew more colorful. They had had twins! He has left for a job in the Gulf! She has left him for a younger man.

None of it mattered. I didn't try to verify any of the rumors. I was reeling from the fact that not only was Rubina two-timing me, but she had done so with none other than my father! And I could not talk to anyone about it. I had to swallow the humiliation on my own. My father! My bad-tempered, unhandsome, ungenerous father. He was more desirable than me? How could that be? It was my natural penury as a fifteen-year-old, I decided. My gifts were nothing compared to what my father with his ramshackle career could offer: a home, a family.

Every human being is a museum of hurts. The curator is a vicious sadist. He knows where the deepest cuts, the greatest blows, the most shattering tremor points are located. And he will pull them out of the secret vault to sabotage every attempt at repair or recovery.

CHAPTER 8

Winter in New York was a tyranny of funneled cold blasts and the long vigil of a humorless sky. Bundled-up, hurrying masses snatched puffs of warmth from steaming grates, heat vents, food carts and humming engines – whatever cubic charge of heat fell in their path. Summer was just as oppressive in an opposing manner; all heat and humidity, the reek of garbage on the streets, the stench of sweat and piss in the subway. Rain came not as a respite, but to further funk up all the muck. Fall provided an interregnum; it came like a beautiful, bowed stranger draped in forlorn colors. The evening light dropped more quickly each passing day, and small downtown restaurants lit up with the convivial canopied glow of taverns from another era. But spring! For me, that's when New York came to life; young couples walking hand in hand past open-air concerts, and friends mingling in cafés with outdoor seating.

We were into the swing of the season now, and Helen and I were off to meet Viktor. Adair had to attend the eightieth birthday party of Aunt Marge. I knew what the lady meant to him. There was no way he could not be there for her on such a special day. Besides, by now I had changed my mind and I agreed with Helen that she might have a better effect on Viktor. She, like Adair, could connect to people naturally. I found it a strain to establish rapport with strangers. In any event, I didn't feel like going alone to this all-important meeting.

I had rented a limousine to travel to Viktor's Upper West Side digs. One could not take the subway to a meeting with a billionaire.

Viktor wasn't a Forbes billionaire. But he was very much in their league. I have always found it a shortcoming of the English language that there are no names for the tenth-base rungs between a million and a billion. 'Multimillionaire' means nothing.

'Hundy,' Adair had told me once when I raised the issue with him.

'Hundy?'

'That's what billionaires call them. Once someone makes their first hundred million, a billionaire will say, "Oh, so-and-so's made it! They have a hundy!"'

I could not vouch for this claim, and it didn't solve my problem: A multimillionaire could in theory have as little as five million or five hundred million. How could wealth levels that were galaxies apart be described with the same catch-all term? And no one was calling anyone a 'hundillionaire'. I had seen the term centimillionaire thrown around occasionally in online sites that talked about wealth. That was, of course, an inaccuracy stemming from the writers' unfamiliarity with the metric system. Centi, thanks to my Third World education, I knew was one hundredth of a measure – not a hundred. So, the precise terminology would be hectomillionaire. Be that as it may, from my vantage Viktor was as good as a billionaire.

Carnivore

Helen wore one of her formal sets, a white and finely textured pantsuit, and knotted her lustrous blonde hair into a tight bun, which made her look like an assassin from a Bond movie. Her only imperfection, a slight crook in her nose that disturbed the symmetry of her face, seemed to complement the part in which I was casting her now in my mind. I had pulled out a treasure from the days of plenitude: my prized Kiton. A charcoal-gray tailored wonder – narrow lapels and kinked pockets, unstitched cuffs and perfect falls and folds. We needed to inspire confidence on sight.

'It'll be fine,' Helen said, as we whizzed up Sixth Avenue. There was a calm about her that I found reassuring. This was something I'd noticed about her in the past; in the face of big decisions or occasions, she was unflappable.

It had been just over a month since the peacock dinner. By now we had catered to another of Viktor's friends; a Nigerian telecoms tycoon who wanted an exclusive dinner with his latest *objet d'amour*, an Angolan-American jazz singer who was starting to make mainstream waves with her *danza kuduro* beats. Apparently, the lady was not faint of heart. The two had talked of going big-game hunting. As a foretaste, there was to be a night of wildebeest tenderloin and giraffe carpaccio. Don't get me wrong, I love wildlife as much as the next Nat Geo fan. But we make exceptions when it comes to our own survival. If I chose to be a stickler for the law, we'd never be able to meet the short-notice demands for super-exotic fare from our burgeoning ultra-ultra-rich clientele. Besides, New York was a hive of buzzing trade in bush meat and other rarities. There was nothing you could not source by reaching deep into the ethnic recesses of Queens and Brooklyn, and of course Chinatown. Hagi, our meat-man, would not deal in anything illegal himself ('risk is too high, buddy'), but he made the introductions. You couldn't walk into these shops as a stranger and ask if they had some bear and gorilla meat or armadillo and iguana parts lying around.

Adair was understandably nervous as we expanded our repertoire. 'What if we get busted?' he would ask me, often from the anxious depths of a hangover.

'Who's going to tell?' I would reply. 'Our guys have spent enough time with the authorities.'

Secretly I wondered, too. The federal bodies most likely to bother us – the Fish and Wildlife Service, National Marine Fisheries Service, even the USDA – didn't have the time or resources to snoop around New York City restaurants, let alone privately catered affairs. But the laws of New York State were busier on this count than most other places. There were specific statutes concerning import and export; possession, delivery, carry, transport, selling or shipping. And even receiving. Still, as long as we avoided the 900 or so animals, not counting invertebrates, plants and insects, proscribed by the broad sweep of the Endangered Species Act, we'd be fine. Except, often that was what our new clients wanted. And why not? There wasn't much point in having fuck-you money if you couldn't enjoy what's out of reach for everyone else.

Thanks to our emerging niche as the go-to fixers for the deviant epicurean cravings of the super-rich, the past month had been the fattest in earnings for us ever. I was able to meet Boris's monthly instalment and make up for a few missed ones. We still owed him a solid quarter million, but I hoped that the amped-up repayments would buy time and spare me any more manhandling.

Apart from the money, I justified our slide into the gray zone of the meat trade in terms of my aversion to regulation. The spirit of freedom that animated our devotion to wild meats was inimical to a world riddled with an excess of rules. I didn't mind if we were in technical breach of the law – as long as we were not easy to catch. But I did care that no endangered specimen be harmed. I insisted that we be supplied only with farm-grown meats, even when the farms were not above board.

To mitigate the increased risk of the authorities clamping down on the illicit flesh that featured more and more on our private dinner menus, I tried to keep as much of the patently illegal stuff off-premises. Kang and I stored things in our own refrigerators. I'd installed a subzero unit at home, the like of which you'd never see in a normal studio-size apartment. And we cooked at the clients' homes whenever we had the chance.

Kang's ready cooperation when it came to storing illicit flesh in one's apartment was a great relief for me; pulling the specific items needed for a dinner and passing it on to him ahead of time was a relief. Kang wasn't at all squeamish about either the cooking or the storing. I had to appreciate this Third World level 'whatever-it-takes' aplomb, since Korea wasn't exactly a Third World country. Maybe it was when Kang was still a child and that had left a mark on him. But more than anything, like his country, I felt he too was just beyond classification.

As our limo pulled up to a corner of the mid-60s and Central Park West, I drew confidence from recent events. We were received by a doorman – possibly a Caribbean ex-fast bowler cooling his heels, to judge by his rangy height – who parceled us off to a receptionist. She was unmistakably Russian, in appearance and accent. The Russian accent was a mystery to me. What torsion of syntax or what twang of phonemes caused this effect I had no idea, but they spoke as if their tongues were laden with the weight of their traumatic history and soured by endless self-disgust. She handed us to a squat, ruddy Englishman tightly wrapped in a double-breasted vest, who addressed us with a chiseled accent and constipated politesse.

The butler led us into a long, chandeliered hall-like room. I believe it was Fitzgerald, forever fascinated by wealth, who said, 'You know the rich, they are not like you or me.' And the master of terseness Hemingway replied, 'No, they have a lot more money.' I could add to that adage: that the rich had more rooms. And more staff. More sofas, too. The long living room was sectioned into sumptuous seating areas. Against a wall I noticed a pair of lacquered Chinese chairs that probably belonged to a long-decapitated king. The walls and surfaces displayed beautiful objects – prints and paintings, old globes and hourglasses, statuettes and abstract sculpture – imitating the rise and fall of the mellifluous notations on a classical scoresheet.

We had been seated beneath a giant painting of a chimpanzee; it sat on its haunches cradling an egg-shaped globe of the world between its prehensile digits. Its manic grin and gimlet eyes did nothing to diminish the surge of kinship that I felt for this ancient cousin.

Helen was tinkering with some chiming bells on a long table running along the back of our white leather sofa.

'Honey, don't touch anything!' I said, with suppressed urgency.

'Why?'

Because if you break anything, it'll cost me both my kidneys to pay for it, I wanted to scream. But there was something so natural about the ease with which she moved about the room, taking in the ersatz representations, checking the texture of decorative rugs and throws, that I had to hold my tongue.

'Look at this, Kash, it's Ming—'

'Kash, is it?'

Viktor's voice sounded as I remembered from the first encounter, when I'd cast Aaron Eckhart to play him. Gentle, gravelly, but with a low timbre that conveyed substance and confidence. When I turned around, he was standing in the doorway. The first time I met him, at the peacock dinner, in the dim lighting of The Hide, his real age was harder to gauge. In the better-lit ambience today, I could see the fine creases on his face. He exhibited the leanness of a well-maintained physique, but the face was the distinctive visage of a man in his late middle age, and richer in experience than most of his contemporaries. His dirty blond hair was brushed back. He was an inch shorter than me but projected a persona that held the room. While his comportment exuded an air of relaxed contentment, his blue-gray eyes were as focused as a homing device on advanced weaponry.

'Yes, sir,' I said stepping forward to shake the offered hand. I didn't expect a billionaire to remember me by name. By face, perhaps. But not by name.

'And this is my partner, Helen,' I said, as Helen came forward.

Viktor ushered us back to the sofa set. 'So, you two work together?'

'And to be honest, also live together,' I added quickly.

'Ah, a working relationship, in every sense,' Viktor said with a chuckle. I didn't think billionaires were given to simple jokes or easy laughs.

'What a marvelous home you have, Mr Karakozov,' Helen said. 'And the art, just fascinating.'

'Thank you,' Viktor said. 'I noticed you were eyeing the vase.'

I have no fucking idea how Helen knew about Ming vases. Or if she did. I guess idle hours and Google are enough to turn all of us into sudden experts in arcane diversions. But I could not help marveling at how at ease she seemed to be amid all this splendor. She belonged in a way that, despite all my ambition, I never quite felt I did.

The butler came in again while Viktor and Helen traveled deeper into the hall, past a baroque red sofa set, to admire the vase more closely. The butler brought in a proper tea tray – porcelain, tea cosy, silver strainer – and behind him an Asian woman followed bearing a tray full of finger sandwiches and little cakes in a delightful array of colors.

I watched the Asian lady pour our tea with the precision of a fastidious grandmother. Soon enough, Viktor and Helen rejoined me in the white sofa area.

I had expected to be met and seen off from a foyer-like station with brisk enquiries about our plans. I didn't think men of Viktor's standing had any time for mere vendors like us. Instead, he was proving to be charming, indeed human – and humane.

'So Yusep says you have an interesting idea for me?' Viktor asked, stirring his tea, blue eyes twinkling with curiosity.

'Yes, Mr Karakozov. We have thought a lot about your Miner's Club, and I believe we can offer something stunning.'

'That's a big claim!'

A foodie blog had named us the 'secret' hideout where the super-rich went for food . . . that no one else dared serve. Nothing as obvious, say, as an ortolan meal, with large napkins covering the sinners' heads, but a more arcane fare, which took real curiosity on the part of the customer and inventiveness for the supplier to provide. The buzz emboldened me; besides, what chance would we have with anything less than startling?

'It's not just about the food for you, Mr Karakozov,' I said, getting up to make our pitch.

'Is that so?' Viktor said, with a twinkle in his eyes.

'You want to make a mark. You want to stand out. In fact, what you want is to deliver a meal to end all meals. To end the Miner's Club!'

I could tell from the sparkle in his eyes, the shifting blue-gray colors, that his interest was piqued.

'And how will you accomplish that?' Viktor asked.

'We go where others don't dare to go. Look at the club, sir, and what everyone's done so far. It's all within the current paradigm of foodism. There are three defining features of this banality. A chef will combine ingredients in new or unexpected ways, which is fine but nothing radical. Cooks have been doing that forever. So, to justify their bullshit they will acquire equipment that most home cooks can't afford, and press things into unexpected shapes and textures. That too can be entrancing, but ultimately, it is what chemists do. For a final Hail Mary, they turn to design and décor, but c'mon, how many times can you admire high ceilings or vintage mosaics? The contents may change, but the parameters are obvious, repetitive.'

'We have been to incredible locations—'

'That's right, sir,' I said, unable to help myself. 'Your chefs and consultants have made you spend a lot, but only to enact the same principles of high dining on a grander scale. It didn't break any new dimensions.'

Viktor straightened his back; he wasn't expecting me to be this bold. 'So, what's the big idea?' Viktor asked.

'You need to hit your crew with something that will not only be new to the palate, but also rattle their souls. They think they own the world, that they control their destinies. Remind them how fragile they are, how easily it can all slip away. Give them a taste of real danger.'

Viktor's face broke into a broad smile, and he stood up. He was hooked. He gestured for me to carry on.

'Men like your friends won't be able to resist a dare,' Helen said.

Viktor smiled again. I felt proud. Women may hate mansplaining, and rightly so. But men loved being told what they did or didn't want – or like – by a beautiful woman. Men loved being told anything by a beautiful woman.

The room was aglow with the unearthly luminescence of a departing sun. The butler came by to turn on more lights, but Viktor waved him away.

'The key to the Miner's Club so far is that everyone thinks it's about the food. But the food is merely the pretext. It's about experience. It's about group dynamics. Don't give your guests the privilege of being judges. Make them the objects of judgment.'

Through my delivery, I had ambled to the window. Viktor was standing in the middle of the rug, arms clasped over his chest, waiting for the specific idea.

'I propose an evening of pure danger. We serve, course after course, items that could kill you – if not handled properly.'

Viktor's eyes widened; I could tell he was surprised – indeed taken aback. Then his face transformed into an approving grin. He had a very changeable face, and this made me trust him.

'We would start off slow and easy enough,' Helen joined in, getting up for her part of our rehearsed pitch, 'with fried legs of the African bullfrog. And a salad of rhubarb, elderberries and ackee.'

'Sounds innocent enough,' Viktor said.

'Any of those items can kill you, if you don't know how to handle them – or,' I added, with a chuckle, 'if you do!'

'You think my friends trust me that much?'

'That is the point, Mr Karakozov. Let's find out if they do!'

'Viktor, call me Viktor,' he said, and walked briskly over to a sideboard near the entrance. An electronic button caused the front panel to roll gently down, revealing an array of bottles. 'Speaking of poison, how do you like your whiskey?'

'Very much,' I said.

Viktor chuckled and began to pour a round. The bottle had Viktor's name on it; clearly a barrel proof batch made to his personal specifications. Viktor could tell I was eyeing the bottle and said, 'From a small distillery in Speyside. A very small batch, triple-distilled, sixteen years.'

I nodded in appreciation. And felt the first sip, gentle

fire coursing down my gullet, spreading shock after shock of delight: a nose of apricot and campfire, followed by a creamy and full-bodied palate of butternut and umami. It was close to perfection; I savored the long finish in silence.

Helen came over and joined me by the window. The honking of passing cars floated up, and a scream came, as if out of the sky. Someone was always calling out in New York; hollering a complaint, issuing an alarm or appealing to God himself with some existential cry. When I opened my eyes and looked down, everything at street level looked smaller than before – Lego pieces on a giant gridded playboard.

Helen had chosen to have a glass of sherry.

'*Salud*,' I said, and we clinked glasses.

'The appetizer would be followed by *San-nakji*, the famous Korean dish of baby octopus. If you don't chew it properly, the limbs can latch onto the inside of your throat with suction cups and choke you to death.'

'And my guests would like that, because—'

'Because you dared them,' Helen completed the thought. 'Because men, even when they have a billion dollars, can't bear to be thought of as unmanly.'

Viktor smiled.

Lesson: You can't explain everything by following the money, but you can if you follow the ego.

'What would one drink?' Viktor asked.

'The pairing will mainly draw on regional inspiration. So, an Amarula shot to go with the African bullfrog. And a biodynamic Vermont white to go with the salad.'

'For the *San-nakji*, we suggest a clear Korean rice wine.'

'Rice wine? Isn't that a little too plebian?'

'Our chef is Korean. He can source rice wine that's as

premium as anything you've ever had. Libations fit for ancient warlords.'

Viktor raised one eyebrow, clearly impressed by how prepared and resourceful we were.

'That *would* keep things interesting,' said Viktor.

'The next course,' Helen continued, 'would consist of sliced *hákarl*, a Greenlandian delicacy of fermented shark.'

'And how is this dangerous?'

'This shark has no urinary tracts. So, all toxins are stored in its flesh. It takes six months to clean it out. The whole thing is poison.'

'Okay,' said Viktor, appreciatively.

'And this we will serve with Ice beer, made with million-year-old Arctic ice harvested from glaciers.'

The butler passed in the doorway with the silky menace of a character out of a Daphne du Maurier novel. That's right, buddy, I thought. Spook me all you want, but I'm in! You better get used to me.

'We will bring out a scoop of *Casu martzu* as a mid-feast reprieve,' said Helen.

'That's the Sardinian cheese with . . . live maggots, right?'

'Yes, sir,' I said. 'And they will tear your intestines out if you let them travel to your belly intact. We will segue into land animals with a serving of monkey brain. Just a scoop, and looking as real as it is in the raw.'

Viktor came back with a fresh round of whiskies for him and me. Helen was nursing her small sherry with deliberate slowness.

'Ichiro, special batch,' Viktor said, handing me a fresh glass.

I knew about Ichiro, but this was different from any of

their vintage I had tried so far. Sublime could barely begin to describe the taut, pure silkiness of this former sake-maker's magic brew. The fact that Viktor had wordlessly picked up my enthusiasm for whiskey told me that unlike many billionaires, Viktor was a people person. He read the room, and possibly played people. And played them well.

'You can get all this in NY? This is permitted?'

'Who says it has to be in New York? We can arrange it in a location where everything will be permissible.'

'Not in the West,' Viktor said, shaking his head ruefully. 'They have lost all sense of fun.'

This remark was revealing; my research on Viktor, and my reading of the man, was spot on. You didn't get to be where he was without a desire to prove yourself. You certainly don't force yourself to the head of the table when you hail from places that are not supposed to be at the table at all.

'The date will be about a month from now, maybe six weeks. But this summer is my turn,' Viktor said.

'Long enough for us,' I said.

'Good. So, what's for the finale?'

'A lion "tartare",' said Helen. 'Given the stringy nature and possible toxicities, you can't do tartare with bush meat, but we have ideas how to make it safe and still give the feeling of eating it raw.'

'And, of course, everything will taste delicious. What we offer is nothing less than the irresistible taste of danger.'

'Good. Very good, my friends,' said Viktor with a quick look at his watch. 'But I'll have to think about this.'

The butler came to hover again at the door. With a flick from God-knows-where, all the lamps in the room came alive in one go, and extinguished the depressing shadows cast by the light of a falling evening.

The next morning, I had finished my routine with Kang and was debating ordering a second macchiato, when Adair burst through the door.

'Shit! Shit! Shit!'

Adair never came by in the morning. This had to be special. He threw down a copy of *New York* magazine, a little bible of all that was worth knowing and doing, shunning and envying, in the city.

'Look,' he said, as if I was somehow responsible for this latest calamity.

It was an article about The Hide. The article was barely half a page, since they had used a large photo of our frontage. It was our dream to be written up in the more prestigious papers, but this was cruel irony: we were finally talked about as saviors of overdone culinary drama, but not as we had hoped. We were portrayed as the gastronomic dirty-work handymen for the ultra-wealthy. While such a mischaracterization of our mission, our personalities, rankled, the bigger problem was the insinuation – nay, claims – that we were trading in illicit items.

The article was titled, 'Dark Meat: Secret Recipes for the Super-Rich'. Subtitled: 'Village Eatery Selling Off-Menu Items from Seals to Serpents'.

Strictly speaking we had served neither seals nor serpents. But journalists aren't the best writers and mistake alliteration for style. Still, the thrust of their claims was true: we were catering to tastes not entirely within the bounds of the law. That's why people paid us; if they could pay anybody else for the fare we were willing to entertain, then we would not get paid so handsomely.

'I told you this private dinner stuff, the funky meat, was bad news.'

'And not having any money to keep Boris at bay was good news?'

I was growing tired of Adair's whining. And a mood of defiance came over me.

'Fuck them,' I said. 'They can't prove shit. And I don't accept any moral charges. The legal ones are . . . well, the law is often asinine. We don't serve anything truly endangered. Only that which others won't. Or prevailing laws don't allow because the laws are written by the cattle and chicks industries. So, yeah, fuck the lot of them. And fuck these New York liberals who think they are so cool but can't handle anything truly radical.'

'Why didn't you just talk to them?'

'I don't think they really wanted to talk to me, or they'd have rung again.'

It came to me now that someone pretending to be a 'New York journalist' had called asking me if we served any 'off-menu' items. I had hung up thinking it was a prank. Ever since the foodie blog that first outed us for our esoteric offerings, there had been more internet sites reselling that story with ever more sensational claims. Who the fuck knew that 'New York' journalist meant a shark from the actual magazine, and not just any odd scribbler from the city's septic tunnels of the talentless?

'Fuck!'

Fucked was more like it. And the assholes had gotten what they probably wanted more than an actual comment from me; they had written, 'the owner, Kash Mirza, refused to talk'. They could get away with such calumny because their readers wouldn't know that *a*. I was a Bengali and *b*. Bengalis never refuse to talk.

I said this to Adair, but he didn't laugh.

'They say all publicity is good,' I said, half-heartedly, to cheer him up.

'That's one of those popular sayings that could not be more wrong,' Adair replied.

I kept quiet, as I concurred. Publicity that has the potential to catch the eyes of the authorities was never good.

The article described the peacock dinner for an unnamed foreign billionaire. It claimed that we had held private events serving 'bush meat' and – this was truly damning for us – endangered species. They didn't have clear sources or specifics; it was shoddy by proper journalistic standards, but it was written less as an exposé, and more to illustrate the perfidies of the rich: how their appetites were still untamed despite the shambolic state of the economy.

What an asinine thesis! From Roman times till now, the rich have never stopped partying. They expect everyone else to eat cake. Actually, they don't think about anyone else.

'I told you, I told you,' Adair said again, without clarifying what it was that he had told me.

I forgave him the repetition and the finger-pointing, because I could see how frightened he was. I think children of the developed world have a lesser ability to absorb shock.

'Don't worry,' I said, as some calm in the face of danger descended on me. 'Nothing will come of this.'

'How do you know?' Adair's face looked pale and drawn, eyes teary.

'I don't,' I said. 'But we will make sure nothing happens about this.'

'How?'

'That depends on who comes looking,' I said.

Adair didn't seem assured by my little act of bravado. Instead, he went into another line of distress. 'What will people think?'

I had never quite pegged Adair as someone who gave a damn about that. But I realized now, instantly, that I was mistaken. Someone whose greatest talent is to smooth-talk people into schemes and investments had to give a damn. He had a society here in a way that I didn't.

'Anyone who's scandalized, if they even see this report, deny, deny, deny,' I told Adair, with feigned authority. 'Anyone who seems intrigued or thrilled, still deny, but do it coyly.'

CHAPTER 9

I was a student of English literature at a college of modest reputation in Dhaka. My brother Hafeez had already started his little *tehari* shop, and I chose a college that was both affordable and close enough that I could go sit at the till in the evenings. I spent my quiet hours voraciously reading books, mainly novels. The self-contained realm of the many concocted worlds was my way of escaping my own reality – until I could do so literally. Why this urge to escape was so strong in me, I cannot fully explain.

One of my teachers, Mr Moinuddin, had been deported from America, and that somehow made him more obsessed with the nation. And he had turned to recruiting people for the mission that had gone so awry for him as his form of redemption. America had rejected him, but he wasn't going to betray America. He was still going to sing its praises. This I later came to understand as the dynamic of America and its allies. Or, perhaps, of all imperial powers and their vassals of different magnitude.

As it happened, I already had my sights set on America too, and so I welcomed Mr Moinuddin's assiduous ministrations. To know the language, its idiom, and perhaps to pick up some of the ethos or mores of the target culture, it all made sense to me.

I attribute my partiality towards America to growing up during the Cold War. The Cold War was good for culture, even for a stripling of a country as Bangladesh was in the Seventies and even on through the 1980s. Both superpowers tried to woo us. The Russians flooded the market with beautifully produced children's books. We had never seen anything like it before: hard-bound and with thick, shiny pages. Amazing tales matched by the equally enchanting and colorful drawings. The Russian largesse came to us in the form of movies, too. I recall one involving an evil midget and a princess; to free the princess one had to cut off the wicked old man's floor-length beard. I fell in love immediately with the Russian beauty who played the princess – and have been hostile to beards ever since.

If the Russians owned my childhood, America colonized my adolescence. It started with a ration of only one daily episode of cartoons – *Casper the Friendly Ghost*, *Popeye*, or *Tom and Jerry* – fragile minions in the fight against Russian ploys to win tender-aged recruits. But the Americans saved their best for the older yet still-malleable crew. It started with the *Wild Wild West* and *Little House on the Prairie*. From tales of roguish adventures to bucolic idyll, something about the wide expanse of the American West, even on our small, fuzzy, black-and-white TV screen, held out a promise of limitlessness.

I belong to a generation that was especially vulnerable to American TV shows: the airing of *Charlie's Angels* in our region coincided with the advent of our puberty. For a year or two, all that my friends ever debated was who was the hottest Angel. I won't rehash that classic; I'm sure you are familiar with its contours. I was in love – no, not with Farrah Fawcett – with Jaclyn Smith. I even liked that Jaclyn was spelled without a 'k' in sight. The lush upsurge of her hair, the high cheekbones, a bosom whose plenitude could hardly be contained by her tight shirts, and above all, the smile: did you ever notice how a hint of sorrow lingered at the corner of her otherwise luscious lips?

What can I say? I was a sensitive child.

Mr Moinuddin began to ply me with his private canon just as my infatuation with more easily consumable ephemera of American culture started to wane. Mr Moinuddin – short, compact, always in a hurry, shock of wavy salt-and-pepper hair – would come into class, spinning an inexplicably large bunch of keys by its ring on his index finger. At the end of class, he would draw me aside and ask conspiratorially, 'Have you read this?' Initially the queries concerned classic noir: Cain and Thompson. Then came the beats: Bukowski and Kerouac.

Once he saw that I digested the offered material with vim and comprehension, Mr Moinuddin steered me towards more literary texts, which he held in the same reverential awe as archaeologists do, say, the Dead Sea or Herculaneum scrolls.

This phase of my education began with the twin pillars, in Mr Moinuddin's estimation, of American modernity – not just modernism (he told me): Fitzgerald and Hemingway. And then more challenging and highbrow affairs: Bellow and Roth. American realism: Updike and Ford. Post-modern icons: DeLillo and Pynchon. Obscure maestros: Elkin and Gass.

Why he was so biased towards male authors – Ayn Rand and Ursula Le Guin being the exceptions – I don't know. And certainly, it didn't occur to me as an issue at the time.

Immersion into voices and visions from a faraway land somehow imbued me with a tremendous yearning to transcend the ordinary. Or, to become extraordinary. This need manifested at first as an overwhelming need to escape. Escape from my family, my surroundings, my city. Only later, or just recently, as meanings crawl out from the folds of my experiences, I realize that I saw home as familiar, and the familiar felt ordinary. So, to be extraordinary one had to leave home, leave it far behind.

Of course, poets and philosophers – and I guess, retirees – will tell you that even the routines and rhythms of quotidian existence can be extraordinary. But I lacked their wisdom or their refinement when I was young and hatching my plans. Even now, I lacked the patience for such sage counsel.

When I first made it to New York, I found myself bunking with fellow Diversity Visa-winning bachelors. There were eight of us crammed into a lousy – as in actually lice-infested – two-bedroom apartment in an old redbrick Sunnyside tenement. The Diversity Visa – DV – was a lotteried visa that America had started giving out in the early Nineties, amped up on globalist euphoria in the first flush of the fall of the Berlin Wall. It allowed the winners to come to America, with immediate pathway to a much-coveted Green Card, and eventually the Holy Grail of citizenship status – the blue passport of the United States of America.

Our landlady, Mrs Zaman, was an older Bengali matron, but the kind who commanded the respect of men and

women, old and young alike, without effort. Even natives –
White, Black or Latino – in the neighborhood submitted to
her natural authority, as if by some deep reflex carried over
from ancient matriarchal orders. It helped perhaps that she
enjoyed a stature, unlike most diminutive Bengali women,
which was quite formidable. She was a clear five feet six and
big boned, but not corpulent. The overall effect was one of
strength. Solid as a brown brick wall.

She, or rather her daughter, was also a DV winner, but
of the first batch. The daughter, being an only child, had
brought the mother over once she was qualified to do so.
Seen as a life-changing blessing for most, the DV had turned
into the most devastating curse in Mrs Zaman's case. The
daughter and her husband, along with their five-year-old boy,
had perished in a terrible crash on the New Jersey Turnpike,
soon after Mrs Zaman's arrival. Everyone thought Mrs
Zaman would go back to Bangladesh at that point. Instead,
she threw herself into tending to Bangladeshis, especially the
younger ones, however she could.

I too had come to America on a DV, but strictly speaking I
wasn't an actual winner of the lottery. I knew by then that I
could not count on luck or chance to deliver anything to me.
So, instead of applying every year in the vain hope of getting
a break, I took matters into my hands. I bought the visa
off someone else. Someone whose details matched mine well
enough. It was long before the days of machine-readable
passports, let alone biometrics, and Nilkhet – the publishing
hub of Dhaka – did a thriving trade in fake passports. My
photo was attached to the passport with the purchased visa.
I landed in America with a new name, or rather one that
wasn't mine, but when asked, colloquially, I always gave out

the name I knew already I'd adopt once I received my blue passport: Kash Mirza.

I retained the family name, Mirza. And fashioned my given name, Kashem, into a formulation that I felt suited my new environment, my new purpose, my mood and my temper much better: Kash.

That was the name I'd given to Mrs Zaman when I first put up at her de facto hostel. I knew enough already not to divulge any vulnerability to anyone – unless it was absolutely imperative.

'So, you have a degree in English?' Mrs Zaman had asked me when I first applied for a berth in her hostel.

'Yes, ma'am,' I had replied.

'And, no relatives here in America?'

I could tell she had appraised me as more well-heeled than most of the young men – and occasionally women (though always in their own separate apartments) – to whom she gave shelter at dirt-cheap rates. And she didn't want someone with better options stealing a bed that might be desperately needed by a more needy chap – perhaps, someone with little or no English.

'No drugs?'

'Never,' I said.

She cast a probing glance at me while pushing her gold-rimmed reading glasses up her nose.

'Drinking? Gambling?'

'Also, no and no, ma'am,' I said, my anxiety rising.

'Smoking?'

'Only occasionally,' I said, thinking it best to be truthful.

'Smoking is okay,' Mrs Zaman said, lighting up a menthol stick herself.

Despite her initial suspiciousness about me, Mrs Zaman came to grow a liking towards me before long. Impressed by my superior English, she placed me at the top of our little totem pole of the unwashed and unwanted. She was both our slumlord and our savior. She introduced us to Dr Hazari, a Bangladeshi doctor, unlicensed, who'd tend to us, the uninsured. And offered us a myriad other life-hacks for the newly migrated – and severely under-resourced.

I was put in charge of paying bills, tallying groceries and any hardware purchases, or calling up repairmen. I also had to make sure no more than four of us were present whenever any outsider came around. Other tasks ran down the ranks according to prison-style cruelty, and the house idiot ended up with the floor mop. I co-opted Samad as my deputy. He was a Dhaka boy; a tousled-haired fellow with an open smile, and the only guy with real curiosity about our new world. The others were too occupied with petty advantages like grocery coupons and phone cards to be of any interest to me.

The ranking within our hostel was replicated in the jobs market. The blokes with no English were handed the toilet brush. A step up were nightwatchmen. The presentable ones from this lot could even snag daytime substitute gigs in nonprime buildings. There was good money, too, in more brutal trades, like selling fruit on street corners. That involved getting up at three in the morning to make it to the wholesaler's and standing outdoors for twelve – or, if you had kids to feed, then maybe fourteen or sixteen – hours, even when an Arctic wind chill forced the temperature to drop.

Fuck that.

I kept managing the hostel, which meant my room and board were free, and I received a small stipend from Mrs Zaman for my services. Very small; but better than nothing. And I got to have a room with only one roommate. I chose Samad for this, too, as he was the only one who didn't exude biohazardous body odor. He was a smoker, which I minded less than any blast of noxious human scent. But I made Samad open the window, even in winter, and he'd stick his head out while he smoked, and we gabbed about the future.

Samad didn't want the jobs that others settled for; he had higher ambitions. Like me, he too had come to America not for a generically better life, but due to a particular passion: cars. Not just any car, but American muscle cars. He dreamed of owning a vintage Shelby Cobra or an Oldsmobile Toronado. He harbored a horror of owning anything as solid and sensible as an Accord or a Camry. In a parallel revulsion, I wasn't going to take any job at either Curry Row or Curry in a Hurry.

'You have the background. And at least you'd be in Manhattan!'

He was referring to my years of work at my brother Hafeez's *tehari* shop back in Dhaka. And also, my well-known wish to be lodged in Manhattan.

'Nah, I didn't come here to shovel buckets of curry.'

'So, you'd rather keep managing Hotel Zaman for less than minimum wage?'

'Yes, I'd rather manage you monkeys than work in a Desi joint serving fake Indian food,' I said.

It was not a practical stance, but I had my reasons. I was ideologically opposed to 'Indian' food. There is no such thing as 'Indian' food, I told Samad. Bengali, Tamil,

Kashmiri, Goanese and many other cuisines, sure. But Indian? No! That's because there was never such a thing as India to begin with. India, in its long history, had never existed in the territorial shape finally forged by the British. It was always a patchwork of kingdoms and fiefdoms with no over-arching notion of one unified juggernaut of a nation. The Brits effectively made up the country for their colonial exploitative purposes, and the natives returned the favor by making up a cuisine for the blighted palates of their former overlords.

What's even funnier is the little-known fact that Indian restaurant food, originating as it did in the UK, wasn't invented by Indians but by a sub-group who hailed from what is today a district of Bangladesh: Sylhet. Many Sylhetis served as cooks on merchant vessels, and a few of them jumped ship in the colonial days. As they plied the only trade they knew to cater to their compatriots and a few intrepid white souls in East London, the Indian restaurant was born.

'Let me know when the Four Seasons comes looking for you,' Samad said, blowing rings into the chilly night air.

The Four Seasons didn't come knocking, but when I finally landed a job, it was as a waiter in a proto-hipster café in Long Island City. It was a good jumping off point. Within a few months I was able to get the job at Brown's, the downtown whiskey bar where I'd also first meet Adair, which felt like a thumb-size grip on the cliff face of my American dream.

I loved that place. I loved Brown, too. That was what everyone called him. I learned his first name – Benjamin – only after I'd left the place. But I had never heard anyone call him anything but Brown both while there and thereafter.

Brown was a burly old man, whose shoulders and biceps had the kind of bulk and density that can come only from years of hard physical labor. He boasted an unkempt reddish beard with flecks of dirty blond and ash gray in the tangle, and he was devoted to whiskey the way I have become a missionary of meat.

We served Pappy Van Winkle long before it gained cult status. Brown, a true afficionado of bourbons, owned an impressive stock of pre-Sazerac distillations, and we sold this most prized, most rare of American whiskey for as much as $180 a shot. We served Willett before it became the consolation prize for *GQ*-reading yuppies who came to the Pappy-hysteria a bit too late. We even knew to serve Old Weller Antique, at a fraction of the cost of either your Pappy or your Willett, because that was where Julian 'Pappy' Van Winkle, the creator of the Van Winkle recipe, the closest thing to a Founding Father of American whiskey, got his start little more than a century ago. At least, that's the kind of thing Brown knew – and I started learning fast.

Brown's was also where I began my acquaintance with the types of people who made up this glorious city, or a certain swathe of them. The bar was a haven for low-grade film and music executives, fashion reporters and PR mavens. But we also got the occasional elderly neighborhood gentlemen, who had clung through the changes in this Lower East Side stretch. On certain days, tradesmen of different kinds popped in. Sometimes a corporate type with loosened tie paid us a visit. There were writers, a miserable lot. The gap between their self-estimation and the value the world placed on them made for hellish torment. Out of this ragtag crew, I liked best the paralegals, receptionists and copy editors. They lived two to a room in the outer reaches of Washington Heights or Flushing and popped in after work for a quick drink with friends. They seemed to be in New York because they wanted to be here. For them, the city was not a launchpad or networking site, a gateway to glory or a passage to fortune. For them, New York was the destination; simply to be here was the reward.

This I could relate to, and respect. I didn't care for the unearned smugness of native-born New Yorkers. It was a privilege to be here. I liked the quiet souls, mercifully free of anxious aspirations or jaunty boasts, who understood that. I shared the feeling, but unlike them I was not content to settle for access to the citadel. I knew already – even if it wasn't clear to me how – that I was here to storm the fortress.

CHAPTER 10

Adair and I sat huddled in my little stockade. We were not in a position to storm any fortresses. Hell, I don't think we were fit to bridge a moat. We were forced to play defense like untrained villagers guarding their little hamlet with rakes and shovels instead of real weapons.

Boris had sent word that he wanted the full amount by Labor Day. There was feedback from Viktor – our last glimmer of hope. But instead of discussing either Boris or Viktor, Adair and I sat in foul silence. A food inspector had chosen this day to pay us a visit. That the man had turned up within a week of the *New York* magazine piece was discomfiting, but 'bureaucracy doesn't move so quickly', I had assured Adair. If the powers-that-be had decided to probe us due to that article, it would not be a busybody from the city, but guys in dark glasses and black SUVs. I kept this thought to myself.

I had left the inspector in Patti and Kang's dubious care. Patti was under strict orders to keep Kang physically separated from the inspector at all times. Last time he had dinged the official with a head of cabbage. Kang insisted it was accidental, but we could not risk the repercussions of a second brassica-based assault on the inspector.

'How do you stay so calm?' Adair asked me.

'It's called numbing, I think,' I said wryly.

Adair rolled his eyes; stress affected his sense of humor. Whereas I relied on wit to cut the stress. And stress was the one thing that was now constant in my life. Even Helen, for so long an unwavering source of solace, had taken the *New York* magazine article badly. She didn't mind if I served exotic and even illicit fare, but she minded terribly that I was up to shenanigans that I didn't share with her. And because of her ire, she had packed up and left for her sister's. It had happened only the evening before, and even Adair didn't know. I informed him now, partly to give him a sense of the multidimensionality of stress I was facing.

'I'm sorry, man. That's really rough,' Adair said.

'Yeah, and for all my troubles there is now only one solution.'

'What's that?'

'Cash. Fast cash. And lots of it,' I said.

Adair laughed. And said, 'Isn't that the answer to all life's troubles? Exactly how much are we talking?'

Taking into account the accumulated interest and fines, we owed Boris $315k as of the first of May. I had used the windfall from the private dinners to reduce the debt to $250,000. That still-daunting amount was now due by Labor Day – and we were at the end of June.

'Then we need to make sure Yusep is on our side,' said Adair.

'Why wouldn't he be?'

Adair looked at me oddly. I'd never previously noticed how his face, the image of eternal optimism, was starting to show some fine lines. These lines were drawn not by time alone but by the late-youth realization of narrowing possibilities and mounting mistakes.

'Everyone's working an angle. Yusep will bat for us, if we offer him a cut,' Adair said.

'Oh, really? He'd sell the gig to someone for a pay-off?'

'Why not? What's the harm in it?'

'What if his uncle thinks we didn't do a good job?'

'Oh, he'll make sure we do. He'd not risk pushing anyone on his uncle who'd not meet the standards.'

'Still, he'd push someone for money? I thought he was devoted to his uncle!'

'No,' Adair said, a satisfied smile spreading across his visage. 'His uncle is devoted to him.'

'Damn!'

'He loves his uncle, don't get me wrong,' Adair continued. 'He'd never cause any real harm to the old boy, but he would not mind taking a gem or two from his Ali-Baba-like cave.'

The door of our de facto brig opened. The inspector was ready for us. I wasn't sure if we were ready for him, but Adair and I trudged up the abbreviated flight of stairs from our sub-basement to the dining room. The inspector was standing in the middle of the room, with an air of dyspeptic satisfaction that I felt was unique to critics. He was shaped like a short-necked soda bottle and swaddled in a cheap, pale green suit. He reminded me of the actor Paul Giamatti, if you can picture him drained of all personality.

'I'm Adair,' Adair said, as he approached the man. The two had not met before. 'Adair White, co-owner of The Hide.'

'Peter Boswell,' said Boswell with a pomposity typical of small men who took themselves more seriously than the world did. They shook hands but I noticed that Adair released the man's gerbil-like paw, small and wriggly, as if without any bones inside, well before it was courteous to do so.

Whenever I stood in the dining room, I felt I gained 360-degree vision. I could sense every little twitch in every corner of the room. Kang and Patti were a tense presence behind me.

'Mr Mirza, it pains me to say this,' Boswell said, 'but we need to make more of an effort in the kitchen.'

I kept calm. 'How so, Mr Boswell?'

This should be interesting, I thought. We had scored a B-grade on our first inspection. There had been a series of citations, mainly to do with how Kang's crew handled food – touching raw chicken before dishing a serving plate, stuffing prep ware and serving ware into the same drawers and failure to maintain proper HAACP logs. And of course, there was the big one, needlessly brought on by the cabbage assault: *Duties of an officer of the department interfered with or obstructed.*

The pettifogger started in on the new violations: 'Outer garment soiled with possible contaminant.' Meaning dirty aprons.

'As you know, you passed the last inspection conditionally. Failing a spot check now can be very injurious.'

Oh, how I'd love to show this little fucker what injurious looked like! I wondered if I could ask Boris for a favor once we were caught up on our payments.

Boswell screwed up his face as he looked up from his notes to deal the final blow, 'And facility not vermin-proof.'

Fuck me! Adair and I made eye contact.

'The exterminator was here . . .' I began to protest.

Adair interrupted. 'You will find everything rectified, totally tip-top next time, I promise.'

'I hope so, Mr White. Or we could be looking at a temporary shutdown even now.'

There are times when a person takes a sharp dislike towards another, and there is nothing anyone can do about it. I felt that was the case between Boswell and myself. The problem was that he held all the power. Malice without power I could live with. But I feared nothing more than when the two came together, as they had with Boris. That fear curdled into hate, which palpitated nowadays in my veins with the feral energy of a cornered animal.

'Oh dear, that'd be awful,' said Adair, in his most ingratiating voice. He was well briefed on our history with the inspector. It was gallant of him to try to deploy his charm against such an impregnable specimen.

'You see, the individual errors could be pardoned, but it's the pattern that's concerning.'

The pattern! Motherfucker, you are the one creating the pattern. The city's supposed to inspect 25,000 joints per year. There's no time to visit anyone more than once a year, if that. We were on our second visit already.

'Ah, I hate bad patterns too, Peter.' Having established a first-name basis, Adair moved in. 'I fell into a pattern in school. I just couldn't focus, you know, in class. All lectures were a drone. All exercises dull as Sunday church. What's a kid to do? I read my own stuff between the covers of schoolbooks. And I talked. I mean talked back to the teachers . . .'

If anyone could strike up a rapport with Boswell, it'd be Adair. He always managed to talk himself out of speeding tickets. No one could say no to him. That was his gift; an ability and willingness to relate to the most distant sensibilities. And his soliloquies had a strange quality of being part stream of consciousness and partly a sequence of abrupt syllogisms that left little room for his prey to get a word in sideways.

I closed my eyes for a second and enjoyed the silky feel of a knife slicing into Boswell's soft gut. As Adair took charge of the conversation, I stepped back. It made me doubt God that the instant we received our biggest chance – a final pitch for the Miner's Club – we were blighted with a visit from a dyspeptic officer of the law.

'. . . they'd give me detention. Like that did anything to dissuade me. You know, it made me cooler. Like these restaurants, you know those stickers out on the windows? With due respect, no one looks at them. It kills me to see how callous people can be. If they had any idea, what troubles you go to . . .'

Adair's voice pulled me out of my reverie. He was on such a roll that even the inspector was thrown off his stride.

'I see how hard you try,' Adair was saying. 'We try, too, but those morons out there . . . they don't care about their own health, own life. Or anyone else's.

'How long's the commute, tell me, please . . . Goddamn, really? And, what's it now, six o'clock already . . . and, what? You're not married? You're kidding me . . . you look like such a dad, like the kind of guy who'd be coaching baseball on weekends or go fly-fishing.'

I knew Adair had no idea what the hell fly-fishing was.

Before long, he had squired the inspector over to a table – 'C'mon, it's after hours, you can have a Scotch now' – waving two fingers at Patti. I was mercifully left out of the count.

'So, tell us, what's the worst you've ever seen?'

'A rat in the freezer! Just last week,' Boswell said, loosening his egregious tie. What's with bureaucrats and the sheer god-awfulness of their ties?

'A live one?'

'Yes, one of the busboys spotted the rat and couldn't go past me to chuck it outside, so he stuffed it into the freezer, with block-frozen shrimp and an assortment of other kinds of fish.'

It was time to open for the evening, even with Adair still whispering sweet nothings into Boswell's ear. Kang had shuffled back to his kitchen. Patti manned the bar, so to speak. The clammy heat of New York's summer daytime gave way to the cooler early evening, with a faint breeze easing its way through the streets.

The first customer was a senior gentleman who always wore a beret and dined alone. Then came the first of the young crew, the ones still with a job and ready to drink to their good fortune. A big-shouldered blond guy and a thin-faced thinker, a folded coat on his arms. And a young lady with them, tumbling forward in her white dress, bright with laughter, perhaps at a joke by one of the blokes, or lifted by the knowledge that she possessed the one great treasure that even New York in its infinite jadedness could never disdain: youth.

Boswell ended up leaving without issuing us any new points. He took Adair's card, and Adair invited him to a private viewing of medieval manuscripts at the Morgan Library. Trust that to be Boswell's thing; illuminated manuscripts made by Middle Age monks. And trust Adair to ferret out that information.

Adair and I stood at the door, watching Boswell slither down Houston toward another evening of the solitude that sustained his surly misery.

'Done and dusted,' Adair said, with an air of well-earned satisfaction.

'See, I told you, it was just a routine visit.'

'And let's hope it stays that way.'

'We didn't finish talking about Viktor,' I said.

'I know, but gotta run now, buddy,' Adair said, putting an apologetic hand on his chest. 'I'll call you.'

Adair always had something to run to. I turned to go back in and noticed that the youngsters inside were being joined by more of their friends. We were busier this evening than we had been in some time at this hour, and that pleased me. Even the asphalt gray sky, with its violet and sapphire, felt oddly auspicious. Inside, I saw young diners in warm, mirthful huddles, not a care in the world, it seemed. Their laughter was unweighted by any worries. Hair tossed back, chinks of raised glasses, the shine of perfect teeth. Oh, how wonderful it was to be so young! I watched the diners and their apparent zest for life, or simply their evening, with an unexpected envy, and realized for the first time that I was no longer one of them.

CHAPTER 11

It was the first time since we began dating that Helen and I were spending Fourth of July apart. The night the *New York* magazine article went viral, Helen and I got into an argument that I thought was silly at first but that somehow spun out of control.

'What the fuck, Kash?'

'We are famous!' I had joked, as I shed my work clothes.

'It's not funny,' Helen said. 'Have you been selling crap that I don't know about?'

'Babes,' I said. I was tempted to take umbrage at accusations of secrecy, if not chicanery, but I had been keeping stuff from her; namely, the full extent of the threats we faced from Boris.

'You know,' she said, 'the one thing I've asked of you, is don't keep shit from me.'

She was right. Despite her involvement at The Hide, she was very client-focused. She didn't come along when we catered private dinners – and wasn't privy to the secret of all the items on the menu. I had been keeping things from her, again. And it made me defensive. And she sensed it, no doubt, growing more inquisitive, indeed interrogatory. And that made me feel more guarded.

'Why are you doubting me?' I shouted back. 'Why are you not on my side?'

'Fuck, Kash! You think I'm not on your side?'

It was the kind of argument which pivots on a faulty premise and thus holds no easy resolution. Both parties are correct in their arguments as they have conceived the premise. And as they talk past each other, the aggravation only intensifies.

'Call me when you're ready to talk for real,' she had said when she left.

I stayed silent. I was clearly not ready. The look on her face as she shook her head was one of pure disappointment. What I most feared, most wished to avoid – her disapproval, I had managed to incur. And even as it unfolded before me, I felt powerless to arrest its fatal uncurling. And I was on my own.

I was invited to Mrs Zaman's. Instead of barbecue, I'd have to mark the day with biriyani. It could have been worse. Mrs Zaman had bought a new house, a lovely two-story affair in Woodside. The celebrations would double up as a housewarming. I stopped by the Crate and Barrel on Houston Street and bought a pair of Laurel Lamps. Not mid-century originals, of course, which were well out of my range, but handsome black, wooden, retro replicas.

Once I got there, I found a group of Bangladeshi men engaged in loud and passionate debate over, what else, but politics. To argue heatedly over matters over which they had no control was the national blood sport. There was also no species other than Bengali men who could get into a state of vein-popping frenzy over a beverage as anodyne as tea.

Mrs Zaman greeted me with a beaming smile. I noticed

that her dyed black hair was showing more whites in the roots than in the past.

'I'll get you a whiskey. On the rocks, right?'

That was what made Mrs Zaman unique. She would freely serve booze where many Bengali households, especially ones belonging to a single woman, an elderly one at that, abjured such luxuries with a horror. It was a sin, but just as strong was the fear of being judged by one's compatriots. Mrs Zaman was beyond judgment by anyone else, or free of such fears. She didn't drink alcohol herself ('makes me gassy,' she said), but was punctilious about indulging her guests. A Muslim of an older vintage; non-judgy and wedded to a private and mystic code of good and evil.

The assembled men were fawning over the guest of honor: a cabinet minister from back home. I recalled him being a minor figure of major disrepute back in the day, but time had been kind, and he was now a major enough figure that his trespasses were regarded as mere bagatelles. That realignment was amply displayed in his personal effects: gold chain, gold watch and, of course, a golden tooth.

By the time I found a seat in this circle of men – the women were tucked away in an inside room, in a classic Desi separation of the sexes – they had shifted to a crowd favorite of Desis: American peculiarities.

'Brother, I never knew dogs needed shampoo! We used the same soap for our head and body – and even laundry!'

The minister chuckled. He occupied a single seat of a paired set. In the other sat a fair man with a sharp glint in his eyes who said nothing. He was familiar, although I couldn't initially work out why. He observed the proceedings with an amused smile.

'Oh, don't speak of manners, these people have no manners,' said yet another pundit.

'Especially the blacks, they're so rude.'

I grew tense, fearing where the conversation was headed. As if on cue, the minister started the wind-up for the fatal delivery. 'It's a great country,' he sighed, 'but their real problem is with . . .' and before anyone could deflect or interrupt his observation as a dispassionate outsider, he landed on the N-word.

Samad entered at this moment and froze.

I took a long draught of my drink: Glenfiddich 15 years, a perfectly respectable single malt.

The ribbing of the host nation that many immigrants liked to indulge in was a pet peeve of mine. I understood that for many of them it was mainly a way to even out the feelings of demotion or slight that resulted from their precarious footing in the new society. The fact that these ingrates were doing it on the Fourth of July was more than I could stand.

'That's not a word anyone uses here anymore. It's considered very rude, very prejudiced.'

The room stiffened. Our ministers were not used to being corrected. Thankfully, I was no longer tethered to the finely graded pecking order of patronage that ruled all lives back home, and thus didn't give a shit if a minister felt offended by something I said.

'Is that so? Isn't that the scientific term for their race?' the minister asked, more out of genuine curiosity than anything else.

The mood in the room was balanced precariously between competing loyalties: keep sucking up to the minister and roll with his relatively innocent, as in uninformed, racism, or be true to one's new affiliations and stick up for its putative ethics.

'Actually, it isn't. It's considered offensive. It's a term that was once used to denigrate them. So, no one uses it anymore.'

'They call themselves that,' said one of the suck-ups. 'All their songs are full of N****r-this and N****r-that, and also Fuck-this and Fuck-that,' he said, and looked to his mates for approval.

'Yes, they have no respect for anyone, not even themselves,' piped up another pillar of this sub-community.

I scanned the council for someone to back me up. There was nothing from Samad. Even Mrs Zaman, usually quick and sharp with her rebukes, maintained a studious neutrality.

'I can't believe what I'm hearing, brothers,' I said, trying to keep the tone amicable. 'If there were any white people here right now, they'd be scandalized. You all know that, right?'

There was no give. Only the man next to the minister, sharply dressed in tailored blue blazer and gray slacks, shifted in his seat, and said, 'Let's face it, if there were any black men here right now, none of you would feel so free to use the N-word. If you know not to do it to their face, why do it behind their backs?'

I realized then that this was the famed importer Askari. The man was a legend in the small community of Bangladeshi businessmen. And it was pure instinct on my part that informed me, as he gave me a wink, that he was the famed importer that I had been meaning to connect with for some time. I wasn't sure why or when I'd need him, but it would be wise to keep a resource like Askari on standby. I had an inkling – or foreboding – that at some point soon I might have to lean on my Desi brethren. I felt I could still call on them for support, especially as we trod into grayer zones, in a way I could not with my new countrymen.

Of course, when I say 'Desi', I'm purloining a Hindi term that encompasses affinities spanning the Indian subcontinent. For my band of Bangladeshi brothers, the Bengali term '*deshi bhai*' would be more apt. But one of the effects of diasporic displacement – and new belongings – is the adoption of more fluid boundaries, and bonding.

What's more, there also existed an unsaid but unassailable code that we came to each other's aid, no matter what. It also hit me that I could ask Samad to do something risky or illicit for me – whether he said yes or no – in a way that I still could not ask of Adair.

'You know a lot about America, it seems,' the politician said to me, appreciatively.

The statement pulled me out of my ruminations. Clearly, the man was looking for a way to disperse the tension in the room, and for this I had to admire him: you don't get to be in his position if you don't know how to pick your fights and disarm your critics.

'I've been here long enough,' I said, amicably. 'It pays to know and respect the customs of the place where you live.'

'Wise. What do you do?'

'I own a restaurant in Manhattan.'

'Indian food? Or do you actually call it Bangladeshi?'

The minister had a twinkle in his eyes. He knew that Bangladeshis running 'Indian' joints were increasingly a sore point for many Bengalis who felt their ethnic identity should be flashed on the signboards.

'Neither, sir,' I said. 'We serve wild game.'

The politician stared at me with a frozen smile of incomprehension.

'He's done well,' piped up one of the suck-ups, changing his tune. 'He's always mixing with celebrities.'

Apparently, puffing up my credentials before the minister would somehow lift the rating of the gathering, or so I surmised was the motive behind this sudden approbation.

'Good, good,' the minister said, turning to the wider circle. 'The young are more in tune with the culture. We should listen to them when it comes to new mores.'

My glass was empty, so I slid off into the corridor where Mrs Zaman had set up the little bar. The mention of The Hide had filled me with sudden dread. Usually, it'd be a source of pride, but today was the deadline to give Boris $50k. I had managed to scour up only $35k. I hoped that meeting most of the demand would hold him at bay.

Samad had followed me to the makeshift bar.

'That was badass,' he said, as I refilled my glass.

'Fuck lotta help you were, you chicken-shit,' I said, still high on adrenaline from the exchange.

Samad grinned as if to say, Guilty as charged. Still, I began to pour him a drink and he put up a hand and said, 'Sorry, I'm driving.'

'Fuck that,' I said, and finished pouring the second glass, also for myself.

By the time lunch was served I'd drained several more glasses. The spread could not be farther from traditional July Fourth fare, but it was enough to fill me with a sense of deep satisfaction, especially on top of the whiskey in my belly. I piled my plate with succulent pieces of lamb, rice and – the best part – the potatoes oozing all the flavors of the ingredients that went into the making of this king of dishes.

After lunch a group of us, the old crew, gathered on the tiny patio in the back. As we sat reminiscing on our harsh early days, now a source of forgiving wonder and chuckles, Mrs Zaman ushered in the most venerable member of our community from those days: Dr Hazari.

Dr Hazari was our go-to guy back when we had no health insurance. He had moved to the new country too late in his years to get properly re-certified for this market, but he ran a solid sideline for us new arrivals and sundry illegals, not just from Bangladesh. Given a sizable group of Desis, you can always count on enough indigestion and weird dermatological eruptions to keep any doctor busy. His hair was white by now, and his skin seemed to hang more loosely off his frame, especially on his jowls and his forearms, but beneath those vestiges of time, he seemed firm-footed and alert as ever.

'So, you're a big shot in Manhattan now, Kash?' he asked with a glint in his eyes that was full of approving affection – not challenge, nor malice.

'Oh, I wouldn't say that. Just trying to get established,' I said.

Samad had gotten up to offer Dr Hazari the most comfortable chair.

'He's being modest,' Samad said. 'He's pals with millionaires and billionaires!'

'Didn't Derek Jeter come to your place once?'

'I heard Reese Witherspoon came there too!'

The enthusiasm of the old homeboys was touching even if it touched a raw nerve. But it was good to know that there was a strange pocket of resources that I could dip into, in extremis. The problem with reaching extremis is that it doesn't always arrive as one fell blow; it can sneak up on you and by the time you recognize your troubles, it's too late!

A swell of summer clouds moved in overhead, cutting the glare of the sun and cooling the smarting from the heat. A stillness took hold of the moment. I felt I'd been here before – or would be again. Like a déjà vu of the future.

I was not the only one who had done well, at least as far as these well-wishers could see. To my surprise, several of the boys with whom I had camped in my earliest days had found positions far above where they had started. One was an area manager for Subway. Another was a certified pharmacist. Even the boy whom we treated as the 'house idiot' in our first days was now a salesclerk at Macy's.

While these old mates looked at me with a mixture of envy and admiration, I was secretly wishing that I had stuck to some simple paths like them.

Perhaps my hidden sorrow didn't escape the old doctor, who suddenly turned to me to say, 'Be proud, young man.' Then with the slightest pause, he added, 'But don't be reckless.'

I looked at the old doctor. He stared back with an arresting stillness in his hooded eyes. His face was all smiles, but his gaze felt serious and portentous. As if he could see into me, or my future. Perhaps it was the whiskey. I had lost count of how many glasses I had drunk by then. But even apart from any distortions created by the alcohol, I knew Dr Hazari's glance was conveying something more than ordinary. I had never seen him as a prognosticator of fates, but his pronouncement today, even on a summer's day, sent a chill down my spine.

After lunch, Samad drove me back to Manhattan, in a black Town Car for his job. He was heading into the city as it was, and I felt that this was a safer passage, in my state, than traveling by subway and on foot. As we crossed the East River, vessels bobbing in the distance like little toy boats, Samad spoke up.

'What's with you?'

'Whaddya mean?'

'You are glum, tense, irritable – and drinking way too much.'

Samad was right. Crossing the 59th Street Bridge always called to my mind the eponymous song by Simon and Garfunkel. But my mood could not be farther from the one expressed in the gentle duo's lilting lyrics. I wasn't exactly loving life lately. And I sure as hell wasn't 'feelin' groovy'. So, my response to Samad's concern also came out sounding irascible.

'Are you my mom or my girlfriend?'

'Don't be a cunt, Kash,' Samad said. 'Something's up.'

'I owe money to some bad dudes.'

'Hmm. How bad?'

'Russian.'

'Faaaaaack.'

The next question he asked was uttered in a soft and almost somber tone; the way one might enquire of a cancer patient the exact nature of their affliction.

'How much?'

'Six digits,' I said, without specifying the actual amount.

And Samad honked loudly and held it for a while. For a second, I thought it was in reaction to my debt amount, but he was warning off a lousy lane-changer.

Samad whistled. And then followed a long litany of expletives, 'Fuck, fuck, fuck, fuck.'

'Thanks,' I said.

It was payday for Boris and I had left a packet with Patti. She had the guts – and the heart – to accept a task like handing an envelope, not as thick as it ought to be – to a character like Snake Eyes. She and I both felt, though, that Snake Eyes would not pick a quarrel with her. He would wait till he saw me again.

It had come to us recently that he wasn't actually part of the Russian Mob. Not that the Russian Mob, even in the Tri-state area, was a monolith. What's more, it was hinted that he might not even be Russian! One source said he was Ukrainian. Another, more startlingly, suggested that he might actually be ethnic Polish! If any of that were true, then did he pose as much threat as he pretended to?

'You have a plan?' Samad had asked me as we slid into early evening traffic. I liked this hour in New York; the warm lights at street level and the shafts of white and blue lights that came down from the sky to illuminate the buildings.

'I do, but as with all plans, it's a race against time.'

Samad nodded in silence, in sympathy. When he dropped me off, he said, 'If I can do anything—'

'I know,' I said, without letting him finish.

Once I got home, I barricaded the door with a clutter of furniture. Good thing Helen wasn't home. It would be too embarrassing to take such measures in the presence of anyone else, even her. As I crashed on our living-room sofa, my thoughts passed from Boris to Helen and what I was at risk of losing with her. I knew I wasn't handling things right. I once again blamed the meager nature of my education for my incompetence in this aspect of my life.

A romantic – and sexual – education, which had begun with the betrayal by Rubina the maid, didn't get much better with subsequent episodes. After that shock, I was sure that no female sympathy could ever reach the wretched recesses of my dark retreat.

These 'never ever' notions of early youth were cured in time, of course. In college I dated a girl who worked part-time as a 'composer'. Not of music. Back then, Bangla newspapers needed specialized typists who could handle an alphabet consisting of eleven vowels and thirty-four consonants, and joint-letter permutations running into the hundreds, on a QWERTY keyboard. She was sweet-natured, and we connected over our love of West Bengali novels, and even went to see theater on Bailey Road. There was no one in my orbit growing up who shared such interests. I kept them well hidden for fear of being laughed off. But she was prudish, like many middle-class girls of Dhaka, at least at that time. Or maybe it was just my luck – or my inability to attract her in that manner. Whatever the reason, even after a year of courtship, she refused to let me close the deal. Because of our different expectations, the affair fizzled; she wanted a ring, and I wasn't ready.

In the end, I graduated to carnal knowledge courtesy of a married woman who lived across the street. I was out of college and had just started working with my brother. She had hired me as an English tutor, having hopes – like so many of us did in the mid-1990s – of winning the DV. Our lessons in conversational English soon turned flirty. To me she was an 'older' woman, but I now realize that she must have been only in her mid-thirties, quite comely in appearance. Not exactly what most young men would consider hot – not Coke-bottle figure or overly sensuous lips or mane-like hair. She was slim, impassive-faced, but possessed a stunning burnished-wood color of skin and beautiful long fingers. Above all, she was the first woman whose body I had full access to, and for me that was aphrodisiac enough. As she became more flirtatious with me, she would ask me about my love life, what kind of girls I liked. And then one day she simply put her hand on my cock. After that first time, brief and clumsy on my part, we set a protocol: a mid-afternoon phone call cut off abruptly with no words was my signal to cross the road to her house. If the composer had been all emo, then this barracuda was pure mechanics. I couldn't complain. To finally experience the engage-all-senses thrill of sexual pleasure and the annihilating whiteness of climax, I couldn't get enough of it.

One time, once I pulled out, still quite hard, she held my cock as if weighing a ripe fruit and said, 'Go wherever this takes you.' I had no idea what she meant and, to be honest, I still don't.

I share this sordid and pitiful history by way of explaining my ineptitude with Helen. Training matters, experience matters. So does instinct. When it came to women though, I didn't trust my instincts, so faced with the predicament with Helen, I asked Adair for advice. 'Just go, man,' he had said. 'Go to her.'

When I first met Helen, I had already left Brown's, and was

busier than ever. I had gone to work for a Japanese maverick intent on shaking up the bourbon scene. My new boss was on a mission to democratize the experience of whiskey. I was hired as a salesman going door-to-door with our unique proposition up and down the Eastern corridor. By the end I was making trips out to DC and Atlanta, Providence and Cleveland. I loved stuffing the trunk of rented American cars and hitting the Great American highway.

I excelled at selling, and soon felt confident enough to pitch a new idea of branding and marketing to my boss. I thought that whiskey was seen to be too strong or too stuffy. There was a class of people – especially among the young – who would shuffle vodka, gin, rum and tequila, but never turn to whiskey.

'So, what's the idea? How do we get them?'

'Lose all arcana, lose the pretense. Make it about the customer – tell them what whiskey can do for them: deliver them to a state of bliss faster than beer or even other hard stuff.'

We would run ads showing construction hunks with the tagline, Everyone Gets It. Harried moms: Everyone Needs It. Off-duty cops: Everyone Packs It.

'But it's the youth we want to get?'

'Yes,' I said. 'But market it as something anyone can enjoy and shed the intimidation factor. Besides, we can shed the whole ageing aspect and focus on flavor profiles. It'll give us more latitude, a broader supply source with better costing, and blends geared to the average or starter palates.'

While I was hired for sales, it didn't take long for me to become the number one Whiskey and Customer-Experience whisperer to my Japanese boss. Funny that he relied on an immigrant, a Bangladeshi at that, for insights into American culture. If I take that as a compliment about my talents, at least half the credit goes to American culture itself and its immense accessibility. There's a kind of outsider who likes to think, churlishly, that American culture has no depth or complexity. Not only are they wrong, but what they see as a deficiency is the true strength of American culture: infinite malleability, endless reinvention and equal accessibility to all who'd take an interest.

I helped design a series of ads based only on images of our models holding the bottle and a one-word caption: Everyone.

Helen was one of our first models. From the first time I saw her photos, sent by the ad agency, I was transfixed. She was tall and svelte, but not starvation-thin like most of the other girls. She was also prone to an affectless self-presentation, again uncommon for the trade, which made her stand out among the regulation beauties. She embodied a kind of realness that might usually prevent advancing too far in the modeling world; but she was just right for our branding needs. She seemed not only approachable but exerted an irresistible pull on me from my first sighting of her image. I felt overcome with an urge to meet her.

I admit it was a little creepy to use the ad agency as a dating service, but I told them I wanted to be present at the shoot. It took place at a studio in Fort Greene, still not a fully gentrified part of Brooklyn in the mid-2000s. We were finished by mid-afternoon. Helen lived out in the far end of Queens, Kew Gardens, but she needed to go into the city, she said, so I invited her to a late lunch at the Cornelia Street Café. To my great joy and mild surprise, she said 'yes'. We shared a bottle of icy muscadet and ate plump mussels that came pooled in a garlic and shallot broth.

I confessed my ploy to meet her much later, once we started dating. She laughed. 'You weren't the first creepy exec to show up for a shoot. I always took a lunch off them if they seemed harmless.'

I didn't know what to do with a girl like Helen. As it turned out, she didn't want to be swept off her feet. She was done with men with smooth moves.

'Look, men – and I mean men, not boys – have hit on me since I was fourteen. My stepfather's friends. Shopkeepers. Teachers. My first was a guy twelve years older than me, and I was only sixteen.' I winced at this detail; some prudery carried over from my Bengali culture, and an inexplicable tenderness for a girl who was still a stranger, sparked a shot of rage. She must have seen it in my eyes, and said with a laugh, 'It's fine, he was actually really nice to me.'

She went on to tell me how she was not one to be impressed by any 'moves' that any guy, no matter how rich or how handsome, could pull. She too – like American culture in the first flush of a new millennia, and perhaps in matters of the heart, like people always and everywhere – was on the lookout for something authentic. And my naivety, apparent to a seasoned operator like her, held out a promise of freshness, innocence, genuineness. She didn't say any of this to me explicitly, but I surmised it from her mere willingness to keep seeing me.

She told me how she had grown up in a small town outside Westchester which, for all its proximity to New York City, could not be farther away in its character. She had one sister. Her father was a deadbeat who walked out when she was nine and drifted ever westwards. First, he stopped sending money, and then started forgetting her birthday. The stepfather was a decent guy. He was a hunter who, given the incorrigibly feminine nature of Helen's sister, decided to make a 'man' out of Helen. She learned how to drive a truck, throw a ball, shoot at ducks and deer and even to drain the blood out of a fresh kill.

'Mostly we slaughtered chickens,' she told me.

'Me too,' I had replied. 'Wrestling a bull, though, that's something else.' There wasn't much by way of practical skills which I could hold over her, so I made the most of the sacrificial rituals of my early years. Despite growing up worlds apart and with vastly different realities, there was some odd affinity that bound us.

Or that's what I had to hope as I drove out to Westchester, following Adair's advice. Go to her. When they won't take or return your calls, you have to turn up. I had asked Chris if I could borrow the green Duster again. I had sent him a fine bottle of bourbon after the peacock trip and was willing to reward him more lavishly, especially if this trip proved a success. If the peacock trip was made in a spirit of adventure, this time I was driving out of desperation.

I arrived at Helen's sister's place in Westchester in the middle of the afternoon. Helen's sister Miranda lived in a lovely two-story stone-and-brick house with a chimney and slate-colored shingles. I rang the bell and waited. And waited. It was too late for lunch, but they could be out shopping or whatever people do on Sundays in the suburbs. I rang the bell again. This time, no sooner had I let the button go than the door opened: it was Helen.

She stared at me. I couldn't gauge if it was a pleasant or unpleasant surprise. But my heart leaped at the sight of her. Even dressed in a simple white linen blouse and well-washed blue jeans, she was stunning. How was this my girlfriend, and how had I done anything to risk losing her?

She stood with her arms crossed over her chest. There were going to be no hugs. That was expected. I could see the tension in her as she debated whether to let me in. Eventually, she turned and went inside but left the door ajar. Progress.

I followed her into the living room. The house reeked of a stolid complacency. Everything was common and well-worn. There was no effort at style. The wall-to-wall carpet in the living area was gray and woolly. A scent of house pets and baby lotions permeated the air. I felt some soft toy crush under my feet.

'It took you a while,' Helen said as she sat in the farthest corner of a sofa, away from me. I sat on a single sofa, leaning forward, tapping the tips of my fingers nervously.

'I'm sorry. I thought you were mad.'

'I am.' She could not help suppressing the tiniest trace of a smile. Knowing she was mad was not a good reason to stay away, and my frank admission reminded her of my ineptitude in relationships.

I took a breath, 'I know I fucked up.'

'Do you?'

'It was stupid not to tell you everything. I should have.'

Helen took in my remorse. She was sitting closer to the window and her hair shimmered golden in the light streaming in. Her blue eyes had never looked so cool, so far away.

'I know,' I said, daring to move over to Helen's sofa. But sitting at the other end. 'I'm so sorry. Things just kept getting out of hand. I was ashamed that I was in such difficulties. I felt like a failure. I never wanted you to see me like that.'

'You fucking idiot! I don't care if you succeed. I mean I *do*, but I don't judge you for it. I don't love you for it.'

What did she love me for? It didn't seem like the moment to ask. I could think of nothing but my super-toned leanness, knife-sharp jawline and an undaunted will to succeed. But all that sounded like good qualities for a fashion model or personal security than for a life partner.

She seemed to be holding her breath, almost as if to restrain an outburst. Her face looked pale and drawn, and her nose reddened with held-back emotion. It quivered ever so slightly, but the twitch was made more prominent by its little crooked slant to a side. Yet, the more I looked at her, the more I knew I needed her.

'I know, I know, I know,' I said, reaching forward. I tried to take her hand, but she pulled away. I drew back to a boundary of penitence, and she clasped her hands between her knees.

'Do you know what worries me, Kash?'

'What?' I asked, dreading the response.

'The fact that you didn't know in the first place that you should tell me everything. That you *could* tell me everything. Who do you think I am? What am I to you?'

'Everything,' I said.

I had never said that to anyone before. I knew I had never felt that way about anyone before.

She sighed.

'I don't know how to be in a relationship,' I continued to explain. 'I fucked up because I don't know that. It's not because you're not important to me. I have never loved anyone more. I can't imagine going on without you.'

She tilted her head to one side, as if assessing me.

'Do you know what that means?' she said, her voice softening.

'I do now. I do,' I said.

A car rolled up the driveway. It was her sister, Miranda. She entered the house with a small bundle of a baby in one arm and a tangle of bags in the other. The baby wore a blue hat. Miranda wore an angry face – at the sight of me. She was younger than Helen but looked older. I jumped up to get the bags, but the look she cast me: I had never seen so much contempt and disapproval in a single glance.

'It's okay, I've got it,' Miranda said shortly, as she hurried towards the kitchen.

Helen stayed where she was. I moved back to her sofa and tried again to take her hand. This time she accepted.

'I am so sorry, babe. Really, really sorry. I honestly thought that this was all my shit, and I shouldn't burden you with it.'

'You stupid man,' Helen said, reaching to touch my face.

Her fingers felt cool on my unshaven cheek. I closed my eyes. I wanted that touch to stay with me forever. It transported me to some fairytale castle in the Arctic wilds, far away from my troubles.

'So, you will come back?'

'Not right now,' Helen said. 'I want to know everything. I need you to make me a real part of your plans. Share everything, let me actually help you.'

'Now? You want me to go into everything right now?'

'No, not right now,' said Helen with a smile. 'Miranda needs me here for a couple more days. New baby, you know.'

'Okay,' I said. 'So, you'll be back, soon?'

'I'll come back soon. Your shit is my shit, okay?'

'I am your shit,' I concurred.

This made her laugh. 'Yes, you are, you piece of shit.'

With that parting assurance, I revved up the Duster and drove off. Helen stood on the doorstep and waved at me. She was a vision of hope. I just couldn't tell if it was retreating or advancing.

CHAPTER 12

That night, after I visited Helen, I went to The Hide and stayed until closing time. It was a good night. A large group of Japanese businessmen descended on us for some big company knees-up. Expense accounts were our best clients. Between elk steak and several bottles of Old Fitzgerald, they rang it up into the five digits. Still, a night like this, I recognized ruefully, wouldn't be enough to raise the full amount due to Boris. Indeed, even a steady stream of nights like this would not be enough, given the tight deadline. Still, as I helped with closing up and walked out with Patti to the F-train stop at the corner of Fourth Street and Sixth Avenue, I felt a spring in my step. No doubt my buoyant spirit stemmed in part from my reconciliation with Helen.

'Just don't fuck up again, Kash,' Patti said. 'You won't find another like her.'

I heard what she said. I wondered if what she really meant was: You don't deserve a girl like Helen. If that was the subtext, I could hardly be offended. She was right. I nodded at Patti to express my assent and future compliance. On bidding her farewell, I decided to take a detour. It felt like a night for walking. I went up Bleecker all the way into the Meatpacking District. I wanted to get a whiff of the salty air of the Hudson. And it was my favorite route, along the river and down to Battery Park. Once I reached TriBeCa, I paused, thinking to turn back. Part of me felt an impulse to call up Adair and see if he might be up for a drink. Before I could make up my mind, I felt two strong arms grip me on both sides and a big palm pressed tightly over my mouth. My feet lifted off the pavement. Within moments I was inside a black minivan. The door slammed shut. The vehicle rolled off smoothly. No hurry, no screeching. Part of my brain marveled at the efficiency of it all. I was laid flat on the floor and pushed down by several heavy feet, and before I could protest, my mouth was plastered with tape and my hands were tied tightly behind my back with what felt like nylon rope.

It had been three days since the Fourth of July. This was the reckoning. The van drove for a few minutes and pulled up. I was bundled out with the same efficiency.

'Sit,' said one of the Russians, as I was ushered into a small eat-in kitchen and pushed into an armless dining chair. The place smelled like a laundry basket. The tape was pulled off my mouth.

My old friend Snake Eyes took up the seat across the small Formica dining table.

'Boris give you many chances.'

This was not something I could dispute. I scanned the room like a cornered animal. I noticed an electric kettle on the kitchen counter, but no other signs of regular habitation. There was also a solitary apple sitting inside a bowl, making it seem like the saddest object ever for a still life.

'I have been paying,' I squeaked.

'Boris say, you insult him.'

'C'mon! How? I fell short, I admit. But there was no disrespect.'

'You give money, not enough, and you're not even there to do it yourself? Or to write a note saying you're sorry?'

Christ! Was this about etiquette now?

'Boris done,' Snake Eyes said casually. There was an insouciance in his tone that hadn't been there before. It wasn't good news. I needed to find new grounds for negotiation.

'I'm onto something big,' I said. 'Viktor Karakozov.'

'Never heard of him,' said Snake Eyes, overturning his lower lip in disdain.

Fair enough. The Russians had minted so many billionaires in the roaring Nineties that no one had heard of them unless they made a big splash in the West. Viktor wasn't even Russian. And technically not a billionaire.

'He owns his own plane.'

I needed to keep him engaged. There was a magic in private jets, the mere mention of which always got people to take an interest.

'And what he do for us?'

'I'll tell you, mate. I'll tell you everything. But could you untie my hands please?'

Snake Eyes shrugged, as if to say he didn't care either way. He said something in Russian and one of his companions, a cruel-faced youngster I had not seen before, came around and undid the ropes binding my hands. I rubbed my badly chafed wrists and wondered why Gruff, Snake Eyes' perennial sidekick, hadn't shown his face yet. Then I heard a commotion in the next room, a sudden rise of foreign voices. I was no longer sure how many people were involved in this operation. Presently Boris entered the room.

'So, you are a storyteller? We bring you in for money, and you give us more stories?'

Clearly, he had heard my last statement. He lowered himself into a chair, though it seemed to be too small for his ample figure. He looked at me with the disdain of someone who had full power over another person and felt no discomfort about it. His skin was more mottled than I remembered. I wondered if he suffered from lupus. He rested one hand on the table; my cherished TAG Heuer fastened around his wrist. It didn't belong there. His hand sat like a giant red toad.

'It's not a story, it's true. Viktor owns his own plane! He's a Russian, but not from Russia. You will like meeting him.'

'What good that do for me? Will I get to ride in Viktor's plane?'

'Maybe! If you get to know Viktor well enough, sure, why not?'

I was willing to give away anything to get out of my present predicament. I was sure Viktor would understand – if I lived to tell the tale.

'I think you're yanking my chain, again. You think we are fools.'

'No!' My voice rose. 'Look Boris, I've said this before, and I'm saying it to you again: I am not going anywhere. You can get to me anytime. I'm not trying to be clever.'

If I understood one thing about Boris, and indeed about all men of power, it was that they hated to be thought of as fools. Criminals, especially ones running an organized outfit of any scale, possessed a highly developed sense of self-respect. I supposed, with no recourse to the law, they banked on reputation more than the rest of us.

'If business is still losing, how are you going to pay us back?'

'This is why doing the dinner for Viktor is so important!'

Snake Eyes said something in Russian. Everyone chortled. I had never noticed this before, but even in my distress it occurred to me that Russians laughed differently. I had never noticed that accents could seep into one's laugh. I wondered if our laugh sounded different to them. Theirs brimmed with a guttural thrust and, to my ears, sounded full of spite.

'How much can he pay for a single dinner? It's not making sense.'

As long as he was trying to understand me, I had hope. As I launched into a finer explanation of how Viktor could change all our fortunes, Boris muttered something and Snake Eyes passed the order to yet another guy, a younger one, part of the larger crew for this night's operation. The youngster moved toward the counter, presumably to put some tea on the boil.

I explained the Miner's Club, as briefly and clearly as I could. Boris perked up a little as I rattled off the names of more famous billionaires. Snake Eyes muttered dismissive remarks – I could tell from his tittering tone, and from the suppressed mirth it provoked in the other guys, who were crowding by the door.

'It's not just the dishes,' I added. 'If we are put in charge of the venue and other arrangements, it could be a lot more. We could rent a private island! Everything would have a charge and a cut for us.'

Even the other thugs grew quiet at the mention of an island. There was something powerful about the word 'private'. Attach it to any asset or service – banks, planes, viewing – and suddenly the value goes up exponentially in everyone's eyes, beyond the material cost price.

'And how much you make from all that?' Boris asked.

'Enough to pay you back in full, Boris.'

That was wildly hopeful. And Snake Eyes said so, finally in English, 'Bullshit.'

Boris barked a reproach. His interest was now piqued.

The youngster placed a mug of steaming tea in front of his boss. Even this minor luxury felt like an expression of Boris's supremacy over me. While I fretted for my life, he could sip a comforting beverage.

'You make a quarter million from one night? We should get into this business!'

The goons laughed. Boris took a noisy slurp of his tea. He stared at me with renewed curiosity, like a botanist examining a rare form of flora in a familiar patch of green.

'Let me explain,' I said and quickly enumerated the scale and nature of some of the previous dinners and the kind of costs that were involved. These were conjectures, but not too far off the mark.

'Besides,' I concluded, 'I have an inside line on this. Someone is helping me from within. We will get the gig.'

'Hah!' Snake Eyes said, with a wave of his arm. He launched into a diatribe. He seemed to burn with a fire that was beyond rage; something elemental, primal, harking back to ancient quarrels that were about to exert some decisive pressure on our present moment.

Boris looked at me with narrowing eyes. Snake Eyes came close to the table and stood by my side. One of the other boys began to move closer. I stiffened, sensing a verdict about to land.

'We think you are not serious, so we help you get serious.'

With this, Boris took a step back. In a flash the other guys were around the table. One of them took my left hand into a hard grip, while another grabbed me from behind and held me down in my seat. Snake Eyes snatched a knife that had been sitting on the counter, next to the bowl holding the apple.

'NO!' I shouted, as Snake Eyes lined up the edge of the knife along the joint of my left pinky finger.

I cast a wild-eyed glance at Boris, who stood aside – it seemed miles away – with a stiff grin on his face. Some desperate part of me wanted to believe that the whole thing was a show, to put real fright into me. That there would be a reprieve at the last second. Instead, I felt a sudden burning sensation tear through my body. My scream filled the room with glass-shattering shrillness, and then I felt a heavy hand on my mouth, and the sound turned to the muffled vibrations of a contained explosion. Before the voice came back inside me, for a second all I saw was blackness, and then the redness of a blooming sun behind my eyelids. The pain began to concentrate at the locus of its origin: the joint of my left pinky.

It felt hot and cold at the same time. A slimy wetness began to pool beneath my palm. Even after they loosened their grip on me, I felt various muscles across my body twitch in uncoordinated spasms. I could see my severed finger on the table. Snake Eyes left it there while he washed the knife over the kitchen sink. The digit appeared smaller than when it was attached to me; and a tiny hint of whiteness peeked from the center of the messy gash.

I didn't understand how we went from what felt like parlay to . . . this.

In my agony, I thought of what Patti had said. No one thinks it's going to go that far, *until it does*.

The men moved about with the composed quickness of medical staff in an operating theater. One guy held my wounded hand tightly in a dishrag, while Gruff – where the fuck did he come from? – fished about in the freezer. And Snake Eyes coolly wiped the table clean.

'Now you be serious,' Boris said as he turned and left.

Every cell in my being trembled in horror and protest and agony. I looked at the severed digit in disbelief: such a forlorn little object!

I didn't know what to say. My back felt damp with sweat, and my heart was still beating fast.

The youngster found a Ziploc bag and packed my finger inside it with ice.

'Take it home,' Snake Eyes said, sitting on the edge of the table. His killer's face was frozen in a rictus of sadistic contentment. Gruff had found some kind of disinfectant which he applied to my wound, and then made a tight tourniquet with a clean washrag. In all our interactions to date I'd have never bet on Gruff being the one with any iota of empathy.

I felt nauseous from the stink of my own sweat. And the sight of my own blood.

'Keep it tight,' Gruff said to me. 'It's important to stop the bleeding.'

The men consulted with one another for a few more minutes. The youngster brought me three Advils and a glass of tap water that I immediately gulped down.

As I drank, a strange equation flashed through my mind. A pinky finger weighed perhaps 2.5 ounces. If this was the price for $15k, the amount by which I was short on the last instalment, the day I went to Mrs Zaman's lunch, then what was the value of the whole of me? I weighed 155 pounds. I had always been good at mental arithmetic: if 2.5 ounces is worth $15k then 155 pounds amounted to a whopping $14.88 million! For one weird nano-second, I felt proud, and then deflated. I felt both worth a lot more and lot less than the estimated figure.

When we went down to the van, the youngster took the wheel. They didn't need to tie or restrain me this time. Out of pain and exhaustion, I completed the ride in the brace position.

When we reached my building, Snake Eyes slid the door open. As I stumbled into the thickness of the strangest night of my life, everything felt different. The steel shutters on the shopfronts, the diffusion of streetlight, the sound of soft music from the sushi joint next door. The seeming innocence of the night, of the world, revolted me.

Gruff walked with me to my door. And as I fumbled with my keys with my good hand, he said, 'Boris give you last chance. Don't fail. No more payments for now, but full amount on Labor Day.'

CHAPTER 13

Most people spend their lives with one purpose: not to get fucked. Little do they know that from the first thumps on their backs out of the birth canal, they are already doomed. The race that begins with the first taunts in school corridors is a great, heaving, heartbreaking sham; it's rigged, of course. Bludgeoned by nature, by inheritance, by demented parents and cruel teachers, fickle friends and cheating lovers, by the whimsies of sheer luck, timing, fate, the innocents hobble forward on crutches of hope. Many will be crushed as early as their youth, the rest subdued by middle age. An exasperated few will arrive at retirement homes full of spirited accounts about that one great missed chance, the one fatal mistake, the one biblical betrayal, which denied them fame, fortune or redemption. There is no hell like the long look back. There is no reprieve until the internal monologue of the bereaved is replaced by the merry sound of bird twitters while a cherub-faced nurse pushes them around on wheelies to water the rhododendrons.

But no one escapes getting fucked.

For me, the instructive event occurred just before I turned eleven. Back then we knew my father was a general manager, quite a respectable position in the corporate world of 1980s

Bangladesh, at a company that made batteries. We enjoyed watching their ads on TV. I have always liked TV people; they are all so senselessly happy. And we, too, felt as happy as the TV people for a change as we moved to Dhanmondi. It was the first planned, modern neighborhood of Dhaka, built in the 1950s when the country first became independent from the British, albeit under the aegis of Pakistan at that time. By the time we moved there, in the 1980s, it was the most prestigious neighborhood in all of the city. Ahead of more traditional areas like Wari or Bailey Road, and yet to be eclipsed by future diplomatic zones farther to the north. The new apartment was located in a compound with two buildings, both two-storied. We lived on the ground floor of the second one. The property and the neighborhood were a step up from our last abode, but the real reward for Hafeez and me were the other kids on our block. There were many of them, and they came out every afternoon to play. We played catch-catch or cricket with taped-up tennis balls. On weekend mornings we got pulled into street-wide hide-and-seek; we'd pop out of roofs or kitchen windows onto narrow ledges, climb into trees and disappear inside storm drains that wend along the streets, and emptied out on a little lake.

I asked my mother anxiously if we would be leaving this place soon, and she tried to ease my mind with kind words whose conviction was sapped by her weary smile. The threat of a fresh displacement was not the only source of anxiety in my small life. Our father's temper hovered over us every day like a black cloud ready to burst at the slightest provocation. My mother and Hafeez were resigned to the sudden outpouring of curses or beatings that were a frequent occurrence in our household. I was better at dodging. I could read my father's moods and wasn't content to surrender to fate. I had to get my own back. One of the methods I came up with as payback involved stealing money from his wallet – not for myself, although that happened, too, in undetectable amounts. Normally I'd stuff it somewhere else, say, within the pages of a book he had been reading or the pockets of pants he had thrown into the laundry. I would watch him fume and fulminate against the household, only to be shamefacedly confronted soon enough with the discovery of his own misplacement. There were countless other similar tricks with which I could disturb his daily peace, and that gave me satisfaction – one that I never shared, except with Hafeez. But there was an innate docility in Hafeez, or a submission to some higher principle of obedience that evaded me, that prevented him from deploying my tactics, with consistency or thoroughness, and left him exposed, to my chagrin, to more frequent abuse.

The basic meanness of the man showed in his temper and in his uncommon stinginess. One of our great sorrows at the time was that neither of us had a bicycle. On days when our neighborhood gang set off on their bikes, we could only hang back and watch. The shame of being so unequipped stung us as much as the tours we missed. In desperation, my brother borrowed the bike of a neighbor's cook to teach himself to ride. My father sat in the doorway cackling when Hafeez fell off the bike and scraped himself badly on the uneven brick surface of our compound. Hafeez tried to pick himself up with dignity and hide the tears of pain. He knew crying would only bring more scorn.

That night, after dinner, I overheard my mother asking

my father to reconsider the decision not to buy us bicycles. It was rare for her to challenge his decisions.

'Look at them,' I heard him say. 'They'll outgrow any bike I get them now in no time.'

'All their friends have bikes.'

'We don't have to spoil them just because other parents are idiots. Give it time; let them grow a bit more.'

My father was a constant source of denial and denigration, but he was not alone in his roughness. Our neighborhood, despite being at the heart of Dhaka, was full of the quarrelsome liveliness of a village. I learned early how shouting has many different characters. Spousal squabbles and a housewife berating a servant were easy to distinguish from other types of altercation. The quarrels of neighbors varied in tone and timbre depending on the topic. An argument over turf issues – branches of a tree reaching across the boundary wall or the length of clothesline on the roof allotted to each tenant – pulsed with a tempo that was different, say, from confrontations over misbehaving children.

In this context, one morning not long after the bike incident, I was awakened by a ruckus that didn't match any of the known sounds. What I heard was the low grumble of a vehicle, and my first thought was: It's the army!

That's what you think of, even as a child, when your country has experienced dozens of coups. I was too small when the bulk of the coups took place from the mid- to late Seventies, but their power to shock and to brutalize meant they cast a pall on the cultural memory strong enough even for kids to be aware of their possibility, their ability to erupt with no notice, and overturn prevailing order.

I sat upright in my bed and heard a rising hum of voices outside our house. Too many voices for our house, for the hour. The voices didn't rise in a steady crescendo, or stay sustained at a high level as they did with most discord. Even the occasional shouts didn't sound like a quarrel, but more like barked orders. I could pick out the sound of my father among the shouting, but it rang with an unusual, syncopated quality. There was a note of plea and submissiveness in my father's voice that I'd not heard before. Then I sensed a different kind of commotion – people moving, things moving.

Hafeez, too, was sitting up in bed by now. I shot him a look across the small distance between our beds, but he kept his head down. Unable to suppress my curiosity, I sprang out of the room and stopped short in the corridor when I saw several men, laborers with rolled sleeves and *lungis*, carrying the sofa from our living room out the front door.

I ran back to the room to fetch my brother. 'Hafeez, look, they're taking our things away!'

I was befuddled by this blatant robbery and that no one was trying to stop it. My brother looked at me with a mixture of pity and sorrow, as if to say, Oh, you fool, you still don't get what's happening!

I sprinted back outside, all the way to the front room, and saw that a mass of our furniture was already piled up in the courtyard. The dining table served as a platform for the TV and other smaller items. Next to it were a cupboard and lampshades, side tables and kitchenware. The things were arranged neatly, but with no respect for category. Items that belonged to different rooms or functions were stacked together.

Neighbors, more of them servants than tenants, began to gather. A few policemen stood around in their blue uniforms. My father, his face slick with sweat, was speaking agitatedly to the officer in charge.

My mother was in the bedroom stuffing her meager valuables – some jewelry, an assortment of documents – into a suitcase. Two men were starting to drag out a boudoir; I was astonished at the swiftness with which things were disappearing. I wanted to strike these intruders; I wished I were big enough to do so. More than the things being removed, it was their impudent presence in our home that enraged me.

And the meek surrender of my parents! It was beyond comprehension.

My mother shot me a glance just for a second, her eyes red and tearful. I could tell she wanted to tell me something – perhaps that it was okay or would be okay, or to pack my things too – but she could not express them in words.

She didn't need to; at that moment I suddenly grew a lot older.

I went back to my room and haphazardly collected my things into a little mound – books, clothes, badminton racquet, a cheap raincoat, a torchlight – and other treasures of an eleven-year-old. When I went out again, I heard my father saying, in a resigned voice, 'You could have given us one more day.'

The officer in charge replied in a voice pitched remarkably between firmness and sympathy, 'Mr Mirza, you were given three notices.'

Later that day, my brother Hafeez informed me that our father had fallen behind on the rent.

As I recall this incident and the strange parallel with my predicament, Boris's notice-to-notice escalation was not lost on me. Of course, where my father's third notice got him booted out of our happy home, mine threatened an ejection from the world itself. My father too had met with such severe consequence eventually, but after how many notices and with what kind of people, I could not know.

'Where will I go with my children?' my father asked pitifully when all his importuning proved ineffective.

There was only one place to go: my grandfather's.

A few of the servants were the only ones who shouted out a word or two in our defense – 'what was the need', 'think of the kids', 'we will watch over the stuff'. They were also the only ones to bid us farewell when we left.

My mother, brother and I left for my grandfather's house in two rickshaws, one of them piled with luggage, while our father stayed with our furniture. It was not the first time that we had to trundle over to my grandfather's like refugees. And it would not be the last time either.

What destiny holds in store for us is so strange, so marvelous, so terrifying that nothing can really prepare you for it. Early trauma is of little avail to foretell future ones. No wonder the ancients valued prophecy to be the finest, most precious and most mysterious of arts. To know what's coming was better than to possess mere forbearance. And what was coming, it struck me, as I pondered the improbability of my disfigured hand, was less of a mystery than everyone made it out to be.

Destiny was desire. Desire was destiny.

Day broke and filled the belly of my white curtains with light. For a second, I didn't know where I was. The gleam of the hardwood floor reminded me: America – New York. There were no wooden floors back home; at least, not when I left.

How long had I slept? The light filtering through the curtain varied in mood and brightness from hour to hour, leaving me no clearer on what time of day it was. I floated simultaneously in a state of delirious haze and a new clarity. Memories from the deep past trundled through my mind: playing cricket with the boys, listening to the beating of hard rain on a tin roof, even the flash of a rare good day with my father – eating cake from Olympia Bakery.

The hours rolled forward with the lethargic diligence of an old waterwheel.

I felt unfit to do anything except take a piss. In time, even the piss subsided. The pain had turned into a dull but constant throb, still punctuated by sudden piercing stabs that blossomed at the joint before scooting off to rattle faraway nerves. The tourniquet had become a dark clotted red, but the bleeding had probably stopped. I felt warm with fever. I was afraid to untie the grisly bundle. Could this turn into gangrene?

I should go see Dr Hazari, I thought. But I hardly had the will to cross the room.

At some indeterminate hour I Googled how to take care of a severed digit or, to be precise, the nub that's left after the severing of the digit. My mind wandered off in far-flung directions. I wondered if Boris wished he had kept the finger. I wanted to go open the fridge and apologize to my finger.

I wondered, too, suddenly, about who had killed my father, and why?

Lesson: People get killed for only three reasons – money, jealousy, and not knowing when to stop.

In my father's case, all three could have applied.

The circumstances in which he was found suggested not only premeditated murder but also a considerable amount of personal vengeance. He was found in a cheap motel, in a cheap neighborhood, hands and feet bound and lacerated with many cuts.

I was already out of the country when all this transpired – and then came to light. Hafeez was so ashamed – ever since our father ran off with Rubina the maidservant – of our father and his misdeeds that he had little appetite to dig up the full details of his sordid end days. He was happy enough for the case to be registered as an 'unnatural' death and be done with the burial before any relatives – the few we were still in touch with – had occasion to ask too many questions.

That fateful event had come to pass a couple of years after I left the country. I can still hear Hafeez's voice over the phone telling me, 'Father is gone!' I didn't know how to respond. It's not like life gives you many chances to rehearse this moment: your father dies only once. It was peak hour at the joint where I worked. Mobile phones were not so common even then. I was on the house phone – a number that I'd given to Hafeez in case of emergencies – and the manager was giving me the stink eye. I was affectless, curt. I could tell it irritated Hafeez, whose voice was heavy with an indeterminable admixture of grief, shock, and a tinge of embarrassment.

Hafeez called me again a day later to ask if I would be coming home for the funeral. When I said 'no', it offended him to no end.

'I, too, am deeply upset with everything he did,' my brother said. 'But you don't skip your own father's burial!'

Yes, you do, I had replied, if the father was as cruel and delinquent as ours.

'You won't get a second chance to attend his funeral, you know,' Hafeez had said to me. But I didn't budge.

Hafeez was furious with me and hung up. We didn't talk for a while after that.

What I didn't tell Hafeez then, or didn't know how to, was the sadness that I felt at the news of our father's demise. The gruesome manner of his death didn't help either. I felt a bit confused too; can one mourn a man one didn't love? Perhaps what I was mourning anew was the sorrow of never having had the father I had wished for: kind, understanding, enveloping me with security. But quarrels with the dead are the most fruitless of enterprises, and my current life overtook all else again before long.

If Hafeez believed in his received wisdom, I was living now by a moral code of my own: if living badly is pitiful, then to die badly is unforgivable.

When I awakened again, light streamed in from the outside; everything in the apartment felt new. The bricks on the part-exposed wall. The Pier 1 lamp with its simple beige shade. A small red pot in the corner in which Helen was trying to grow some sprout-like plant. Where did all this come from?

I missed Helen. And, oh god, there was more to explain now!

It was rather late in the night, I could tell from a shift in the quality of street sounds. Not just quieter, but differently paced. Ordinary sounds became more audible, sirens more piercing, and a hush that fell on the towers and pavements as soft as snow.

I turned on the TV. It was cued to a news channel. US researchers announced that they had made a living cell powered by manmade DNA. Good! In Oakland, police arrested twenty-six members of the Ghost Town street gang. The arrests capped a five-month operation dubbed 'Ghostbusters'. This made me smile. BP conceded that more oil than it had initially estimated was gushing into the Gulf of Mexico as heavy crude washed into Louisiana's wetlands for the first time.

I grew tired of the news, and switched to Turner Classic Movies. It was the best of channels. And on this night, I hit jackpot: *Butch Cassidy and the Sundance Kid*. I have probably never mourned the deaths of two movie crooks as keenly as I did those of Cassidy and the Kid. That heartrending final freeze shot! They really should have gone to Australia! And Katharine Ross! She was my personal definition of hotness; her lustrous disheveled hair and the slow unbuttoning of her white linen blouse – the trusting innocence of her limpid eyes – I wanted to save her! What moved me also is a little-known fact that I had actually bothered to look up: while Cassidy and the Kid are enshrined in criminal history, Etta Place – the real-life character Ross plays – disappeared without a trace. No one knows what became of her. Where she went, how she died – no trace. The fate of most of humanity. Once the last person to have personally known us leaves this earth, we too in most cases become a mere notation in official papers, if that. But the unknown fate of Etta Place, to be connected to so notorious and charmingly memorialized a pair as Cassidy and the Kid – and still move out of time without a mark – filled me with a unique sense of dread, and poignancy. Call it sentimentality if you like, but there was a lesson in the erasure of her life for the rest of us, certainly for all the graspers like myself, who make up, let's face it, basically all of humanity (bar one in a million who are truly touched by the gods): anonymity in history is not necessarily the sign of a life without meaning. But I wasn't ready yet to simply aim for and be happy with some form of quiet plenitude. I took a long swig of a Diet Coke spiked heavily with rum.

Then I rose to my feet humming 'Raindrops Keep Falling on My Head'. I moved to the kitchenette, placed a skillet on the stove and poured a generous quantity of olive oil into it. I pulled the Ziploc bag that contained my pinky finger out of the freezer. Once I drew it out of the ice, the finger didn't look like anything that had ever been a part of me. I placed it on a cutting board and carefully removed the nail. I washed the digit in cold tap water. Once the oil was ready, I dropped my finger – is it still 'mine' when it comes to one's digits, if it's become detached? – into the oil and drizzled it with a dash of herbes de Provence. A sprinkle of salt and a solid dose of freshly cracked black pepper. I hadn't bothered Googling how long it took to stir-fry human flesh, but I felt it should not take much longer than chicken. It pleased me to see the finger slowly turning brown. But added a small cup of water, just for safety. I could not stand to have Boris find any fault with my cooking, too. And in a flight of inspiration, I pulled out a dried tamarind pod from the cabinet and added a dusting of dried ginger powder. The smell started to feel right – a sweetish curry with a hammy scent – and all it needed to finish was a flick of lemon zest.

The dish was ready in about fifteen minutes, and gave off a lovely fragrance. I found a blue-top Tupperware, nice and clean, and transferred this little culinary marvel into the receptacle. It had to be delivered by courier. I'd have to call up my one true pal from Queens, Samad for this one. He'd know the right person for such a job. I'd call him first thing in the morning. They say, you call a friend when you need to move, and you call your best friend when you need to move a body. Here was a variant of that rule: when you need to deliver a cooked human finger, you called up a fucking Desi brother.

CHAPTER 14

I had asked Samad to come by at 10 a.m. No one would be at Boris's office before then. I had put the Tupperware inside a cooler with a couple of ice packs. When Samad saw my hand, he said, 'Holy shit! What happened?'

'Kitchen crap,' I said.

Samad cocked his head to one side as if to say, *Really?*

'What's with the dishrag? Why don't you get a proper bandage?'

'Did it last night. I'll go today. Don't worry.'

'Take proper care of that,' Samad said as he left, pointing at my wounded hand.

Soon after, I fell into a slumber, but before long I was awakened by a loud rapping on my door. Jesus! I sat up on the sofa with a start, then calmed down. Boris would not be knocking with such impatience. He was in control; this was the knocking of someone anxious.

It was Patti.

'What the fuck, Kash!?'

'I'm all right,' I said. 'Just taking a break.'

'The fuck you are!' Patti said. 'What's this?'

'An accident,' I said nonchalantly.

We moved into the living room. Patti didn't sit down.

She stood in the middle of the room, wary but reproachful. Her tattooed arms were crossed across her broad chest. Her boots sounded heavy on my wooden floor.

'Accident? You don't come to work for days. Don't even answer your phone. And you look like you lost a fight with a coyote.'

'Yeah, it's not been the best week,' I yielded.

'And I thought I was coming over with bad news.'

'More?'

Patti pulled a chair from our small dining table, turned it around and sat before me, arms crossed over the back of the chair.

'Looking at you, I'm thinking maybe it's not that big a deal,' Patti said.

'Why? What happened?'

'An inspector came around,' Patti said.

'Oh, that. He's a pest. Did Kang ding him again?' I asked, half hopefully.

'It wasn't Boswell. It was a woman,' Patti said.

'Oh? What did she want?'

'She asked what kind of food we served. If we had anything off the menu. But something wasn't right about her.'

'You sure she wasn't shopping for a client?'

'No, Kash. I know the type. I asked her if she was from the health department and she said, no. But she didn't say anything else about where she was from.'

'Maybe she's an undercover journalist. We've got some crazy write-ups, you know.'

'Nope. That's not it either. I'm telling you now, you don't want people like her to turn anything into an official investigation.'

'Hmm,' I said. So, in addition to the lawless, now I have the law coming after me too? Jesus!

'Once they get on your case, they don't stop until they pin shit on you.'

'There's no shit to pin,' I said. This was bravura on my part. We had served many items that were not kosher; what I meant is that there was no contraband to find on our premises – unless one were to raid it at the moment of preparation or service. We didn't keep any stock there. Patti and Kang, for a little additional compensation, had agreed to keep things in extra-large subzero freezers in their apartments.

'Ri-ight. So, what's this then?' Patti asked again, pointing at my improvised bandage. 'You got fucked, didn't you?'

It was a bright morning. Even though my white curtains were drawn, the room felt alive with outside energy. A truck was beeping as it reversed. You'd think people would see such a big thing moving in any direction. The infantilizing protectiveness of this culture and its increasing compendium of laws felt like a betrayal of its original frontier spirit. The frontier had shifted back to the rest of the world, I supposed, as they shook off centuries of slumber to claim a place back on the world stage. Back home, in Dhaka, nothing beeped when it reversed. People would only honk to go forward – recklessly, heedlessly, ceaselessly. I guess I was still, ineradicably, from my Bengali Muslim culture, in more ways than I cared to admit.

'Telling me I fucked up, that's not helping, Patti.'

'Would telling you you're a genius help?'

'It would if we didn't worry about my intelligence or my character.'

'Then do the smart thing.'

I looked at her quizzically, sure that she had some notion of what that smart thing was.

'Go see a fucking doctor!'

'Right. Of course,' I said, finally heaving myself from my couch. It was time to shake off whatever trauma had befallen me and re-enter the game with a new plan, new vigor.

When it came to a doctor, there was only one choice for me: Dr Hazari.

He had moved to Kew Gardens, the area where Helen lived when we first met. She was subletting a room from someone in a large 1940s, post-depression, post-war, brick-and-mortar complex, with an arched entrance and terraced courtyard. Her place was a stone's throw from where Charlie Chaplin had once lived. Where Dr Hazari lived, however, turned out to be a patch of Kew Gardens that was starkly different from my previous experience of the neighborhood. His little clapboard house by the tracks of the Long Island Railway resembled a recidivist's shack in some corner of an abandoned factory town. If it was Kew Gardens, it was so only by some trickery of city mapping and codes, not in terms of its essential character. One had to climb four flights to reach his 'chamber', which was in effect the front room of his tiny and sparsely decorated apartment.

'So, what have we here?' he said, once we exchanged greetings.

I was seated at a narrow table which served as his consultation desk. A metal lamp with a strong bulb blazed on my exposed wound and reflected off his cropped cap of white hair. The doctor was wearing the kind of white half-sleeved shirt that used to be the uniform of his profession back home. Thin-rimmed reading glasses perched at the tip of his nose.

'Hmm,' he said, pensively. 'It's a few days old now.'

'Yes, it is,' I said.

'How come you didn't come right away? Or go to ER?'

Dr Hazari stared at me with a penetrating gaze. I'd never seen him look at me this way. His usual affability had given way to seriousness – and suspicion.

'Are you into gambling, Kash?'

'No, sir! Not into that nonsense,' I said. Though, in a sense I was all in, wasn't I?

'Surely, not drugs?'

'Of course not!'

'You know when I've last seen wounds like this?'

I was sure I didn't want to know.

'In the village. Back when they'd do things like chop off a thief's finger. At least, they did once when I was a medical student. And then came the war. I saw all kinds of wounds in the war.'

He was referring to the Liberation War of Bangladesh. It took place in 1971, just a few years before I was born. The war began with the Pakistani military unleashing a brutal genocide on the rebellious Bengalis in the eastern wing of their country, and the Bengalis – till then not known for their martial qualities – quickly formed a resistance force composed largely of defecting Bengali officers and soldiers, and ranks of civilians from all walks of life – students, farmers, professionals. In 1971, Dr Hazari was in the final year of his medical school and working as a 'field surgeon' at a guerrilla camp. Given the scant resources available to our freedom fighters, they were lucky to have a medical student at hand. I knew that he had 'fought' in the war, though technically he was not so much fighting as mending people, but I'd never looked at him as what he was – a freedom fighter.

There were men back home who made much of having been a freedom fighter, and I didn't hold it against them. If you fought a war and won it, you have bragging rights. But there were many like Dr Hazari, who had never bothered to pick up a government certificate testifying their contribution and never brought up the topic to extoll their own virtues. The period after the country gained independence was chaotic. Many fighters, like Dr Hazari, hadn't belonged to any political parties; they had joined the war out of their general sense of patriotism. It was unfathomable already for my generation; but some we personally knew still came from a time when people risked their own lives for an ideal. As the party that had led the political movement for independence seized control, many like Dr Hazari felt sidelined – and even slighted. I didn't know the details of his case, or why he nursed such a deep sulk, if he did. But there was an intentness about him as he attended to me that jolted me.

I had always felt pity for him that a bona fide freedom fighter should be reduced to the status of a backstreet doctor so far from home. But I sensed a deeper pride, an internal compass in him, which suddenly made my 'pity' feel like insolence.

As I sat there and contemplated the fate of the man ministering to me, for the first time my struggles, my sacrifices, my ambition felt tawdry and trifling. It was as if the world, weary of real wars over ideals that mattered, had consigned us to inferior struggles over scrappy little personal ambitions.

Be that as it may, my wound was real.

'Fine, don't tell me,' Dr Hazari said with a fleeting smile. He turned the lamp on my stump-like limb.

The doctor folded and stashed his glasses into the breast pocket of his shirt. He studied the wound with the impassive concentration of a philatelist scrutinizing a stamp of familiar provenance but deserving attention. He cleaned the finger and re-bandaged it with care. And as he did so, he spoke to me again, 'Your business is your business, but whatever it is, Kash, I hope you find a better solution soon.'

He was looking into my eyes. I had not met with a stare like this in a while; perhaps not since my interactions with my grandfather: a look brimming with as much reproach as it sparkled with compassion.

He said he was giving me some painkillers and some ointment for dressing the wound at home, and a dose of antibiotics. He said that he could take another look later. If the skin seemed to be resealing in a particularly grotesque manner, he could help snip off corners – with local anesthesia, of course.

'It won't be the same as what a real cosmetic surgeon would do, but they'd also charge a hundred times more than me.' That was true and fair enough.

Once his treatment finished, like a true Bengali, he offered me a cup of tea. Part of me was tempted to soak up his reassuring company. But there was business I needed to get back to.

'Thanks, doctor. Another day,' I said meekly, while he wrote out his prescriptions.

'If you need anything, you can always come to me. But I hope you won't need my services again anytime soon,' Dr Hazari said, casting a meaningful look in my direction. The metal lamp was still the only light in the room. Backlit by that narrow luminescence, the doctor, always a benign presence in our circles, took on a new aspect that seemed balanced precariously between authority and ghoulishness.

I too hoped that I'd not be needing his services again anytime soon. But today, he was a lifesaver. He wasn't qualified to write official prescriptions in this country. 'I am too old to take exams,' he would say, if ever asked why he didn't get re-certified. But ethnics like us tend to enjoy the benefits of full-blown black markets in almost everything. You had to know the right people. The meds he prescribed, I could get from a grocer in Jamaica, who 'imported' various cheap Bangladeshi generics under the radar. The trick was not to get too greedy. Get too big or too loud, and you're busted. Sell to blabbermouths, and word spreads to the wrong people. The trick was to keep it tight, keep it tidy.

By the time I got home it was late afternoon. I came out of West Fourth Street station and the funky smell of New York summer hit my nose. A mixture of rotten fruits and damp clothes pervaded the air. It was just short of rush hour, and yellow cabs zoomed north at full pace along the broad expanse of Sixth Avenue. At the corner of Carmine and Bleecker, I stopped at Joe's Pizzeria for a slice. Like every New Yorker, I believed my neighborhood joint to have the best slice in town. But after the past several days, this slice really did taste like the best pizza I'd ever had.

The fact that I could relish such a minor pleasure again said something about the shift occurring inside me. Despite the freshness of my trauma, I felt all my nerves releasing themselves from the knots of pain and fear to form new coils of clarity and intent. It filled my body with a rush of energy. The loans, Boris, Boswell; after this, I would be able to handle whatever the city threw at me. The wound would heal. Even if I couldn't see the path ahead, in that moment I knew I'd have the energy to walk it.

When I reached the apartment building, I bounded up the stairs. No sooner had I hit my passageway, than I noticed the glimmer of light under my front door. Did I leave the lights on when I left? I could not remember. Surely, Boris's guys would not come by at this hour? The street outside was full of people.

I reached the door and turned the knob gently. It was locked. This was interesting. Intruders might shut a door, but surely would not need to lock it. I opened the door with trepidation.

The TV, left on mute, was tuned to Turner Classics. I could see it through the small parting of the door. I could even tell what was playing: *When Harry Met Sally.* Definitely not what Boris's bloody-minded oafs would be watching. I opened the door wide and, sure enough, seated on the couch was Helen.

She turned to look at me and smiled, and it felt as if all the lights in the city had come on at the same time.

CHAPTER 15

I rushed over to give Helen a hug, but before I could grasp her, she rose with a start, eyes widening in horror, and shouted, 'Oh my god, Kash, what happened?'

I wanted to tell her everything. But I didn't know where to begin. As I sat there, I realized that there is a particular kind of shame, a sense of humiliation, to being subjected to violence. Helen possessed an uncanny ability to read the slimmest shifts in my moods.

'It's okay, Kash. Whatever it is, just tell me.'

I looked up at her and was struck newly by the delicacy of her features. Her high cheekbones, her jawline, everything seemed thinner than I remembered. Her eyes were a pair of opalescent mysteries, fixed on me with a world of curiosity. I was falling in love with her all over again. And at the same time, I felt more unworthy of this love than ever before.

'What's the worst that can happen?' Helen said. 'I'll just leave again!'

Her laugh made a crystalline sound – crisp, unadulterated.

I lifted my bandaged hand, and said, 'This was Boris.'

'OH MY FUCKING GOD!'

Helen put a hand on her mouth, then her eyes filled with tears. 'Oh, you poor baby. You poor, poor darling.'

She took me in an embrace and touched my bandaged hand, gently. I felt relieved that her reaction was horror and sympathy. What else would it be? What did I think? Any sense of humiliation, of diminishment, was in my head.

'The assholes! I'll fucking kill them,' Helen said, on releasing me. Her eyes burned with rage and her face became contorted in disgust – not at my deformity, but at the cruelty of my assailants.

I drew breath and began to narrate the events of that fateful night. The abduction. The interrogation and the threats. And then the butcher. 'I'll fucking kill them. Who do they think they are? Where do they think they are?'

'In Russia, apparently!' I said, unable to resist the joke.

'Well, they're mistaken,' said Helen, no smile on her face. 'They're in the Wild Wild Fucking West. Out here, you take a finger, we take an entire fucking arm.'

I looked at her with amazement. She seemed to read my mind and said, 'Wait.' She walked over to the small desk at the other end of the room and fetched something from inside it.

When she came back, I could see what it was: a silver-barreled revolver.

'A Colt .32,' Helen said. 'My stepdad's.'

She handed me the weapon. It had a black handle, grooved for ease of grip, and a stubby muzzle. As I weighed the piece, careful not to point it at Helen, she said, 'I've had time to think things over too.'

She had never seemed sexier. Her rage was incandescent, radiating the heat of determination. I knew that she came from gritty stock, full of mettle. Her father had been imprisoned for dealing methamphetamines out West. A pioneer, if you like, in the nefarious field of synthetic addiction. That had explained the missed birthday calls to his daughters, perhaps. Even her stepfather grew weed in the mountains. 'It's just a hobby,' he'd say. Something he did with the 'boys'. The boys being rough individuals with colorful rap sheets. Even her mother's side wasn't without history. There were men who worked as bouncers in second-rate casinos, and men who ran illegal poker rings. And then there was Uncle Ben, who had beaten up a veteran from the first Iraq War because the man, despite multiple warnings, kept hitting on his girlfriend at the local bar. This was a complex test for the town's sense of morality; root for the man who stood up for his girl – or support the man who'd served?

I had heard these stories from Helen over time, but I had never done the calculus of what it meant for her moral and tactical resources. I wondered if our shared experience of miscreant fathers was one of the reasons we were drawn to each other.

'I'm going to teach you how to shoot.'

She walked over to me. I leaned into her with my head resting against her taut belly. She stroked my hair. Her shirt smelled like it was fresh out of the laundry. Clothes never smelled like this back home. Tide, the detergent, to me was the smell of America.

'No more secrets, okay?' Helen said. It was posed as a question but received as a dictum.

'No more secrets,' I said.

'Let's get some food,' Helen said. 'I'm starving.'

We ordered takeaway from Kelley and Ping, our favorite Asian joint. Not too fancy, but much nicer than any typical Chinese takeout. I filled Helen in on the whole scene, while we waited for the food. Not just what had transpired with Boris, but also the developments with Viktor. We were this close, I said with a pinch in the air, to getting the Miner's Club gig.

'God, it's like you've lived a whole other life while I was away,' Helen said. Her legs were slung over my thighs, and I loved the feeling of their weight, their warmth.

Once the food arrived, we found *Death Wish* with Charles Bronson on TV. I liked Charles Bronson. I liked that entire generation of actors, who seemed to spend much of their careers either in Allied Forces uniform or in cowboy outfits. I liked how men back then looked like men and acted like men. They could go from suavity to savagery in a blink. I'd watch anything with those guys – Gregory Peck and David Niven, Anthony Quinn and Roger Moore – anytime. But on this night, Bronson's unrepentant vigilantism felt apt.

We were well satiated after our Chinese meal and buzzed from some beer I had found in the fridge. Helen was lying curled up against me, and my breath landed softly on her neck. I felt safe and sufficient. The two of us ensconced in the ghostly blue balm of TV light. The sounds of New York, a distant din that didn't touch us.

I kissed Helen lightly on her neck. She turned to lift her face towards me. As I kissed her cheeks, her brows, her lips, I shifted a little, resting almost on the blade of my hip and giving Helen room to turn more towards me. The desire swelling up within me was a different kind of ardor; a longing to hold and to be held as tightly and as closely as two people could ever be. To become lost in a state of sweet oblivion.

Helen's mouth tasted of beer and salt and her tongue pressed against mine with a willful thrust. The way I was positioned, my good hand was pinned under her. If I wanted to caress her, I'd have to do it with my bandaged left hand. For a second, I felt self-conscious about it, but the compulsion was too great. I traced her warm skin with the tips of my fingers – how the bandage and the tape tickled her skin, I didn't know, but she didn't seem to mind.

She placed a hand on my bandage and pulled my hand out from under her shirt – not in alarm or disgust, but with affection. She stared at my hand in silence and then fixed me with a gaze and asked, 'Where's the finger Kash? Did you throw it away?'

'Sort of,' I said.

'Sort of?' She looked intrigued. 'Didn't you go to the ER?'

I'd never told her about my DV-scam. This didn't seem like the moment to unspool that early sin; there's a limit to how many confessions one can make or receive in one session.

'Fingers are hard to reattach. And I don't have insurance.'

'So where is it? Did they keep it?'

'No, they gave it back to me.'

'What do you mean, gave it back?'

'In a Ziploc bag filled with ice. I brought it home.'

'So, what'd you do? Where is it?'

No more lies, I had promised. I took a breath, and then said, 'I . . . sent it back to Boris.'

'You . . . what!'

She sat up. It seemed unlikely that we'd proceed to sex tonight now. But I had to tell her the truth.

'Actually, I did something crazy.'

She looked at me expectantly. 'It felt wrong to throw it in the garbage. I thought, if Boris wants a piece of me, that's what I'll give him. I cooked it and sent it to him.'

Helen put a hand on her mouth. The look was a mixture of shock, wonder, hilarity, disbelief – not these feelings mashed together, but like fast-moving clouds that showed different qualities of light as they scurried across the sky.

'You did not! You're crazy!'

'I did! It felt like the perfect "fuck you" to Boris.'

'You're a complete freak. You know that?'

She wasn't going to leave me. I could tell that much. So, I said, 'I cooked it in herbes de Provence and ginger. And finished it with a touch of lemon zest.'

Helen started laughing. 'You fucking maniac!' As I watched her laugh, it hit me that what united us was not ambition for money or fame or status. We were two nobodies in the big city, but we were not just another pair of clichéd dreamers hoping to make it in New York. We wanted to rip the script to shreds. We weren't Bonnie and Clyde. To go on a killing spree would be too easy. We were a new breed, for which a name was yet to be coined.

I took her into my arms again. My hunger for her was raw. I didn't bother with her shirt anymore. I pulled down her jeans, her black panties. I kissed her on her thighs and between her legs, and crawled up her belly, across her breasts to her lips. I kissed her face the whole time that I was inside her. I didn't think I'd ever fucked her that hard before. She didn't seem to mind. It felt like an intense embrace of unity. When we finished, I fell off her to the side. We lay there a long time, with the TV on but neither of us watching.

Helen took my hand and kissed my bandage, once, twice

and many times. 'We should move to the bedroom,' I said. Neither of us moved.

'This is what we should do,' Helen said.

'What?'

'For the Miner's Club.'

'Do what, honey?'

There was a strange look in her eyes. She held up my bandaged hand and said, 'This. What you did for Boris, that's what we should do for the bloody Miner's Club.'

'Serve the rest of my fingers?!'

'Not your fingers, dumbass,' Helen said, and then, 'but, yes, somebody's fingers.'

'Fingers?'

'Or other parts.'

'Wha . . . Viktor wouldn't go for that!'

'Why not?' Helen challenged me.

'It's . . . crazy! Who eats people? Where do you even find the flesh?'

'People sell kidneys, don't they?'

'If we pitched this to Viktor, he'd say—'

'Unprecedented!' Helen said, finishing my sentence. She was sitting up on her haunches, her eyes big with excitement.

'So, we serve this instead of the Evening of Danger?'

'Or as the capstone of that menu!'

'Right, what could be more dangerous than eating other humans,' I said, thinking aloud. 'The moral hazard is certainly maxed out.'

'Nothing new comes into the world until someone does something wrong,' Helen said, and rose to move towards the bedroom. I followed her. We changed, brushed our teeth and slipped under the covers. Now that the idea had been planted, I could think of nothing else. The gambit was unprecedented, without question. It appealed to the side of me that wanted to make a mark on this world.

Would Viktor dismiss us as lunatics? Or would he be intrigued?

She fell asleep before me. I could hardly believe that my sweet Helen was proposing cannibalism. Yet, as I looked at her face, so soft in sleep, mouth slightly open, it seemed natural that she should suggest that, and that it made a kind of sense. What trickery of fate brings two twisted souls like us together I didn't know, but for once it was on my side. My circumstances had called for something extreme, and at that moment I happened to have by my side a fierce, loving woman with a dark genius. I didn't care about Boris anymore – or, at least, the gig was no longer just about earning enough to pay him off. I realized that it didn't matter if The Hide survived. Not really. The gangsters and the authorities would do what they do. I didn't need to succeed as a culinary impresario in New York. No, what I wanted was to be responsible for one unforgettable act. In that moment I understood something about how great art is created, and great crimes are committed. It didn't matter if people admired me or condemned me; the only thing that mattered was that they could not ignore me.

CHAPTER 16

By the time I met Adair again, I had a new clarity about cannibalism. Humans have treated it as the most heinous act in all of recorded history. Herodotus pinned it on unknown and unseen tribes, albeit without judgment. It is the thing that others do – the complete, unassimilable other: the barbarians. It's a most useful attribution – it can pave the way for acts that are otherwise difficult to do or justify. When the conquistadors realized there was no gold in the new world, they started labelling the natives as cannibals. That made it possible to start carting them off as cargo, to sell and use as slaves. The poor Caribs have the dubious honor of giving this act of barbarism its name. It is thought that the word root 'canib' derives from the term Carib. As if they were the only people ever to indulge. As white colonizers spread across continents, it didn't take long for them to find other offenders. From the jungles of Africa to the islands of the Pacific, from the Amazonian heartland to remote corners of India, allegations abounded. Tagged as cannibals, natives everywhere became fair game. Their lands were ripe for the taking, their lives begging to be transformed. And while the white man expressed horror at the sins of the heathens, they perpetrated the greatest violence history has known.

Yet it was their victims who bore the stigma of being the barbarians.

It is odd that it should fall on me, Kash Mirza, a figure of no consequence from a country of no great repute, to mount a challenge to this self-serving narrative of 'civilization'. That's how I felt now about serving the ultimate meal for the Miner's Club. To do it furtively, with no artistry, would amount merely to a wretched satisfaction of a perverse need. But to be upfront about what one was doing, consciously – and with conscience – and with all the craft of the highest exponents of the culinary world, now that would be something else. It would be less of an escapade and more of an arrival.

If you looked at all modern iterations of this transgression, you would find that it is attributed to actors who are as much of an Other as a barbarian. Or acting in conditions so extreme – war, famine, lost in the Andes – that the act of eating one's fellow beings is normalized for that context. Either the person or the context has to be extreme and alien enough for it to transpire. In my childhood, a man called Khalil had captured the national imagination for his habit of exhuming recent burials to consume human livers. He was thought to be deranged, even though there was no abnormal behavior in the rest of his life. The act of eating dead people was repugnant and scary enough for the public – even the state – to label him as 'mad' which, apart from barbarians, seems to be society's way of containing behaviors that it finds unacceptable.

I asked Adair to meet me at Brown's. When we reached the bar, it was past five o'clock. Officially Happy Hour. But there were no merrymakers in sight. There was a new girl behind the bar. She was covered in intricate and richly colored tattoos. Some mythical beast rose out of her skimpy blouse and reared its fierce blue head on one side of her neck. A spiritual sign of unknown origins was emblazoned on the upper part of her spine. A commotion of images and letters were etched on both arms. And, in case these weren't enough to declare her individuality, there were metals: pierced into her eyebrows, nose, lower lip and, I was willing to bet, either a nipple or a labia or both. She introduced herself as Orange. People didn't have real names anymore and I was fine with that.

I ordered two Scotches. Doubles on the rocks.

I could have gulped down both shots myself.

There was no word from Viktor yet. And the initial slew of private dinners seemed to have dried up too. I felt Adair was slacking. It was an awkward moment to question his performance. But our survival was at stake, and I could barely hide my frustration. Adair sensed it. And said, with a bristly tone, 'Finding rich douchebags isn't as easy as you seem to think.'

'I don't, but you have to be doing something hard, don't you think?'

'You think you're the only one doing hard stuff, don't you?'

'I'm the only one who has literally taken a beating so far,' I said.

'Fuck man, don't bring that up again.'

I shrugged. We downed the first round in silence. And then Adair asked me again where things stood with Viktor.

'We're good,' I said. 'We need to pin down a date. I've spoken to Yusep.'

Adair shot me a look, as if to say, I didn't know you had gone direct with him. I understood now why he would guard his gatekeeper role more closely. 'He called me. He wasn't able to reach you.'

Adair nodded and loosened his black tie.

'So, what does the uncle want?'

'Never mind what he wants. Or thinks he wants. It's what he needs!'

Adair seemed intrigued. I was glad to see a spark of the old twinkle in his eyes.

'Something unprecedented, right?'

'Okay,' Adair said. Waiting for me to say more.

A couple of new customers walked into the bar. A man in a suit, tie undone, and a much younger woman. An old tale that will never die. When I turned back to Adair, I noticed the hint of a smile. I paused, staring into my glass; the mercurial colors of the drink, glints of gold and red and honey, flickering even in the dim light, and sluicing around the ice, made me think of a cave full of riches. The idea was clear by now inside my head. The logic of it – moral, practical, tactical. By now the proposition was not only shorn of qualms, for me, but starting to gain momentum. But Adair would be hearing this for the first time. I decided to coax him into the subject with a little preamble.

'Atahualpa. Do you know the story of Atahualpa?'

'Is it a place or a person?'

'He was the last Aztec king. When the conquistadors asked him to submit to their religion, do you know what he said?'

'Fuck you?'

'Yes, but with good reason. He said that they – the

Aztecs – sacrificed humans at the altar of their gods. But the Catholics—'

'They had sacrificed their god for their own salvation.'

'Bingo! What's worse, they continued to repeat that sacrifice in the grisliest form, by consuming his body and blood, again and again, in the form of the Eucharist.'

'And Ata-Ata wasn't into that?'

'He thought *Catholicism* was the barbaric religion. Imagine his dismay that he and his people were accused of being barbarians for a crime – cannibalism – which his accusers committed as a sacred ritual!'

'He was right. The Catholics are one fucked-up lot. So much illogic, and so much power.'

'Right, but that's not how Atahualpa's captors saw it.'

'Okay, so, what happened to Atahualpa?'

'They executed him.'

'The man died for his beliefs,' Adair said.

'Yes, though there are other versions where it's said that he was not nearly as heroic. He was baptized as Juan Santos Atahualpa. And his own people killed him for that betrayal.'

'Poor fucker was doomed from the moment he lost his empire.'

'Indeed, and it's the victor's prerogative to label the losers as savages.'

'So, who are we in this scenario?'

'We are the third party – the redeemers.'

Adair leaned forward, his long bony fingers clasping his glass of whiskey as if it were a sacred chalice. The bar had filled up by now; the faces were different from my time, and yet the effect of the assembled was much the same: gregarious youth brimming with hopefulness.

'Redeemers?'

'Yes. Do you know the date Atahualpa was killed?'

'Of course not.'

'August the fifteenth.'

'And this is significant because—'

'It's the same date on which Father of the Nation of Bangladesh, Bangabandhu Sheikh Mujibur Rahman, was killed.'

'Whoa! That's some coincidence!'

'Nope. Centuries apart. Continents apart. Two heroes, who were also victims. One lost his war, the other won it, but ultimately, they suffered the same fate. Atahualpa was killed by the Spaniards for challenging their religion, and Sheikh Mujib for the impudence of standing up to strongmen – Pakistani generals, Nixon, Kissinger.'

'Hmm. And all this connects to our dinner . . . how?'

The dinner, I explained to Adair, was no longer just a moneymaker, a gimmick. It was about making a statement. To reclaim what it meant to *be* a barbarian. To wear that name proudly. To recognize the value inherent in rites that were once deemed barbaric.

'There is value in cannibalism?'

Very much so, I explained to Adair. My theory was gaining clarity with surprising speed. Where we had gone wrong as a species, I told him, was to think of ourselves as special. We did it because we could not face death. Or rather, we could not stand the curse of being endowed with a consciousness capable of conceiving eternity while being trapped inside bodies that were perishable. So, we made up tales and tried to believe that we too could be coeternal with all of time, with God. What hubris! What heresy! As if the tales even served their purpose. How many of us came to peace with our own mortality? We needed a new understanding to help us become reconciled to our lot as accidental organic chaff spat out by galactic churning.

I was pumped up. I asked Orange for refills. She was prompt and attentive. I had asked for extra ice the first time, and she served my drink with three large cubes, whereas Adair's contained the standard two. This pleased me. Brown's, even if the man himself didn't come around so often, as I'd heard, was holding up to his punctilious standards.

Adair raised his glass and said, 'To Atahualpa.'

'To Bangabandhu,' I replied.

The shared date of their deaths no longer felt like a mere coincidence to me, but a sign, a harbinger, a divine guidance. To defy, to dare, to dream.

With new fortification at hand, I resumed telling Adair my theory of cannibalism as an act of self-realization, even self-purification. Our challenge, I told him, wasn't with the idea itself, but the fact that we were presenting it as a secular proposition. If we were to give it a religious cast, we would not have so much to explain or justify.

'How do you mean?'

'Look at butchery! The meat industry has it under wraps. Laws are such that it's practically impossible for any ordinary citizen to slaughter their own dinner – but the minute you claim that it's a religious sacrifice, everyone backs off!'

This was not only true at home where, as I knew so well, millions of people turned into giddy-eyed butchers and left even a modern capital like Dhaka awash in the blood of sacrificial animals. But in the hyper-regulated world of the

USA, men could cart off their prey for ritual slaughter – but would be forbidden from conducting the same act for mere consumption.

'It doesn't matter how old or new the religion. From Judaism to Santeria, everyone gets the same privilege.'

'You know followers of Santeria would say their beliefs predate even monotheistic ones, as they draw on pagan roots from the dawn of time in Africa.'

'Of course, they do. If we formed a new religion, we'd also have to find sinewy roots to a foggy past.'

'So, what are you proposing – we start a new religion?'

I leaned against the short back of my high stool.

'We could, but we don't have the time. Besides, I lack the evangelical spirit.'

'Oh, I don't know about that, Kash. You seem fairly hell-bent on this "eating our own flesh" business.'

'Yes, but I am not delusional enough. I think to start a religion, or even a cult, you need to have a burning, psychotic vision that's a step too far even for me.'

But Adair's question had tickled some speculative knot of my neurons. I began to extemporize. 'You know,' I said to Adair, 'the real lesson of all the great religions is humility: Buddhism, Christianity, Islam. To think we have lives after death is the original sin. This is why we treat the human body as sacred even after its death. By losing that piety about the human form, we could return to real humility. We have no right to eat other species when we won't subject ourselves to that ignominy.'

'So, we want giant farms where human corpses are sent for processing?'

'Of course not! Don't be preposterous. If anything, we

should end our dependence on farmed meats altogether. Only wild games are honest. Only things that are hunted, fished, caught – but without causing a free fall depletion of any species.'

'Such puristic policies would make it hard to run The Hide,' Adair said with a sudden and rare concern for pragmatism.

'Well, that's why we depend on farmed meat. I'm not an absolutist. We have to make pragmatic concessions.'

'And what would that be?'

'I think to earn our right to eat other species, especially farm-raised, humans should be required to have a taste of ourselves. You could do this, for example, by making a ritual bite of one's kin a burial rite again, as it was for many ancient tribes.'

'I believe they exhume the body sometime after burial in Madagascar. But putting a piece in your mouth, that's something else!'

'Look!' I said, holding up my damaged hand. I kept the nub of my severed digit swaddled neatly with skin-colored tape. I had told Adair how Boris's goons had taken my finger. But I hadn't told him the second part of the story. I told him now how I had cooked it and sent it to Boris. Like Helen, Adair's eyes widened with a mixture of horror and astonishment.

'Okay,' he said, and let out a long whistle of wonderment. 'So, what makes you think Viktor will go for it?'

'Just a feeling,' I said as I placed my empty glass on the tabletop. It was still light out, but it was a soft light, the mellow iridescence of the earth slipping into its daily retirement.

'A feeling?' Adair said, raising one eyebrow.

'Don't scoff at feelings. They can harness the truth, fast as lightning, out of all the billowing clouds of obfuscation,' I said, signaling Orange to bring us a last round and the check.

CHAPTER 17

I wanted a source for our proposition firmly in place before I pitched to Viktor. The moral hesitations and customer queasiness could be overcome. Legal jeopardies dodged. But any great idea could founder on the shoals of execution. Most people – and their plans – went nowhere because they could not solve the logistics and supply. So, I had gathered my brain trust – Helen, Adair, Kang and Patti – at The Hide. In the dim, smoky, after-hours lighting, the dining room felt as small and cozy as a living room.

'Look,' Helen said, taking the floor. 'Every food has its own name. Like pork, ham, sausage, bacon, beef. No one says, I'll have some pig.'

'Right,' I said. The first album by the Strokes played in the background; to me it was the sound of New York at the start of the twenty-first century. 'It's the only white people music I can stand,' Patti had joked, when we first discovered our shared fandom for the band.

'Beef. Not cow,' Helen continued.

'Venison, not deer,' Adair said, picking up the theme.

'We need a name,' Helen said.

'A name that'll help put them at ease,' Adair added.

I took a bite of Korean fried chicken that Kang had

rustled up for this late-night confab. I liked the toothiness of this kind of meat. As I pondered its texture, I wondered if human flesh would prove to be tough or tender.

'Think of veal,' Helen said. 'It's got a bad rap now, but for the longest time the name helped disguise what people were eating.'

'This can be the new veal!'

'La nouvelle veal,' Helen said, laughing.

'A French-sounding name is half the solution if you want to pass something off on the public,' Patti said.

'I think it needs to be two words, *Le nouveau* something,' I said. 'It needs a little more lilt to it.'

'*La nouvelle—*'

'I think it's best if we give it a masculine gender.'

'*Le nouvel?*'

'*Le nouveau morceau!*'

Adair was the only one among us who knew French, or enough of it to get everything in sync, gender-wise.

'We have a name!' Helen exclaimed. 'This we can sell.'

'I don't know about that,' Patti said. She had been the most skeptical so far, although I felt it was more out of squeamishness than any deeper-rooted objection.

'There's no reason why it can't work. People eat placenta,' said Helen, trying to normalize the idea.

'There are vampire clubs now, underground, where they drink blood,' Adair said.

'Fine, let's say demand is not a problem. What about supply?'

Patti had hit the crux of the matter. This was going to be the real issue.

'No one gets killed. That's rule number one,' Adair said.

Everyone looked at him with reactions ranging from bemusement to what-the-fuck's-wrong-with-you. Adair grinned at everyone with an impish charm that reminded me of the early days when I knew him. In the relative darkness, his fine wrinkles were not visible. The mood harkened back – fleetingly – to more innocent times.

'We are not barbarians, after all,' I said. Adair laughed the loudest.

'Seriously guys, where are we going to get this rare meat?' Patti was all business.

'Ask Google!' Adair again. This time, no one laughed. Helen and I had researched this topic. It was time for me to speak.

'So, we've looked this up. There are forums on the dark web. But you never know who's on the other side. What they'll send you. Or if it isn't an FBI scheme to entrap you.'

'I thought cannibalism wasn't illegal,' Patti piped up.

'There are no laws per se against the eating of the flesh, as it is deemed so unthinkable that no one ever bothered to prohibit it.'

'But?'

'But procuring human flesh in any form or for any purpose, on the other hand, can fall foul of laws governing the handling of human corpses.'

'Hmm,' said Patti. It made sense for her to worry the most. She was the only one of us who had seen the inside of a prison – and was understandably reluctant to risk another stint. She looked like someone who was worried about what she was getting into.

'But there's always a workaround. Maybe not fully legal, but not exactly illegal, either.'

'Something in the gray zone,' Adair said sagely, as if the gray zone were a specific category.

'First, as Adair said, we can't have anyone die. We can't even harm anyone. It has to be donated. Most likely for a fee. There are no clear laws about anyone willingly selling their flesh. Against selling, or rather buying kidneys, or other transplantable parts, but not explicitly about flesh.'

'Didn't that guy in Germany go to jail for trying to cook and eat another man's penis, even though he was a willing donor.'

'Which is why we won't be doing this in Germany,' Helen said.

'Where then?'

'In international waters.'

'Viktor has a yacht,' Adair said with a trace of pride, as if he somehow enjoyed a stake in it by mere acquaintance.

'Fine, we stage the dinner out there on pirate lanes,' Patti said. 'But we still have the problem of where the meat is coming from.'

'Bangladesh,' I said.

There was a moment of silence. Helen knew about my plan so was inured to the idea. Kang never reacted to anything. But the other white people in the room – Adair and Patti – needed a moment to digest such a brazen proposal. It would not be easy for decent white Americans to consent to an idea that might violate the same people who had been brutally exploited by their forefathers. After decades of denial and suppression, their culture had now embraced the admission of historic crimes as a form of virtue. They knew to show special sensitivity to once-subjugated societies. Hailing from one of those societies myself, I was free from the burden of such guilt – or the duty of being forever vigilant about my political correctness.

'It's okay, kids,' I said, allowing myself a moment to enjoy their unease. 'People sell their kidneys there already. Even if we don't buy it, the donations will still be going ahead – their need is as great as that of their clients.'

'Capitalism at its purest,' Adair said. His booze was slipping down faster than usual tonight.

'And how will you find these people?' Patti was having chamomile tea.

'I'll ask my brother,' I said, playing my trump card.

'Really? He'd do that for you?'

I had been running from home all my life, but in a sense I was right back there. From Samad to Hafeez, even Dr Hazari, and back when I first came over, Mrs Zaman, also Askari, at all my moments of most critical need, and now for my one-off, life-changing – indeed life-saving – scheme, it was folks from back home who I turned to, again and again.

'He'll do it for the money, if not for me,' I said in a deadpan.

'With Viktor in our corner, the money isn't a problem,' Helen added.

'So, you've thought it through,' Patti said.

'I have but we need to put the wheels in motion. I need to contact my brother. And also, someone who can bring frozen products over from Bangladesh – secretly.'

'You have someone in mind, I'm guessing?' Adair said.

'I think I do, but we'll see,' I said.

'And we have to pitch this to Viktor,' Helen said, with a nervous laugh.

'Kash will do the sourcing. You guys will do the pitching. What do we do?'

'I'll work on the nephew to make sure, hopefully, that the uncle goes for it.' The room knew about Yusep and the role we were trying to recruit him for: our man on the inside.

'Kang doesn't have anything to do until the ingredients are in place,' Helen said.

'He can start sourcing the other products. The Dangerous Meal won't just be man-meat. That'd be too much. We still need a multi-course extravaganza to meet the Miner's Club's exacting standards. *Le nouveau morceau* will be the—'

'*Coup de grâce!*' Adair was flush with energy now.

'And me, what do you want me to do?' Patti asked.

'Select the serving crew. We don't want outsiders. Reduce exposure to any outsiders as much as possible.'

'But the ship will have its own crew?'

'For the sailing, yes. For the meal itself, it'll be only staff from The Hide. I told Viktor it has to be so, and he accepted. So, make sure they're groomed to the point where they can be trusted to be part of a shindig this sensitive. Then coached to perfection for serving.'

'Gotcha,' Patti said. It was the first clear affirmation of her involvement. I was glad to have won her over.

Once everyone else had left, Adair said to me, 'A word, mate?'

Helen looked at us and with a smile said, 'I'll give you boys some space.'

'What's up?' I asked.

We both sat back down at the table, which was strewn with used cups and dishes. Julie came around to clean up, but Adair motioned her away. I noticed only now that Adair was looking a little dried out; the pouches under his eyes a little heavier than usual.

'I've been thinking,' Adair said.

'Good,' I said.

'Asshole,' Adair said. 'Look, it's about the money.'

'Yeah?'

'I'm getting worried,' Adair said.

'What's the worry? We are going to do this. We can pull it off.'

'It's not that,' Adair said. He seemed uncomfortable, shifting. 'Okay,' he began again, apparently attempting to get to the heart of the issue. 'I'm worried we have too many people involved now and there won't be much left for us.'

It was a valid enough concern, but how were we going to pull this off without paying everyone we needed to pay?

'We need the people we need,' I said.

'Right,' Adair said. 'And then there's Yusep's cut.'

'Correct. There'd be no dinner without his assistance.'

'And there'd be no Yusep without me!'

I finally sensed what he was getting at, and I felt a throbbing in my temple – temper rising with anger. I could not believe the gall of this guy. He was angling for a bigger cut.

'Sure,' I said, keeping my calm. 'Why don't you spell out what you want?'

'I don't know, I was wondering if there isn't some logic to a slightly bigger cut for me. You and I are fifty-two and forty-three, right? And Kang has five percent?'

'Yes, and after everyone's paid off, we'd split according to that ratio.'

'I was thinking, maybe Kang doesn't get the five percent. He gets paid like everyone else.'

'And we pocket his share?'

'Maybe after everyone's paid off, we split fifty-fifty?'

I had not seen this greedy side of him before – not so nakedly. It wasn't a good look for him. Somehow it felt more unbecoming precisely because his charm and handsomeness had been so prominent for so long.

'Ahh,' I said. 'And I'd give up a little of my portion so you can have more?'

'I was just thinking that there'd be no access to the Miner's Club—'

I could not hold myself back anymore. At least, I held back an irresistible urge to punch him in the face.

'Okay, so why don't you take over? I'll step back. The sourcing is all on you. And why should Helen not ask for a cut for what she's doing to help source the material, without which there'd be no dinner – no payout?'

'Hey man, don't get all worked up! We're just talking.'

'No, we are not!' I said, my voice rising. 'You're acting like a *chuut*' – I used the actual Bangla word which would translate roughly to *fucker* but, given the venom with which I spit it out, it rang more with the resonance of *cunt* – 'a typical, over-entitled, white-ass *chuut*.'

Adair put up both hands as if to say, Okay, done. He was clearly just taking a chance. He wasn't committed enough to the ask – and that somehow irked me even more.

This was the problem with money. The moment people sensed a serious amount coming their way, suddenly their sense of what was owed to them changed.

I'd need to be careful. I'd have to have a word with Yusep and make sure the cash was delivered to me directly – into my hands, on the boat. Or as soon as we docked.

CHAPTER 18

As-salamu alaykum Kashem: I have had time to mull over your abnormal request. It is possible, but I am worried that it may prove to be a step too far even for here. I can initiate earnest exploration if you really want it. But before we proceed, please consider the risks. For me, but especially for yourself. You know how things work here. There's a lot we can do. And get managed. But it's different where you are. Is the risk worth it? Surrender yourself to Allah, brother, He will guide you. Khuda hafez, Hafeez.

I was touched by Hafeez's concern for my welfare. But I knew him, and I knew to read between the lines. He wasn't so much trying to dissuade me as asking me to persuade him. I didn't think it would be difficult. Hafeez had not only survived but flourished in the most densely populated of Third World countries. Dhaka, last I checked, housed 135,000 people per square mile. When you jostle for every inch at every turn, it brings about a kind of intensity that even New Yorkers could not fathom. When every person performing every transaction, from cabbies to meter readers, grocers to doctors, tries to get one over on you; when people

189

are constantly measuring the social pecking order, looking for any weakness to seize on, your instinct to be on guard, to defend, to bite back is pitched to a high degree of sensitivity. I knew not to underestimate Hafeez. I'd get what I wanted from him, but at a price.

And what I wanted was human parts: flesh, preferably from the calf or buttocks. Anyone willing to sell a kidney could be persuaded to sell some modicum of muscle that was not directly vital to their survival. I didn't know if muscle grew back, but you'd be surprised what people were willing to do for money. In a world where people sold their own babies, would their own flesh be so unimaginable? I was ready to pay twice the going rate for a kidney. And two times more than that for actual flesh.

It was telling that Hafeez had voiced no concerns about harm to the potential donors. What a pure Third World reaction. Centuries of subjugation and brutality had inoculated my kind against excessive sympathy for our fellow man. The world is rife with this kind of callousness. Think of trafficked labor, say, from Central America. Sure, most of them came to be exploited in North American farms and brothels, but their own people had no qualms about parceling them off to such grisly fates. One could procure child brides in parts of Muslim Africa, or sex with children in Cuba or Cambodia. So, there was no surprise that countries with vast swathes of subsistence-level population would be open to even grimmer practices: the infanticide of girl children in India, or voluntary kidney-selling by poor families in Bangladesh. In China, they had turned 'organ donation' – in truth, organized culling – into a virtual industry. Against this backdrop of practices which the world had been tolerating for generations, I didn't see how our careful use of human flesh, voluntarily sold, was so beyond the pale.

As I saw it, the human condition was simple and obvious: to be consumed by other humans, one way or another, was the fate of most souls to tread this earth, and then to perish without trace.

Let philosophers quibble about the salvation of the hapless billions. For my purposes I could trust my colleagues in Bangladesh to procure the goods without protest. Now I needed someone who could bring the goods over safely.

I met with Askari at his office in Astoria, a neighborhood that was tonier now than when Bangladeshis first started flocking here. His room was handsomely appointed, as one would expect, with wood panels and ebulliently colorful Persian carpets. He made me a creamy latte – trust him to have a coffeemaker of suitable caliber for the job, and that too resting on a rosewood console table of vintage quality.

'So, what can I do for you?'

He knew I had come on business. I had kept in touch with him since the meeting at Mrs Zaman's. I'd given him a big discount when he came to The Hide soon after, dessert and port on the house. My sixth sense had told me I'd be needing him at some point.

'I want something brought over from Bangladesh.'

'Easy,' Askari said smiling, as if to say, 'let's move on to the real issue'. I admired, almost envied, the sheen of health on his smoothly shaved face. I saw it as the rude glow of success. Once I boasted such radiance. Lately it had been dimming.

'It's an unusual product,' I said.

'As long as it's not drugs or arms, I'm listening.' Askari's eyes twinkled with intrigue. He was enjoying a palaver that didn't involve the usual haggling over prices or the tedium of administrative issues like L/C's or shipping times.

'Of course not,' I said. 'It is far more exotic.'

Askari chuckled; I thought he'd appreciate my reasoning. I was about to ask him to do something that would probably be in violation of a litany of rules. Money alone would not be enough to entice him. I needed to get him interested. I needed to make him feel essential. To make the mission worth being part of.

'Is it safe for me to know what that is, or better if I don't?'

The fact that he'd even ask that question proved I was right to come to him with my proposition.

'Perhaps I can place you within a vicinity of the product, and then you can decide how much you'd like to know.'

'You know, Kash,' Askari said, 'from the time I met you at Mrs Zaman's, I knew we'd meet again, or I hoped we would.'

'Oh?' I said with a hint of genuine surprise.

'I had a feeling that you would not be dull,' said Askari with a little chuckle. 'You see, most Bengalis I meet seem to have the same story: misery back home, struggle here. Complaints about racism. Well, if that's so bad, why leave home in the first place? Look, I have great sympathy for them, and help out whenever I can. But these tales of immigrant woes bore me to death.'

'There is a big swathe of enlightened Americans with whom that shit sells well,' I said. And we both chuckled. 'Indeed, but as an immigrant,' I continued, 'tell them another story, and they won't know what to do with you. Foreigners, especially from the Third World, either need to tell tales of discrimination and overcoming, so they can be tucked away as good immigrants. And the hosts can be reassured of the ultimate superiority and justness of their culture. Or, the immigrant must narrate epic sorrows of war and fratricide, or brutal repression, among other horrors, of their old country.'

Askari laughed, and asked, 'What's the pleasure in reading about misery?'

'It helps affirm the White folks' notion of their world being a better place; morally sound if not superior, a refuge. Tell a story of any other kind, from your mouth, and they are befuddled. You're then of no use to anyone's purpose.'

Askari laughed at my little rant, approvingly. Perhaps not fully convinced but certainly amused.

His double espresso was long gone, and I was drawing on the dregs of my piccolo latte, remnants of the foam clinging to the inner sides of my little clear glass receptacle.

'One more?' Askari said, getting up.

'I'm not going to say no to espresso coming out of a Faema,' I replied.

'Oh, a connoisseur, I see,' Askari said appreciatively. 'It's an E61 Legend, vintage!'

I whistled in admiration. I knew that 1961 vintage machines could easily run into the thousands.

'And the beans,' Askari added, 'are from a co-op in Costa Rica, single-farm, hand-picked!'

'Oh, you should have told me before,' I said. 'I'd have asked for a black then.'

'Here you go,' Askari said, handing me just that.

Most Bangladeshis grow up with tea and lack any taste for coffee. For that matter, most of them also possess little knowledge about truly good tea. The culture had been too poor for too long to develop a true gourmandizing spirit, except in the case of own-culture delicacies: biriyani (*Dhakai dum*-style above all); fish (hilsa, forever); sweetmeats (*rasgullas* made with molasses and *cham chams* from Porabari). I could extend the list. But Askari, like me, was willing and able to go into new branches of delectation that required a re-training of one's palate. Indeed, mindset. We were kindred spirits.

'You know, "assimilation" has become a dirty word,' he said, as if reading my mind. 'I think that's a mistake for both the host culture and their guests. There is no harm and no shame in fitting in with the norms where you are. I switched to coffee, among many other changes, when I moved to America.'

'True enough,' I said. 'I have no patience for folks who come here and then become obsessed with retaining their Bengali or Muslim identity in some pure form. They'd never be so devoted to the articles of those identities – real or imaginary – if they'd stayed home.'

'I still enjoy many Bengali elements of my life – fish curry, Satyajit Ray movies, cricket,' Askari said in response. 'I don't get the anxiety about staying true to one's ethnic roots. It's not as if you could erase that if you tried!'

'Of course, Americans aren't helping matters either with an excess of their new pieties.'

'Meaning?'

'You know, they need their immigrants to be properly ethnic. They don't know what to do with a foreigner who is here but who isn't an immigrant.'

'Hmm,' Askari said, pensively. I could tell this was not

something he had thought about before. He was comfortable in his identity and place as an immigrant. I, on the other hand, didn't see myself as an immigrant, but as an adventurer. I had chosen America as my frontier, but I could have just as easily tried my luck in Turkey or Japan.

'So, you don't think you're an immigrant?'

'I am for practical purposes, yes,' I replied. 'But in terms of identity. I see myself as no different from, say, White folks who make homes and careers in other countries. They're never called an immigrant. They're expats. So, think of me as a Colored Expat!'

'Interesting,' Askari said. 'Then why choose America?'

'Because it still has more room for someone with a frontier spirit! It's still a good place for experimentation, for adventure. For someone like me, starting from scratch, to make a mark.'

'Fair enough,' said Askari. 'And how exactly do you intend to make this mark?'

The aroma wafting out of the cup Askari handed me was so fragrant with a leathery richness that it felt intoxicating. Askari sat back in his plush, black executive chair, with its finely calibrated tilt and swivel, with a fresh double espresso.

'So,' I said, in a more serious tone, 'I have branched out from the restaurant into high-end catering. I have a dinner to host for billionaires. I mean that literally; every guest will be a billionaire. It's a little club they have. For anyone catering private dinners, it's the ultimate gig right now in NY. And they wouldn't be who they are if they didn't seek – and get – what no one else can have.'

I could tell that I had his attention. Nobody, at least nobody in the moneymaking business, can resist wanting to be associated, even if only indirectly, with any project tagged to a billionaire.

'So, let's say there's a special item on our menu this time that'd be best sourced from Bangladesh. It's not technically illegal, but it may be frowned upon. It's so rare that it's not on the list of your approved products, but nor is it on any list of prohibited items.'

'Okay,' Askari said. He was sitting still now, no more micro-swivels on his chair. 'If it comes as part of a larger consignment of frozen foods, then there should not be a problem. Even if customs stop the container for a random check, they are unlikely to open each case.'

'It's also unlikely anyone would know on mere sight what it is.'

'You have someone on the ground there to source it? And they can give it to my guys freeze-packed?'

'Yes. That's all taken care of. Your guys simply need to tuck it into a case of regular items.'

'Sounds doable,' Askari said.

'There's one more issue. Time is of essence.'

'Ahh,' said Askari. 'We need to air-ship it.'

'That's why I came to you. I felt you'd not only have the discretion that's needed, and the solutions, but that you'd also understand the special nature of this need in a way that others wouldn't.'

'Of course,' Askari said. 'Always happy to help a fellow Bangladeshi. Especially one who's doing such interesting things.'

'Thank you,' I said. 'And this will pay more than what you earn when shipping an entire container. Much more.'

You could never underestimate the financial incentive.

'How well do you know these billionaires?'

I chuckled internally. While the profit mattered, an easy windfall with seemingly low risk, the real hook for him was the mention of 'billionaires'. Once I left, his mind would be racing with fantasies of how I might introduce him to such lofty figures, and how it might lead to opportunities beyond his wildest dreams.

'Well enough to get such a gig,' I said. 'I can't say I'm friends with them, but I've gotten to know the man who's hosting this pretty well.'

'I don't suppose I should be asking who it is,' he said.

I smiled. Someday, I said, once the sensitive dinner was behind us, I'd be happy to make introductions. It was always good to have some cachet. Lots of interesting people came through The Hide. I could stage natural-seeming introductions with regulars on Wall Street, in other avenues of commerce, in glamorous arenas of culture. I knew I'd have to dangle all this to cement the deal, to keep Askari hooked. The offer was this: do me this one turn, import a dodgy product for me, and I'll open doors for you that you couldn't on your own.

The deal he offered me was simple; he would charge the price of a twenty-foot container of prized Black Tiger shrimps. The transport should have cost no more than US$3,000, but air-shipment cost more than twice, and given the high and unspecified nature of the risks, he had to add a premium. We closed the deal at $30k. A tolerable amount for me, especially given that there was no 'market price' for what I had in mind. And a handsome earning for him for ultimately little hassle – though a gamble in terms of risk. It helped that we felt kindred on other levels.

I sensed that Askari, like me, was here to make a mark as well as a buck.

'Tell me, Kash, what do you see?'

I had come to meet Viktor at the rooftop bar of a new midtown hotel. 'You'll have exactly fifteen minutes with my uncle,' Yusep had told me. 'That's long enough for me,' I had quipped, projecting confidence (and a secret prayer). Viktor was attending some gala at the hotel and would meet me for one drink beforehand. A gala! Why couldn't they just call it a fucking party? Since the rich preferred to have their own names for things, I could only hope that after tonight *le nouveau morceau* would start finding a place in their louche lexicon.

Viktor and I were standing on the edge of the sixty-seventh floor roof. A running glass-board made an infinity wrap-around. A glass wall guarded the precipice, making us feel safely suspended above reality.

The rooftop was buzzing with a scented crowd that consisted of men who were too corpulent to make a good meal, and women who were too lean. Ever since we conceived of *le nouveau morceau*, I found that I could not help but size people up as potential meals.

Viktor had appeared to break my reverie. He looked dapper as usual in a slim dark suit. I wasn't sure what his question meant. *What do you see?* It sounded like the kind of crypto-wisdom quiz that the moneyed like to spring on the penniless, the elderly on the young and masters of arcane arts on their apprentices. What did I see? I could play along by giving an honest answer – Buildings! Lights! Or make more of an effort and hazard more cunning guesses – Hubris!

Futility! Instead, I decided to take the challenge full on with an enigma of my own, and said, 'I see Icarus – landing safely.'

Viktor smiled. 'Good,' he said.

It's not easy to get the attention of a sub-billionaire. So, I felt pleased with my counter-gambit. A waitress who looked as if she had walked off the runway of a Tom Ford or Alexander McQueen show – alien-tall and skeleton-thin – brought over our drinks. Martinis served not in the customary glasses, but in long, conically shaped receptacles designed probably by a solitary Zen master in a Japanese island of eternal fog. You needed a story to charge $30 for a martini.

I looked again at the view. You never saw starlight in New York. Only city lights. As if a giant had snatched all the blinking dots off the night sky and trapped them in the rising towers and spires of the looming skyline. They blinked in the windows and off-street lamps, on spikes and antennae and on the fronts and backs of endless vehicles.

'So, tell me Icarus, where and how do you intend to land?' Viktor asked.

'Rewrite the rules,' I said. 'That's the way. Icarus's mistake wasn't flying too high but imagining that he needed to. Fly higher than all others – that should have been his goal. Go where others haven't, yet. But don't burn yourself for fuck's sake.'

'And how does that translate for my dinner?'

Viktor was almost halfway through his drink, whereas I had taken only a few sips. Parts of our fancy martini glass were opaque and full of internal twists that were hard to read.

'Your pals want something unprecedented. You are

worried that even our meal of danger can be argued with. Well then, let's really give them what they want.'

'OK! What's the idea though?'

'You serve what none of them have had before. You serve the wildest game of all.'

'The wildest game of all?'

'The riskiest. One that is both endangered, by itself, and is a danger to all other life forms: the planet itself.'

Viktor whistled. There, I'd said it. Viktor's expression was inscrutable. My heart pounded. This is the moment where he could decide I was a lunatic – or that I was his man. To my relief, his eyes sparkled. Viktor's well-scrubbed and finely creased face cracked into a friendly smile.

I could see Yusep tapping his watch at me from a distance. Yusep no longer looked like an eager student. He had cropped his hair. Our boy was coming into his own, as Adair and I had learned. Yusep had agreed to bat for us afterward, when his uncle spoke to him. What he wanted in exchange was not any monetary cut in the deal but something subtler: he wanted a role in Adair's corporate coaching business. He didn't want to work in the embassy or go home. 'Fuck that!' he had said to us, putting a lifetime's distaste into the landing thud of the 'that'. He wanted to strike out on his own; make a way in the world, and in New York. Away from the spider's web of his Kazakh family.

'Okay, tell me more,' Viktor said, suddenly somber.

I quickly explained the work I'd already done. We could 'safely' source organs and some flesh from healthy and willing donors – compensated insanely well by their standards – in Bangladesh and have them shipped out through super-safe channels.

'The people who do this work, you trust them?'

'The man on the ground is my own brother,' I said.

Viktor raised an eyebrow in surprise – but also as a sign that he was impressed. No matter how much more power or wealth someone may possess, you can always achieve an ersatz parity with them in terms of capacity or performance, if your perversity is deep enough.

'But we don't want anyone to get hurt,' Viktor said. 'I mean, people are of course incurring some damage if they're willing to spare even a pound . . . but no taking of a life. Right?'

We were negotiating. 'Yes, of course,' I said. 'Damage only up to the point that it can be compensated with cash.'

My job now was to assure him. Ever since I had floated this idea, everyone from Patti to Viktor, even Adair and Hafeez had needed coaxing towards its acceptance. Only Kang had been unperturbed. I had always liked his pathological pragmatism. It could come across almost as amorality. I had seen back home, especially in people of older generations, grandees and clan-heads – who were in charge of the survival of the many against improbable odds – possessed such severe practicality and a corresponding lack of sentimentality.

Kang had also shed some opinions on which parts might be best to serve: pectorals, glutes and calves. Maybe shoulders, triceps and biceps. Thighs too. Stomach muscles for their tensile strength and texture. Organs, of course; Kang never said no to organs, no matter the species. I told him I could not guarantee the parts; we could not be sure we'd have a whole specimen to work with. So, he would need to be ready with recipes for whatever became available.

Helen, of course, was the real originator of the idea. And, to my surprise, the only one who could handle the kind of conversation around this topic that Kang raised with such blitheness. Adair was squeamish. Patti wary. And Adair had told me that Yusep didn't flinch when he heard what we had in mind either. It was too small a sample from which to generalize, but I could not help suspecting that Yusep still retained enough of a hardy Third World instinct for getting on with the necessaries to take the horror of our project in his stride. Or, not see it as such a horror.

'Exactly. We are building on the earlier idea of "Danger". But posing physical danger isn't enough. This group, they need to face moral hazard.'

'They won't see this coming,' Viktor said approvingly.

'And they can't top it – nothing can. They wanted "unprecedented"; you will give them exactly that.'

'Their rules said nothing about things being legal,' Viktor said.

'It won't be illegal. No action we are taking in the course of this meal is itself fully illegal,' I said. 'There is nothing explicitly in the books about cannibalism. There is prohibition against using body parts without consent. Against even consensual murder. But in our case, there would be no murder. And the use of body parts would be with consent. They even have laws about kidneys. But not flesh.'

'But you are proposing to use kidneys?'

'Hence, the need to be on international waters. It'd be a novel enough setting. No one in the Miner's Club has staged a dinner there yet, even if many of them go there on their yachts. With our offer, the blue waters won't be just a scenic setting, but a theatre for our gesture of radical liberation.'

A tall blonde assistant approached us and hovered within our peripheral vision, to remind Viktor that he was running late. Viktor signaled to her with an almost imperceptible gesture that he was aware, and he would be on his way soon.

'Custom,' Viktor said, 'is as important as the law.'

'Selling our bodies is what all physical labor, including sex work, or even wet nurses from another era, is all about. And there are underground Vampire Clubs these days. Ordinary people think nothing of eating placenta. And eating human flesh when in dire need, like the footballers who crashed in the Andes, has always been accepted by everyone. Anything that is accepted in extremis should also be permissible *de jure*.'

'You're giving me something to think about,' Viktor had said. 'That doesn't happen every day.'

'I can bring you all the details soon,' I said. 'Menu and recipes. The legal angles and precautions. But I need to know the exact guest list. And anything that's worth knowing about their tastes; any allergies, preferences for wine, and all that. I'm sure Yusep can secure that from their assistants.'

'Of course,' Viktor said.

I said goodbye feeling more confident that Viktor would give his consent. I shot a glance at Yusep as I raised my glass to his uncle in response and caught the young man – sly and alert bastard that he was – doing the same from his perch at the bar. There was a look on his face that said: we're all in.

CHAPTER 19

Before I left Dhaka, a strange mood beset me. In those final days, I fell into the habit of wandering the city without purpose. I felt a premonition that I might not see this city again. Despite my conflicted feelings about it, I needed to construct a private farewell. I sought out the places I knew. Neighborhoods where we had once lived. Parks where I'd played as a kid. I visited favorite old restaurants: Star Kabab and Chilli's, which in Dhaka was a Chinese place. I strolled around Dhanmondi Lake and went around to my grandfather's old house. It had been sold off after his death and obliterated by the new owners as if in a vengeful erasure of all my memories.

I began to lose myself in unknown parts of town. I didn't care for the new areas so much; they felt boring in their grim, concrete homogeneity. I visited Old Town and the *ghats*. The river was among the dirtiest in the world, but the busyness of boats loaded with crops and goods was mesmerizing. I found a little shop, a green-tiled hole-in-the-wall, where the head baker sat cross-legged on a raised platform and tossed out the lightest, flakiest and most flavorful *bakarkhanis* on his tandoor. I cruised the wider boulevards of the colonial era, bought pastries at the old Intercontinental, and stopped at the legendary bar, Sakura. The bookstores in Shahbagh. I went to the New Market, which was no longer new by any standard, and brought home a wheel of Dhaka paneer.

'You're going to take that to America?' Hafeez had asked me with a mocking smile.

It was during these wanderings that I found myself one day in the Farm Gate area. It was one of the busiest intersections in the city. More people congregated there in any given hour than you could get into any town square in Europe during a proper revolution. A dictator had built the city's first 'foot over-bridge' there in the late Seventies or early Eighties. This feat was celebrated back then, in the tragicomic way of a Third World dictatorship, as an achievement almost on a par with the moon landing. To make much out of meager, even laughable, achievements was one of the hallmarks of all Third World dictators of the Cold War era. And General Zia, during whose term this bridge was built, was no exception. He dug canals throughout the country to help with irrigation, and got the cowed population to applaud his hard work – even though most of them never saw the expected water-flow due to technical errors. He hosted a fellow dictator from an African nation, and the government-owned TV, the only single-channel station available in Bangladesh of the late Seventies, broadcast it as if it were a top global summit.

Where the dictator did excel, however, was the one area about which the entire media, and he himself, was studiously quiet: the hanging of real and suspected challengers. After one of the two dozen or more coups during his few years in power, it came to light much later, he had hanged over six hundred army officers. Many of the orders were signed, sometimes as a batch, as if the sentenced were a fungible commodity, while he ate his lunch. Like many army officers of his generation, he ate with knife and fork, and that allowed for extreme efficiency in signing off on executions.

For all his other faults, and unlike many members of the middle class, my father was never fooled by Zia or his propaganda. He was steadfast in his admiration of the Father of the Nation, Sheikh Mujib, whose brutal assassination had paved the way for Zia to assume power. He rejected Zia's Islamizing of the country as an abomination. And thus, he never took us to see the over-bridge or any other developmental landmarks. But during my anticipatory nostalgia walkabouts around Dhaka, some perverse curiosity pulled me to the blighted Farm Gate foot over-bridge.

It was the middle of a sun-blasted afternoon.

The railing was splattered with bird shit and stains from spit-out red betel juice. The passersby who chose this path were mostly middle-aged men, who had perhaps lost the agility or gumption to dart across speeding traffic. I leaned over a rare clean spot on the railing to enjoy the chaos of traffic and the tumult of the people below.

Buses raced each other to the stop; whichever got there first would get to load more passengers. In this competition the buses would over-park, causing major congestion in the remaining lanes. Yet vehicles still tried to edge past each other with drag-racing techniques: cutting each other off, never giving a pass, bullying lighter vehicles into retreat. And still, through all this madness, people traversed the wide boulevard in an unending stream, while intrepid hawkers of items – from newspapers and glass bangles to fresh-cut fruits, woven bamboo mats and stools – plied their trade on the street, often in the middle of the traffic, to passengers and pedestrians.

On this day, I spotted one such passerby, an office-goer out on a midday errand, chatting with a peddler of pirated books. What book could be so urgent for him that he had to procure it without the pair removing themselves to the safety of a sidewalk? A gaggle of nuns with their pillowcase headdresses crossed the street in a great hurry, arm in arm, but without breaking their chain-link bond. It could be a sport, I felt.

In the middle of this commotion, my vision registered an anomaly. The kind of information that the brain picks up before the consciousness can process it. I realized that among the great ferment below there was a figure who was known to me: my father. He was dressed simply in a white shirt and his hair was brushed back in his old style, slightly off to one side. He had aged since I'd last seen him. There were streaks of gray in his hair, and a subtle stoop to his shoulders, which I could detect even from this distance. But what surprised me most was his little companion: a boy, about seven or eight years old, held by his hand. The boy was in his school uniform. A cheap backpack hung from his shoulders. I studied his face; his complexion was lighter than my father's and his features were as sharp and slender as those of Rubina the maid.

We knew they had had a child together, a boy. My half-brother. But we had never seen him. I was still taking in the shock when a bus arrived and hid them from view. When the bus left, they were gone.

I don't believe in the supernatural, but it was hard not to

feel that the city I had so conspicuously failed to love had decided to bestow on me an astonishing parting gift, which I received gratefully. My father had managed to love another boy the way we never felt loved by him. Surprisingly, it didn't spur any feelings of rage or bitterness. I felt oddly soothed. I never told my mother or my brother what I saw that day. I feared that their reactions would spoil any tenderness I had from this serendipitous revelation. I was content to take it as a secret farewell from the city of my birth.

Three days after my meeting with Viktor, Yusep came to The Hide to tell me that it was a go: An Evening of Danger, featuring human flesh as the *pièce de résistance*! Adair had overslept and missed the meeting. This presented me with the perfect opportunity and I raised the issue of the payment.

'You know, I need a guarantee.'

'You think Viktor won't pay?'

'No, I think you will run off with it!'

We both laughed. We both knew that there was nowhere either of us could run to where Viktor would not be able to locate us.

'Seriously, though, man,' I said. 'It's a lot of money.'

'What do you want?'

'I want you to have the money here, at The Hide, from the moment we board. I'll have a trusted associate here to receive it.'

I was thinking of Samad, of course.

'When the trip ends, I'll come straight here and you will release the money to us.'

Yusep pondered this in silence for a moment.

'Once we board, you know shit is going down. We can't

not deliver at that point. So, our end is all but guaranteed. We need the money secured too.'

'Okay,' Yusep said. 'I'll bring it in a portable safe, and chain it to something in your office. Something that can't be moved. And the key will be with me.'

He was hardly the greenhorn being schooled by Adair anymore. He was capable of making his own decisions, and with an air of crisp confidence.

'Fair enough,' I said.

'I'll have to run it by my uncle, of course.' Clearly, he also knew his place and didn't over-promise. All his moves I found reassuring.

'Please do,' I said. And we shook hands on this little understanding.

Knowing I'd have my hands on the cash before anyone else left me with a feeling of deep restfulness; I wasn't about to get fucked over again by anyone in any manner.

But by now I had also heard from Hafeez, and parts of the planned '*pièce*' had met with not entirely unexpected '*résistance*'. Hafeez had managed to secure sources for two human kidneys. The advance was paid, culling assured, delivery guaranteed. But even the kidney brokers were reportedly appalled when Hafeez raised the topic of human flesh. Hafeez said he had to quickly change the topic lest they back out altogether.

In my desperation, I had broached the topic with our meat-seller, Hagi. At first, he thought I was joking. That's why I had lubricated his brain-motors with generous doses of cognac in the little cubby of my office first.

'You crazy,' he said with a laugh, when he realized I was serious.

'It's for a group of billionaires,' I replied, and filled him in on the Miner's Club.

Once I invoked that benighted clique of Ubermensch, Hagi did not question my seriousness anymore. Billionaires were capable of anything; they lived in a space beyond the trappings of ordinary laws and morality. I wanted to know if he knew any sources who could prove useful. He shook his head. It could not be done. I knew my secret was safe with him, but he too was a dead end.

If pitching Hagi was one act of desperation, then my moonshot was to go see Dr Hazari. I had the inklings of a most extreme possibility start to take shape in my head, and I felt that having someone like our community doctor on hand, perhaps even on board the ship where we intended to hold the dinner service, might be a notion. But one can't just blurt out a pitch for cannibalism. Illicit proposals require a soft, silky approach. Besides, I was overdue for an assessment of my wound and a dressing. When I entered Dr Hazari's dimly lit chamber, to my surprise I found my friend Samad there.

'Oh hello,' I said.

'Hi Kash.' Samad was as ever all smiles.

It was a hot, late summer afternoon, and the curtains were drawn shut. A window AC unit, seemingly from the Soviet era and perhaps of such dubious make, made strange noises, like an animal being throttled or a small car backfiring, while blowing out only a modest stream of cool air.

'Come,' said Dr Hazari. 'Samad just dropped by with some sad news.'

Samad didn't look like he was carrying sad news, but at the mention of it his usually beaming and dark-as-teak face recomposed itself into a semblance of somberness.

'It's Mrs Zaman,' said Dr Hazari.

'She has cancer,' added Samad.

'Oh my god, that's awful!'

I sat down on the other side of the shabby sofa occupied by Samad. Mrs Zaman was like a mother to us all. She had housed us when we first arrived – and no one else would have. She allowed anyone hitting a bad patch to go on residing at her makeshift hostel. And came by with soup or oranges when she heard someone had fallen sick.

'That's not all,' said Dr Hazari. 'She got hit with a very large amount of back taxes and had to sell the house.'

'The one in Woodside?'

'And the apartments in Sunnyside,' added Samad.

'Holy crap! When did this happen?'

I had been too preoccupied with my own troubles to stay in the loop of community news. A sudden choking feeling gripped me, like when I first heard that my mother had suffered a stroke. And panic gripped me that we might lose our surrogate mother. Losing my real one was hard enough, but the thought of New York without Mrs Zaman made me feel unmoored. I didn't see her so often anymore, but simply knowing she was out there helping new batches of hopefuls was comforting.

'She must have some savings?' I asked with faint hope.

'She had sunk what she'd saved into the Woodside house,' said Samad.

'But she owned several apartments in Sunnyside, didn't she?'

'She didn't own them,' Dr Hazari said, with a sigh of exasperation. 'She rented them, and then sublet to hapless buggers like you guys.'

This was, for all my savvy, unknown to me. 'And the rents she charged—'

'Barely paid for the rent she paid,' Dr Hazari completed my thought.

'Why do it then?'

'Who else would rent to you guys? Who else would take the risk of over-stacking them to keep the rent cheap?'

'So, it was all for . . . charity?'

'You could say that,' said Dr Hazari, as he rose to leave the room, and motioned at Samad, indicating that he should fill me in. I knew he was going to make tea. There was no point protesting. Trying to stop a Bengali making tea for their guests is as futile as telling a bull in Pamplona not to charge at a waving red flag.

What I learned from Samad cast the bad news of the disease into a more depressing light. Mrs Zaman was diagnosed with Stage 2 colon cancer, which apparently was not the most dire of diagnoses as cancers go. It was a more treatable type of cancer, and still at a curable stage. But the cure was expensive and, like so many immigrants, even well-heeled ones, she had not acquired the kind of insurance that would have covered its costs.

The conjunction of her tax problems meant she was also now short of cash to pay out of pocket; and bills could easily run into the tens of thousands, perhaps more.

As it happened, there was no dearth of well-wishers for Mrs Zaman. People had already pulled together to support her. A family in Jackson Heights was putting her up in their spare room for now. And medical bills were being paid ad hoc by weekly fundraisers by whomever was willing to cough up something. Samad, not surprisingly, was running the funding drives.

'But this is not a solution,' Dr Hazari said.

'Right,' I said, unsure though as to what would be a solution.

'If we could persuade her to go to India,' said Dr Hazari, 'that'd be an idea. Health care there is very good and much, much cheaper.'

'Does she know anyone there?'

'No,' said Samad. 'Any other place that fits that profile, say Turkey or Thailand, she doesn't have people. We don't have people.'

So many Bangladeshis everywhere, yet not where you need them sometimes when you need them the most.

'Then our only option is to raise a lot of money. Askari is willing but no one man can raise the kind of funds one needs to raise.'

They both stared at me, and I understood their meaning.

'I'll do whatever I can,' I said.

Samad shot me a look. He knew what critical straits I was facing myself. But it wasn't just concern for me; he didn't want me making any promises I might fail to keep – not on this score.

I knew what I owed Mrs Zaman. So, I meant what I said, as if it were for my own mother.

The rest of my visit was whiled away on ideas – good and hare-brained – of how we could raise funds. There was the delicacy too of getting a proud woman like Mrs Zaman to accept charity.

'We have to convince her that if she takes this help now,' Samad said, 'then she can come back to help others again.'

It was a highly optimistic angle, but I could not think of any better. The real reason for which I had come, to see if Dr Hazari would be willing to come on board, literally, for my on-the-ocean dinner, I had to postpone for now. But the commitment I got drawn into, in his presence and at his behest, meant we were now also bound up in a new bond of implicit mutual obligations. I decided I'd come back another day to ask and felt it would not be in vain.

I got a call from Boris the next day. It had been a long time since he had called me directly. The digital inscription on my screen – BORIS – beamed with the menace of a red light on an oncoming train.

Boris wanted me to come see him at his office in midtown. This was unexpected, but the venue and timing felt safe enough. Even Russian mafia would surely not choose to dismember their victims on Tenth Avenue at noon. But you can never feel too sanguine about meeting a person who has already taken off one of your fingers.

'You need backup,' Patti said.

I didn't tell Helen that I was going to see Boris. I was worried she'd insist on coming with me. I was also hoping she would not find out, or I'd have hell to pay – for not telling her.

'Hmm, I guess I do.'

'Take Dolores,' she said. 'I'd come myself, but we have the training—'

I put up a hand as if to say, *No need to explain.*

Dolores was the hardiest of the whole lot of convicts who ran our kitchen. And also, had been with us the longest. She was a small, squat Guatemalan woman. Short hair, tattoos, and smiled as little as Kang.

'She'll know what to do if shit goes south.'

I didn't doubt that she would. She used to work as a mule for a Mexican cartel in the Texas border. One time, when one of the *siccarios* tried to rape her, she punctured his thorax with a hairpin (she had long hair back then) and left him to rot under a cactus. She moved to New York and changed her name. She went to prison for other crimes – stealing copper wires from a construction site.

On the morning of my appointment, I found Dolores skulking under the awning of a nearby bodega. She wore a multi-pocketed jacket, clearly to conceal weapons, and heavy military boots. I rehearsed our plans again.

'If anything happens, I'll press this beeper. And you come running up. If you can get in, great. If not, call 911 – and tell these fuckers you're doing that. And tell Patti.'

Dolores gave me a cold look as if to say, *You don't need to tell me anything twice.* I wondered what kind of weapons she was carrying, but thought best to let that be her secret.

'And *do not* call Helen.'

'Yes, yes, I know,' she said at last, impatiently. And I took that as my cue to go.

I took the elevator, as instructed, to the nineteenth floor. Boris's office was at the end of a hallway, and I was received by a matronly Russian woman whom I recalled from my visits in more halcyon days. The elderly receptionist accompanied me inside; Gruff was sitting outside Boris's door. And on seeing me, he flashed the fulvous grin of a diseased soul.

I was ushered in momentarily. Boris's office was large and simply adorned with an old wooden desk, an out-of-place button-tufted settee against one wall, with a pair of matching sofas. A pair of aquamarine Gardner porcelain vases sat atop a mantelpiece; but the fireplace was merely decorative. Rich red Turkish rugs covered the floor.

Boris's taste in decoration was both more refined and staider than I'd expected. His window framed a slice of the midtown skyline. The only Russian touch seemed to be a gleaming bronze samovar, albeit a modern electric one, that sat atop the center table of the sofa setting.

Boris didn't stand up and didn't offer his hand. He looked ruddy as always but seemed to have lost weight. In fact, he now looked like he would have perfect marbling. He also looked a little thinner on top, as if his hairline, like a trained battleline, had suddenly retreated.

'Good morning, Boris,' I said.

I didn't know how I might feel seeing him – nervous? angry? – given that at our last encounter he had cut off my finger. Surprisingly, I felt nothing; just the tension that one feels at a business meeting with an especially obdurate counterpart.

I had come prepared. I had taken a chance and carried the Colt .32 strapped to my ankle. My bet was correct; they held me in too much contempt to pat me down. I had started going to a firing range.

'Sit, sit,' Boris said, appearing somehow a bit subdued.

'Thanks,' I said. 'I take it you want to hear about your money,' I said.

'Of course. I want to hear about your big dinner. It is happening or not?'

'Oh, it's very much happening,' I said. 'Before I share the good news though, Boris, can I ask you something?'

'Sure,' Boris said, with a hint of irritated weariness. He leaned back in his chair.

'What was it like?'

'What was what like?' Boris seemed puzzled.

'You know, what I sent you.'

Boris's face darkened, as much in confusion as in distaste.

'You received it, right? I was curious myself but didn't take a taste as there was so little to begin with.'

'You make fun of me?'

'Are you kidding?' I said, raising my good hand to my chest in a show of sincerity. And then I pointed at my missing finger. Or to be precise, the joint where it once was affixed. And said, 'You think I'd dare?'

Boris grimaced and waved his hand, as if to swat away the offending evidence and said, 'You crazy, Kash. You fucking mental.'

The feel of the gun against my right calf imbued me with a feeling of confidence that I had not felt in Boris's presence for some time now – predating even the encounter at the gym. I understood, in a flash, the American obsession with guns. You don't have to fire it to feel its power; simply knowing you had such annihilating potency in your possession was enough.

'Seriously though, Boris, what did you do with it? My finger.'

'What I do? I give to my boys and tell them to throw away.'

'That's a pity,' I said, feeling a twinge of sadness for the unceremonious casting away of something that had once been literally a part of me.

The door to the room began to open. I felt myself tensing up, and my good hand reached for the side of my calf where my gun was attached. False alarm. It was the tall blonde assistant who appeared at the door. In response to a gruffly delivered order, she went over to the samovar and began fussing with it.

'Tell me about the dinner,' Boris said.

'Six billionaires on one yacht,' I said with an air of mystery and maybe a touch of hauteur.

Boris held on to his grim expression. I knew he was being coy. Meeting a billionaire is like meeting the Pope or the Queen. You don't have to believe in their holiness or their divine right to be awed by their presence. Money was the religion of our times. No state and no army, no borders and no strictures commanded a final sway over money anymore: capital was the ultimate sovereign. As inexorable as water, money could break dams, overflow lands, run around all obstructions. Anyone who possessed money in ungodly amounts appeared godly to us pitiful avaricious souls.

'Good for you,' Boris said, finally.

'Good for you, too,' I retorted.

The blonde was beside us, placing ornamented cups with gilt edges in front of us. A single biscuit rested on the saucer. I thanked her but she vanished with no reply. The fragrance of the tea was soothing. I took a deep sip.

'Good, how?'

'With this gig, and everything that comes with it, I'll have your money, the full amount.'

'So you say,' Boris said. 'How I know any of this is true?'

'I know what's waiting for me if I fail,' I said.

'Look, what good it be for me if I hurt you? I want my money.'

I was struck, momentarily, by the accidental properness of Boris's speech – 'what good it be' – and felt it in synch with his glum mood. This felt like the perfect moment to broach a bit more of my plans, and extend an invitation to the boat.

'Come with us,' I said, without any further feints or circumlocution.

'You inviting me? You have power to invite?'

Boris looked skeptical. I reverted now back to my 'humble' routine. 'Boris, if you come to the dock and I can't get you to board the ship, what happens to me when I come back on shore?'

Boris seemed not only convinced by this logic but pleased with my newfound submissiveness.

'Look, I have become friendly enough with Viktor that I'm sure he'd grant me this much leeway as a favor. I'll tell him you're a good friend. I can't promise you a place at the table with the billionaires – that's up to him. But a berth, that much I can guarantee. And of course, tastings of every course of the fine, fine meal we are producing.'

Boris kept staring at me, and then shook his head. It occurred to me that for a sadist of his caliber, to have power over another person was the ultimate pleasure. So, while he no doubt wanted his money back, and was thrilled to be invited on the boat, he felt his hold over me suddenly slip. The closer I got to making him whole again, the closer I was to escaping his grip for good.

'I believe when I see,' Boris said, perhaps in the hope of extending the torment of my unequal status a little longer.

'Fair enough,' I said.

The window behind him was aglow with the light of a bright New York morning. I could not tell how much of his pine-needle hair was silver and how much simply bristling in the sunshine. The skin on his face looked a bit drawn and full of special peptides of disgust at the state of the world, or his place in it. If humans did appear regularly on menus, he would not be a prized piece. He'd get crushed into keema or burger patties at best.

I rose to take my leave, and Boris emitted a snort by way of farewell. That was good enough for me. He was not only on board with my ideas, but was now committed to being on board with me on our vessel. If he had been the master of matters on land, the sea would belong entirely to me.

CHAPTER 20

Protocols of Ethical Sourcing and Consumption of *Le nouveau morceau*

To freely consume other animal forms for one's sustenance or pleasure is an act of human arrogance and places the species in a relationship to the living world that is injurious to both.

To call for the suspension of this practice is impractical; but to continue as a flesh-eater one should recognize that the power of consuming other species does not make humans special or superior.

To continue this form of consumption, in an ethical and responsible manner, one should restrict one's source of meats only to animals killed or slaughtered by one's own hands – or by expressing one's humility through a ritual partaking in the flesh of one's own kind.

This ritual should be conducted as per the following protocols –

1. No human can be killed for this purpose. And no minor, elder, disabled or diseased person may be considered a suitable subject for this purpose.
2. Any flesh that is sourced or secured for this event must be received from either a willing donor or an unclaimed body.

3. The healthfulness of the flesh must be ensured by a medically sound professional.
4. The amount consumed by any Ethical Consumer during this event may not exceed 2–3 morsels or 4 oz per person in quantity.
5. No sexual organs nor any part of the human face may be consumed for this event.

I came up with these guidelines in response to a request from Viktor. He felt such a radical enterprise, one sure to cause some moral issues (if not outright commotion) among its participants, especially those consuming human flesh, would need some justification.

I had been called to a final meeting with Viktor before all of us – crew, caterers and guests – boarded the yacht. We had barely a week to go. I still didn't have any human flesh, aside from the kidneys we had imported from Bangladesh. Those organs were inside a Tupperware box, in the freezer in my apartment. If law enforcement were tipped off and raided our place, I was sure the presence of such contraband would be enough to send me to jail. But it was still safer there, where only Helen and I knew about it, than it would be at The Hide.

Viktor had taken an interest in me since our last meeting. He had called me over on several occasions: once to have a working breakfast at his midtown office, with an unimpeded view of the Hudson River and the gigantic sprawl of Queens; the next time to visit a downtown gallery for a new photo exhibition on life in the steppes; and another time while he was doing some private shopping at Barneys. I imagine that these were moments that he normally shared with Yusep, but now I, too, had been conscripted to the role of a pseudo-nephew, faux-friend, proto-confidant, trusted underling. As much as I enjoyed this access and thrived on his attention, I could not tell what he hoped to get out of these meetings. Did he enjoy my company? That seemed flattering, even for my newly restored – or expanding – ego; surely a billionaire has no problem finding people who'd be glad to entertain them. Everyone hated the super-rich, but almost no one said 'no' to them.

I sure as hell could not.

We were at the gallery. Yusep was there too, and Viktor had set us loose to scour the gallery during a private preview, for photos that he might like to have in his collection. The gallery owner, an Upper West Side princess who'd normally never have the time for either of us, and probably appeared in the party page pictorials in magazines like *Vanity Fair* or *New York*, fawned over us as if we were the billionaires. The perks of being a favored companion to a billionaire were sometimes tangible – and sometimes satisfyingly material. The time we went to Barneys, I came out with a blazer and a handful of shirts and ties, all for barely an hour of telling Viktor if this fabric or that cut looked good on him.

I could not fully fathom why he was choosing to indulge me. I had to believe I was interesting enough. Viktor asked me what it was like to grow up in Dhaka. I figured this was a higher form of due diligence, to go beyond what a private eye can compile into a dossier: a real sense of the person, based on the nebulous, minute yet telling details that get revealed only on close interaction. I could not blame him; given what was at stake, I too would want to get a measure of the man on whom I was relying to pull off such an uncommon and risky stunt.

Viktor was amused by tales of how my childhood was filled with books and other trifles that came our way from the Soviet Union. Even for someone who had grown up in a part of the USSR, Viktor wasn't surprised to learn that the Cold War had extended as far as Bangladesh, but he was tickled to learn that the superpowers were desperate enough to vie over tiny souls – future proxies in their great ideological tussle. He listened to my account of my father's cruelties without comment. I even felt free to confess my visa scam. Since he had opened up to me to an unexpected degree, I could not resist the urge to reciprocate with some significant matter of confidence. He asked me about how we got the idea for The Hide, and how I arrived at the idea of *le nouveau morceau*.

'Really, it was Helen?' He seemed genuinely surprised and impressed. 'And Adair, he's on board too?'

'Yes, of course,' I said. And added, 'But you know, with white-folk queasiness.'

Viktor laughed with understanding. His laugh lines made his face look kind, and indeed avuncular. When he laughed, or even smiled, he did not feel like a super-rich man whose reality was miles apart from mine, but like an older mentor figure.

Two weeks before the dinner, Viktor summoned me to his apartment and handed me a slim dossier with a profile of all the guests. Five members of the Miner's Club, in addition to Viktor, had confirmed their attendance for Viktor's Evening of Danger. The Chinese and the Indian, whose competition led to the formation of the club in the first place. The Englishman who had set the rules. The Frenchman whom Viktor wished to bring down a peg. And the Mexican, who was one of the nicest people in the group, according to what Yusep had told me. Out of these principals, the Indian was the only one missing. 'Son's wedding,' Viktor had told me. 'You know how Indians are with that; goes on for bloody weeks.' I knew.

There were several pages on each man. They were a relatively young bunch, as billionaires go. The Englishman alone was in his seventies. And the Chinese man, at forty-five, was the youngest. The rest were in their fifties and sixties. There was more than such basic information in the dossier. Dietary matters: allergies and intolerances. Even minutiae, like who hated a particular color on their plate, who didn't like their plates hot (or cold), who didn't like wines from specific vineyards or vintages. Even who didn't like what kind of music (heavy metal, for all of them, it turned out, except the Chinese man).

No matter how ridiculous the parameters, I was ready to please.

'They don't know what's for dinner?' I asked Viktor one evening, sitting in the living room.

'Of course not! It's always a surprise.'

'You are not worried about how they'll react?'

'They set the bar at "unprecedented". I won't stand for any other qualms. Eat or don't eat, I don't care. But they have to judge on whether the meal was "unprecedented".'

'Amen to that.'

'I am so sick of these guys,' Viktor said, suddenly and unexpectedly. 'Their pretense and their arrogance, their rules and their rubbish. I don't care to be a member of their club anymore. I am going to smash it to tiny little bits.'

'I hear you, sir. Loud and clear.'

'And I have to thank you, my young friend, for opening my eyes to that option.'

We chinked our glasses of Scotch.

'You know, all my life I have tried to fit in. It's funny, you'd think the money would set you free. It's not so easy. It comes with expectations. You think that now that I'm at this level, I must act this way or behave that way. It takes time to break free of those notions.'

I imagined that he felt safe saying these things to me because I was a nobody. My lack of station rendered me harmless. Besides, most men cannot resist playing mentor to a willing protégé. And I was ready to play any role Viktor needed me to play – novice, amanuensis, footman, faux-ward, part-time confidant, task-monkey, ever-willing factotum – it didn't matter. I just needed the job. And to do it well enough to impress the hell out of him and get paid.

'Aunt Marge died.'

That was the text from Adair. I called him back, but he didn't pick up. I didn't know where he was, whether at home or in the hospital. I didn't know where he lived. He had never taken me to his place. He was always a bit vague about his living arrangements, but in time I gathered he lived with Aunt Marge. I was sure that for Aunt Marge having her only nephew – one she had raised like a son – by her side was a source of great comfort.

Unable to reach Adair on his cell, I called a landline number I had for him and was greeted by the voice of a distinctly older man.

'Hello?'

'Hi, is Adair there?'

'He's busy right now.'

'I'm his friend, Kash. His business partner.'

'Oh, I've heard of you. You see, there's a bad—'

'Yes, I know. He texted me.'

'Adair is talking to the guys from the mortuary.'

'Can I come over? I'm so sorry about Aunt Marge.'

My one encounter with the lady had not been a success. But I knew how much she meant to Adair and so my sentiments were sincere.

'Sure, please come over. Adair would be glad to see you.'

I had never been to Aunt Marge's place. The building where my cab stopped looked unremarkable. The lift rattled like an old tram car. Aunt Marge's place was at the end of a narrow, cheaply carpeted passage and the chipped blue door was forlorn in the pale light of the corridor. It didn't seem like the kind of place where Adair had grown up, at least not according to his own accounts of his life.

The man who opened the door introduced himself as Adair's 'Uncle Eddie', the same gentleman I had spoken to earlier. He let me into the small two-bedroom apartment. The place was cozy – to put it in flattering terms – and daintily decorated. The sofa set was upholstered in faded floral material. The walls were adorned with watercolors of New England scenes – colorful fall foliage, waterfronts and tiny yachts, ducks. It was fitting for a lady of Aunt Marge's age and comportment, but there was hardly a trace of Adair.

'Have a seat, Kash,' Uncle Eddie said, waving me toward the living room while he shuffled into the adjoining half-open kitchen area. The comforting scent of coffee permeated the air; I heard a percolator make gurgling noises.

'Adair just left.' Uncle Eddie shouted over the din from the kitchen. 'The funeral home has taken her away.'

This was a relief; I didn't want to see the beldam lying in state.

In recent weeks I had gradually grown more accustomed to the idea of cannibalism. In fact, I had even become comfortable with eyeing my fellow citizens as prospective meals. I didn't trust myself to not have unacceptable thoughts cross my mind at the sight of a corpse. I didn't think Adair would appreciate any such thoughts; and even if they occurred only in the privacy of my mind, I felt I'd be somehow disrespecting my friend and his feelings.

'I'm so sorry, Uncle Eddie,' I said, extending my formal condolences as we sat down. He had graciously handed me a mug of strongly brewed coffee.

'I'm glad it happened this way,' Uncle Eddie said. 'Peacefully in her sleep.'

I thought of my father's unseemly end, and my brush with violence, and I agreed. A death like Aunt Marge's, well into her eighties, was no small mercy. Uncle Eddie looked to be well into his seventies. Perhaps even into his early eighties. But despite his age and the circumstances, he presented himself smartly. Dapper in a rust-colored cardigan and green corduroys. He drank the coffee with long sips.

'If I may ask, how was she related to you?'

'We are first cousins.'

'So, you are from Adair's father's side?'

'Yes, I am also a White. Edmund White. But Ed or Eddie to my friends and family.'

'I am sorry,' I said again. 'I know she meant a lot to Adair.'

230

'Yes, she was a mother to him. Raised him in this very apartment.'

I nearly spat out my coffee but managed to keep my mouth closed. Adair grew up in this dingy little apartment? *Fuck me!*

'Are you okay?'

'Yes, sorry,' I said, collecting myself. 'Didn't Adair grow up on Fifth Avenue?'

'Fifth Avenue?! Why would he be there?'

'I don't know,' I said. 'I thought he had relatives . . .'

'No, we are not Fifth Avenue people. Adair's grandfather, my uncle, suffered during the Depression. Years of no work. He never recovered from that humiliation, especially the handouts. I think that's partly why Marge turned out how she did. Always feared poverty. Always acted like she was an heiress.'

'Huh.' Was all I could say.

'To be fair, she never claimed she was an heiress. But she carried herself with such dignity. Others would say airs, I suppose. I liked it. Her accent. Her manners. I don't know where she picked it all up. Her taste for higher things – the opera and high teas, her French and her gloves – I thought it was all so fine.'

I sensed the residues of a distant crush in the man's voice, but what affected me more was the discrepancy between the world Eddie was describing and the image that Adair had been projecting through all the years of our friendship.

'So, she wasn't rich?'

'No! None of us were rich. I mean, she was married briefly to a guy who was quite rich. A banker. Took her to Paris. Took her places. Some nice jewelry, even a minor Miró, just a sketch,' he said, pointing towards a piece of art that had escaped my notice until now, hanging in solitary pride on a wall behind the dining table. 'But that was it.'

Uncle Eddie noticed my befuddlement.

'Why – what made you think she was rich?'

'Oh, it's just how Adair always talked about her. And the family. I thought your clan was old money . . .'

Uncle Eddie coughed a small fine spray on his sweater. His rotund figure rippled with tiny jiggles of laughter before he composed himself.

'Adair always had a lively imagination! And it's his gift that he can make that as charming at his age now as he did as a boy,' he said, indulgently. 'What else did he tell you?'

'I thought his great-grandfather was pals with J. P. Morgan.'

This sent him into a new fit of laughter. With the back of one hand, he wiped a tiny drop from the corner of one eye.

'Pals? Oh, that's good! He worked briefly as a clerk in the bank. I seriously doubt that Mr Morgan knew his name. Adair's exaggerations, I guess it's an only-child phenomenon. Marge's affectations of being highborn must've also rubbed off on him.'

'He seems to know a lot of people in high places,' I said, partly in defense of my friend and as an effort to salvage some kernel of Adair's story as true.

'Yeah, Marge spent all her money on sending him to good schools. She was amazing that way. She could have lived more nicely, perhaps. But she adored that boy. Doted on him. He'll be sad now she's gone.'

'I am sure he will be,' I said to Uncle Eddie, standing up and getting ready to leave the apartment.

As we said our goodbyes, Uncle Eddie said, 'Look, don't tell Adair what I've told you about the family.'

'There's no need,' I said.

Uncle Eddie's eyes filled with sympathy, and he said somberly, 'To you, he is who he says he is. And always was.'

CHAPTER 21

On the morning of our big day, my phone rang early: 6:23 a.m. Patti.

No one calling too early or too late bears good news. I pressed 'receive' on my screen and walked out of the bedroom.

'Kash?'

Patti's voice sounded raspy, bereft, ghostly. I had never heard her sound so distraught.

'Hey Patti, what's wrong?!'

'Kash, Kash, I'm so sorry.' Patti sounded tearful.

'It's okay, whatever it is,' I said. It was disturbing to hear the invincible, always-knows-the-score Patti, so distressed. I was standing in our living room, the morning light filling the space with a warmth in stark contrast to my caller's mood.

Helen appeared at the bedroom doorway and cast me a worried look. She was supposed to pick up Patti, Kang and Julie from The Hide.

'I'm sorry Kash, but I can't do it.'

I stiffened for a second. Fuck's sake! What a time to tell me.

'I'm so sorry, Kash. I know it's terrible timing. But I just can't. I didn't sleep all night. I thought I could, but I realize that there are lines I'm just not ready to cross.'

'It's okay,' I said softly.

'I'm not judging you or anyone else. You guys do what you gotta do, but I just can't be party to it.'

'It's okay, Patti. I understand.' And I did.

'If you want to let me go, I get that. But you know, right, that I'll take your secrets to the grave.'

'Let you go? Are you crazy? Why'd I do that? For fuck's sake, Patti.'

'Thanks, Kash. You're a good guy.'

'Really?' I said, with genuine surprise in my voice.

'Yeah, really. Totally twisted. Utterly fucked up. But not evil.'

'Man, that's a helluva endorsement – not evil!'

Finally, there was a small laugh at the other end.

'Listen, there's one little thing you can do for me.'

'Sure. What?'

'Yusep was going to bring the money to The Hide. I had Samad receiving it. But now—'

'You want me to receive it?'

'Yeah, and I'll take Samad on board.'

'Sure, that I can do. Okay if I keep Dolores with me?'

'Absolutely,' I said. If Yusep tried to pull any stunts, between Patti and Dolores, he – and anyone he brought along – would have a lot to handle.

Helen crossed her arms and raised her eyebrows questioningly. I gestured at her with my free hand by way of saying, 'Don't worry, it's all under control.' Helen seemed assured and turned to go back into the bedroom. She had yet to shower, and her departing figure, a cascade of uncombed blonde hair, a confusion of curls and long, slim legs beneath the baggy sleeping shirt, evoked a sudden tenderness in me. This was someone I had to take care of. I'm not given to spasms of sentimentality, but the notion struck me powerfully in this instant, perhaps in anticipation of the adventure ahead. She turned back, sensing my eyes on her back and smiled. I returned the smile as I waved her goodbye.

I had to make hurried calls as we drove to the pier. I had told Yusep that my crew and I would not be boarding until Patti confirmed that the funds were in place. That was going to be Samad's job but now it was on Patti.

'Why the switch?' Yusep asked me.

'Not your concern, mate. You deal with whoever I say is my person.'

What I didn't want to tell Yusep was my growing discomfort with Adair. Ever since the death of Aunt Marge, Adair was acting a bit different. More aloof, less enthusiastic. He had also become more direct, especially about money. He had asked that he be the one to receive the money from Yusep. 'He was my find, after all,' he had said by way of justification. I didn't know that I could trust him with so much raw cash.

The fact that we had never talked about my visit to Aunt Marge's, right after her death, and everything it would mean in terms of what I knew by now about him, was a sign of our growing distance. There was always an outside chance, though, that Uncle Eddie had never mentioned my visit. And I didn't bring it up either. So, I could not be sure what he did or didn't know – only that I could not trust him as I once did.

Being a long weekend, it didn't take much time to reach Brooklyn Heights. Once I reached the pier and saw our boat – the *Analise* – I felt I suddenly understood why all sailing vessels were feminine in the English language. There was something bewitchingly beautiful about the slender, long white ship, and soothing in the soft lapping of waves against its hull.

It was a sunny September day. Across the mouth of the East River, the towers of downtown Manhattan rose like shining knights, guarding a citadel of mysteries, and longed-for riches. I was noticing the beauty of the city more and more as the sense of an impending separation grew stronger. In the other direction, a low gray sky fused with the seemingly still and steely surface of the wide waters.

The *Analise* was the largest boat on the dock this morning. A sleek triple-decker, its steel and chrome fittings glinted in the sun. It seemed narrower than it should be relative to its length, and the bow had a peaked quality.

A group of seagulls circled over the boats. I always wondered about seagulls – you guys can fly, so why don't you go to the most beautiful place on earth? You don't fucking need visas! Turns out 'free as a bird' is another false apothegm. The reason we humans huddle around congested centers of finance is also why colonies of seagulls flap around piles of garbage – a better chance to make a living.

With the corner of my eye, I caught the approach of a van. Hagi! I knew his service vehicle well; apparently it doubled up as his weekend chariot too. Hagi was not refined enough to handle the front room or other people as Patti would have. That would now fall on me. But he'd be perfect to give Kang a hand in the kitchen.

I greeted Hagi and we did a faux chest-bump, mainly due to his eagerness. I called Samad again to see how far he was.

He was the one guy I could call up. And the one guy who'd join me on such short notice.

By now, Dr Hazari was also part of the crew. I had gone back to his place since the meeting where we learned of Mrs Zaman's case to invite him. To my surprise, he agreed readily. An old ally. The way my plans had changed, he was now a critical part of the whole scheme – as critical as Kang.

'We gonna board that thing or just stare at the birds?'

There was something about the desultory gliding of the seagulls that was quite mesmerizing. By comparison, the flitting about of the terns and skimmers was more fitful, less graceful. I realized with a little start that I could tell these seabirds apart. A result of my many walks down Hudson River Park with Helen. Having grown up in one of the world's most merciless concrete agglomerations, even such elementary knowledge of nature was an attainment for me.

'Patience, mate,' I said.

Hagi brimmed with his customary cheerfulness. He was dressed in his characteristic red tracksuit, CCCP emblazoned on the breast. The opposite of billionaire chic.

'Are we waiting for Helen?'

'No, but a couple more crew members. I can't board without a posse.'

Hagi chuckled but rooted himself next to me without protest. I had gotten to know him well over the years. I could trust him. He didn't flinch when I told him what we were planning. 'We need someone in the kitchen who can handle meat,' I had said, adding that the project was too sensitive to share with the rest of the yacht staff . . . I needed people who would keep quiet.

'Whatever I owe you, I'll pay you four times as much. In cash.'

Most people don't say no to four times their dues. And almost no one says no to cash.

My bargain with Samad and Dr Hazari was similar. Spare me three days of your time – also do my bidding, ask no questions and forever keep quiet – and I will make you richer, and do it faster than you ever imagined possible.

I knew Samad was plotting for a while now to start his own limo business. Dr Hazari, at his age, was anxious to become a homeowner. But both of them, I also knew, would be donating heftily to Mrs Zaman's treatment fund.

Presently, a green Dodge Charger with white racing stripes pulled up. I knew Samad had bought it used; not quite the vintage models he yearned to win. But a half-step in that direction was still progress.

The doctor was dressed in a blue blazer and stone-white khakis. And Samad looked sharp in a James Dean leather jacket.

'Motherfucker, whaddya need a leather jacket for?'

'It might get cold out there,' said Samad, pointing at the open waters.

Bengalis and sailing! It's not as if our ancestors didn't sail. They were among the world's finest boat-makers. But our generation, growing up in a city like Dhaka, we were firmly land animals, and possessed little experience of life on the water.

At this point my phone rang: Patti.

'It's all here,' she said.

I felt relieved and indicated to my crew that we were now ready to board. It wasn't long before Helen and the rest of the crew got there either. Adair arrived almost at the same time and, to my small surprise, with Yusep.

We were greeted by the first mate, a blond man in his thirties, and heavily tanned. He led us to the captain. Captain Lewiss was a ruddy complexioned, bearded and portly man, who reminded me of good old Brown – owner of the bar that in some ways set me off in my errant journey into the world of high cuisine, and I suppose now, high-water crimes.

Once we were introduced, I asked the captain, 'Why is your last name spelled with a double "s"?'

Without losing a beat, or taking his eyes off the horizon, he replied, 'My ancestors came from France. An ignoble line of Louis'. My grandfather didn't like the silent "s". So, to make up for the lost years of sibilance, he added an "s" to our Anglicized name.'

This was a man I could trust! Captain Lewiss exuded an aura of assurance, not just about being on the water but about the world at large, in his own skin.

Presently, we were taken on a tour of the ship by the chief stewardess, Marianna. She was an Italian lady of striking looks and presence, sporting long black hair and a full-focus way of looking that was almost unnerving. But despite a daunting veneer, she could be warm, and laughingly told us that she was trained to be anything her over-pampered passengers needed her to be: waitress, cleaner, nurse, dog trainer, therapist and God-only-knew-what-else. Right now, she was our guide.

The top deck boasted a helipad and a swimming pool. These were not services we would get to use, or need to manage. So, promptly Marianna led us to the lower deck. This was where the kitchen and staff quarters were located.

There was an even lower level, which housed engineering and mechanical units of the ship, and had nothing to do with us. Apparently, there were a few cubicle-sized rooms down there, which would have to be used on this trip. It was clear that on a super-luxury vessel, even the service quarters were lavishly appointed: the rooms, although small, were rich with wood trim and leather armchairs. The deck above ours contained the main guest rooms, which were each double the size of our rooms, and adorned with vintage lamps and original Renaissance-era miniatures.

'You know, the rich park their paintings in offshore sites – ships to warehouses – to dodge taxes,' Adair said, as we inspected the master suite.

I had no idea about the veracity of this claim. But I was aware of Adair's need to feel he knew the rich better than I did. So, I nodded in a quiet assent. 'And I delivered them to you, the richest of the rich,' Adair said again. Others had left the room; it was just the two of us now.

'That you did, buddy. That you've done.'

'So, speaking of that, I was thinking . . .' Adair said, and paused meaningfully.

Even before he said what he was thinking, I could guess it. Still, I wanted him to actually say it.

'Do tell,' I said, deadpan.

'Look, I hate to bring this up again, but what can I say, I really feel this. I know we now have fifty-five/forty-five in terms of share. But for this particular project, the split should be more even. Hell, no disrespect, but maybe I should get even a teensy bit more.'

'Oh yeah, how much?'

'Fifty-five/forty-five in my favor?'

I could not believe the sheer gall. I looked at Adair and felt as if I didn't recognize this person. Only the small lamps in the wall sconces were lit, and in that dim, moody, yellow light, Adair looked, momentarily, like a ghoul. A face full of dips and shadows and a smile as broad and frightening as a skeleton's.

'Really?' I raised my amputated hand in front of his face.

'Ah yes, I'm really sorry about that,' Adair said. 'But strictly speaking, that's not my fault, really. And this would not happen if I couldn't rope in a guy like Yusep—'

'And if I hadn't found a peacock with one week's notice. Which I even had to drive up to go slaughter! Or, if I didn't source the ultimate dish to make this dinner unprecedented.'

Adair went silent. He didn't seem to have any good counters. Only a claim. A claim born of entitlement, and where that came from, or how that had increased, was frankly a mystery to me.

'Look, steal a miniature,' I said. 'Compensate yourself. I won't tell.'

He cast a nasty, how-dare-you look at me. But I had heard enough, had enough. And without giving him a chance for any retort, I walked out of the sumptuous chambers into the dark, narrow corridor.

I returned to the top deck once our tour of the boat ended. And caught Viktor, arriving in his white Rolls-Royce Corniche, a little to my surprise, driven by himself. I took this as a sign of his mood – upbeat, maybe even pre-triumphal. The Englishman and the Chinese man arrived together, right after Viktor, in a latest-model Maybach. Their buoyant mood suggested that they had made good use of the champagne cooler in their car.

They all knew the *Analise* and thus needed no tour, and repaired, as the old-fashioned term goes, to the closed upper-deck lounge.

During our brief encounter, as we received the first of our guests – in this instance, Viktor, I felt, was both the host and partly a guest – I was struck by how ordinary the other two billionaires seemed. If I found myself standing in line with them at, say, Ess-a-Bagel or the Second Avenue Deli, if billionaires ever visited even such iconic but basic eateries, I'd never guess that they were billionaires.

The Englishman, sporting a thin mustache, vaguely resembled a less anemic version of former British premier, John Major. And displayed a wryness characteristic of his race. The Chinese man, the youngest of the group and with a round and happy face, spoke, thanks to his Stanford degree, in a distinctly American idiom. While we had studied their files, and also googled them extensively, even in our brief encounters we picked up new details not found in our research.

Once the three billionaire friends were seated in their custom-made Boca do Lobo leather sofas, Adair presented them with his welcome cocktail: the New Grog. It was his own rum-based invention, inspired by a nineteenth-century British admiral nicknamed Old Grogram, on account of his penchant for wearing coats made of grogram cloth, and his role in introducing the original ration of watered-down rum as a staple for shipmates. Shortly the last of the billionaires arrived, also by helicopter, a miner from Botswana. The man was in his sixties, but somehow looked baby-faced and clearly a person who was liked by everyone. He too was introduced to the new libation, and we were all set to venture out to sea.

* * *

The *Analise* eased out of its berth with a gentleness that belied its massive tonnage. It was 10.15 a.m., and if all went according to plan, we would be back in exactly forty-eight hours. I could hardly believe that the captain and the first mate, and an engineer tucked somewhere in the bowels of the vessel, was all it took to steer such a large craft.

I signaled Adair to gently steer the billionaires into the enclosed lounge. Earlier, I had ushered Boris up to the boat separately from the billionaires. If he had taken any offense at being made to stay quiet, he was mollified by the fact it was me personally escorting him up. I used a back stairway to take Boris down to the staff lounge.

I could tell what was on his mind. 'I'll introduce you once the others arrive, in one go, before dinner.' Whether he was satisfied with this plan or not, being off his territory – literally and otherwise – had rendered him more docile than usual. He followed me without any protest.

'Don't worry, man, your bags will be delivered to your cabin. Have a seat,' I said.

'Okay, I take seat here,' Boris said dully, as we sat on the tan-colored sofas of the staff lounge.

'Adair's made a cocktail. You'll like it. He calls it the New Grog. It's rum-based.'

'Grog? Why it is called Grog?'

'I don't know. You'll have to ask him.'

The story behind the Grog felt too obscure to share with Boris. Boris didn't even know who Steve McQueen was. I glanced at his wrist; my precious TAG Heuer snugly wrapped around it. You took one of my most cherished possessions, I thought, and didn't appreciate its value. I wasn't about to waste time explaining the boozy legacy of some British admiral.

The staff lounge didn't get any sunlight, but the lighting was so sensitively done it felt as if our room was suffused with afternoon sun. Boris was dressed uncomfortably in a blue block-patterned suit. He didn't want to risk being underdressed to meet the plutocrats.

Hagi brought us our drinks. I thanked him and invited him and Samad to join us.

'Who's that? A billionaire?' Boris asked with a snort.

'Yes, I summon them when it pleases me,' I said wryly. 'They fetch me drinks.'

Boris made his own sarcastic comments, but like a true narcissist never laughed at other people's jokes. Especially if they were made in a spirit of retort.

'Boris, why don't you take your tie off? Relax, it's just us.'

'I'm okay,' Boris said, by way of guarding his autonomy.

I raised my glass and said, '*Salud.*'

He issued a customary grunt but took a sip when I did. We sipped our drinks in silence for a minute, and then I broke the awkward silence with a question that had been on my mind all along.

'Boris, can I ask you something?'

'Ask,' Boris said, loosening the knot of his tie.

Good. He was starting to relax. I could only hope that'd make it easier to have a frank chat with him.

'What exactly is your business? Is moneylending your main thing?'

'You want to know my business?' Boris seemed taken aback, and unsure as to how offended he should be.

I didn't care. He was no longer on land. I was new to the sea, but this boat and this journey were mine. Lulled by the temptation of meeting billionaires, and the gauzy hope of some kind of vague but extravagant gain, he had agreed to come alone.

'What is it to you?' Boris came back, finally. 'You know you owe me money. That's my business.'

'Well, you know,' I said, raising my amputated digit, 'for me it isn't just business! It's also a little bit personal.'

'Ahh, that! I am sorry. But look . . .'

Boris paused, as if to search for the right words. I could see consternation on his face; he had not computed having to answer for this episode. He must have assumed it was a closed business, something solidly in the past. And didn't anticipate the super-luxury billionaire ship turning into a scene of personal reckoning. The readiness with which he had slipped out the 'sorry' was telling; he knew he was on a weak footing here against me.

'Look, I could have done so much more. But what I do? Just cut a little, and not even from thumb or—'

While Boris stumbled around in the vocabulary part of his brain, Samad and Hagi came by holding growlers, filled with Adair's concoction.

'The number one finger,' Boris said, giving up on the nouns that eluded him. He meant the index finger, I gathered, since he held it up as exhibit number one in his defense.

'Ah Samad, meet Boris, a friend of The Hide. And Boris, this is Samad – a dear friend from home.'

Boris tried to rise, but the handshake ended before he could complete the motion.

'And this is Hagi,' I said. 'He's a good friend from the city.'

Samad and Hagi sat down on a bright orange leather settee next to Boris and my paired single sofas.

'Boris was telling me how it was so kind of him not to take off my whole finger.'

The boys laughed nervously. Boris was startled by my proclamation. 'It's okay, relax,' I said. 'They know everything.'

Boris looked flummoxed. I noticed the redness of his skin, the flaring of his nostrils. With effort or suppressed rage, who knew? Who cared anymore? All I could sense was my rage. It flapped like a broken sail inside me. I was the wind. I was ready to rattle the whole house. Rip doors off their hinges, slam windows against their frames until the glass shattered.

'Tell me what else could you have done? I'm very interested.'

Boris shrugged. As if to say he didn't care to elaborate on such matters. Or because he could not come up with ideas, or specific acts that he felt would have been permissible punishment for me. He took long and angry drags of his drink. To a Russian any rum-based cocktail probably tasted like juice.

'Take the whole finger? An entire hand? What should I be grateful to have been spared?'

'Kash, you invite me as guest, and now you interrogate me.'

Ahh! A new line of defense. Appeals to my sense of decency – and obligations as a host. Suddenly Boris looked smaller. It is astonishing how when a person you have long feared loses their menace, their stature also seems to shrink.

'Yes, I invited you. I didn't kidnap you.'

There was a silence. It seemed only now to dawn on Boris

exactly how vulnerable he was. For the first time he was alone with me, without any of his goons to back him up. He had agreed to such a circumstance, assuming there could be no physical danger to him in the company of billionaires. But sitting now with me and my two tough enough buddies, perhaps the shadow of a new thought crossed his mind. And his tone softened.

'Look,' Boris said, 'I make up to you.'

Samad and Hagi sat silently, the way uncomfortable guests do when a couple suddenly break into a marital spat.

'How?'

'I give you big discount on what you owe me.'

'Okay, but you know what's the problem, Boris?'

'What?'

'No amount of money, not even the billions' – I said this pointing upstairs with an intact finger – 'that's sailing with us today can restore what I have lost.'

Samad coughed. I gave him a sharp look. I knew he was tempted to object; one could always acquire prosthetics. But that wasn't the same. My neck muscles stiffened at the thought of the irreparable damage done to me.

'I know,' Boris said, solemn and subdued. 'But what I can do? I can give you some compensation. I'm not God. I cannot grow you new finger. True. But you knew what the deal was. And you broke it repeatedly. And now you ask me,' he said with a rueful snort, 'what's my business? I ask that myself. You want to know what it is? It's not just lending money. It is lending to people who cannot get a loan from anywhere else. No banks. No investors. Not even friends or family. They come to me, so sorry, so pitiful. They are the meekest people. They are willing to promise anything. Hold my feet. Agree to any terms. And then, as time goes by, they grow used to, they think it's okay, to take more time, and then they start feeling they don't even owe me. But my real business isn't lending. It's collecting. That's the business. I have bosses too. They give me the money to use because they believe I can collect. You lost a finger. I'd lose all my limbs, all my organs.'

I stared at Boris. I had given a lot of thought to whether one can make reparations for certain crimes. Violent crimes. And especially when the violence causes an irremediable loss. I had concluded that even such crimes can be forgiven. You must. To hold onto the hurt and anger is to let your aggressor win. Almost anything can be forgiven. But the culprit must ask for forgiveness.

And it didn't feel like I had heard an apology.

Lesson: You cannot forgive those who don't know they need to be forgiven.

'What then? What else I do in my line of business?' Boris said, as if to himself.

'I am in the hospitality business,' I heard Samad say, apropos of nothing. It broke the spell woven by Boris and my mutual accusation.

Boris asked Samad which aspect of the hospitality industry he was involved in. I heard Samad mumble something, and Boris exclaimed, 'Ah, you own hotels?'

You can always count on a Desi to present their position in a complimentary light. From concierge to owner was not a big leap.

'I help manage one,' Samad replied.

Hagi kept mum through this pointless prattle between Boris and Samad. He fiddled with the zipper of his red tracksuit top. Boris was trying to listen to Samad with interest, but his attention was drifting. Hagi cast me a look. We knew what was coming. That knowledge had helped me rein in any rage I had felt during my discourse with Boris. Besides, I had realized that one of the problems with harm, meaning harm that comes from other people, is that if the aggressor is morally and intellectually less equipped than the victim, as may often be the case, then there could be little satisfaction to be had from any reconciliatory dialogue.

In such cases one had to explore other options. And I had done that. Momentarily, Boris leaned back into his sofa, almost dozing off. Samad reached forward and grabbed the growler from his hands before it could fall. Boris turned in my direction and tried to say something, but it came out mumbled and fizzled off without finishing.

Samad and I looked at each other. He was fully in the know. We had spiked Boris's drink with a little help from Dr Hazari. The potion had acted exactly as the good doctor had predicted: no effect at first – but when it hits, the bloke will sink, as the seamen of yore used to say, like he's rushing headlong for Davy Jones's Locker.

I cast a look at Samad and Hagi. They had been briefed already and knew where to take the knocked-out Russian. Hagi hooked his arms under Boris's shoulders, Samad gripped the torso, and I lifted his legs. We only had to walk down the corridor to the last room. Thank God, there was no need to hoist this heavy luggage up or down any hatchways.

It's been said that living well is the best revenge. Whoever said that was a complete fucking pussy. It's the kind of homily with which the powerless reconcile themselves to the indignities of being human. They are told to take the high road. That karma is a bitch. There's always a price to pay. It is better to forgive than . . . what? It's not as if we have any other option but to forgive, in most cases, do we?

This was no longer most cases.

This case had another option.

CHAPTER 22

'Looking a little green there, mate,' Captain Lewiss said to me with a chuckle.

It was the middle of the afternoon, and we were well out of sight of any shoreline. We, meaning Yusep and I, stood on the upper deck with our reassuringly big-gutted captain. The captain was regaling us with nautical information: our position in relation to the coast, our plans to hold a steady course for now and expectations of the weather.

I was a land animal through and through, and prone to motion sickness. I didn't feel it so much in cars, not at all in trains, but the wobbliness of the boat, the constant bobbing, was starting to take a toll on my equilibrium.

'Take one of these,' the first mate said in his reedy voice, as he handed me an anti-nausea pill, a chewable kind.

'Set your gaze on the horizon,' the captain said to me. 'It'll help.'

I did as I was told, training my sight on the long, slow dip of the arcing blue sky to the water's distant edge. The sky was shockingly clear of clouds. To be so ensconced between the blue dome of the sky and the brighter blue surface of the ocean, even with their vast expanse, made me feel trapped.

Suddenly the captain cocked his head, shading his eyes with a saluting palm. Captains of the sea are like dogs: they sense any disruption in the environment long before we mortals do. We caught sight of a black dot in the sky that grew steadily larger, along with an increase in the *budge-budge* noise of its approach.

'They're early,' Captain Lewiss said.

The first mate, who had joined us by now, whistled as the helicopter carrying the remaining billionaires drew closer to the ship. 'It's a beauty,' he said, apparently a connoisseur. We were all focused now on the steady advance of what looked like a large and menacing black bird.

Other members of my crew came out from different parts of the ship to welcome the guests. A large black helicopter was about to touch down on the helipad. At this juncture, Viktor himself emerged from the enclosed upper-deck lounge and joined us on the open deck.

The new guests emerged from the belly of their super-luxury 'copter as the *gud-gud-gud* noise of the rotor subsided. None of them looked like billionaires, like Aristotle Onassis or Gianni Agnelli. Having grown up in the Third World in the Eighties, my idea of billionaires was heavily influenced by the typology of those Mediterranean *bons vivants*: lush, back-brushed hair and rude tans, striking features, legendary tempers, and arm candy of the stature of Jackie Kennedy and Rita Hayworth. Those were fucking billionaires; these guys looked like professors of chemistry or certified actuaries.

And yet, there was still something distinct and mysterious about them. The unfathomable wealth commanded by them was testament to some knowledge or ability that so far outstripped us mere mortals, it was impossible not to feel daunted and captivated at the same time.

The Frenchman flaunted Richard Branson-like long hair, but not the latter's charm. Rather, his loping, wolf-like gait suggested a lack of human qualities. In contrast, the Motswana, with a tight cap of salt-and-pepper hair and heavy-lidded eyes, was the most subdued of the lot.

Out of this whole group, the Mexican came closest to fitting my notion of a billionaire, with his shock of black hair and strong jaw and a golden-glow tan. The Mexican, more than the others, evoked a classiness and a brashness that recalled a time when people lived larger.

Viktor and his buddies greeted each other with the exaggerated bonhomie of false friends. I saw Helen and Marianna fixing their hair, ruffled by the air whipped up by the 'copter's blades. The only other woman on the open deck, Julie, quite well-seasoned as a waitress by now, had a tightly wound kerchief to keep her lush blonde mane in check.

Everyone stood to attention as the men made their way away from the landing circle towards the center of the deck. Viktor introduced the captain with fulsome praise, 'If I had to cross the Drake Passage, I'd trust no one more than Captain Lewiss here for the journey.'

The guests nodded in approval and shook hands with the reactionless captain, while the first mate stood back, expecting no such courtesies. Next, Viktor introduced Yusep as his nephew, and then the ladies – Helen and Marianna. I was the one holding open the door to the saloon, and Viktor paused before the party proceeded indoors to introduce me as the 'brains behind our exceptional fare tonight'. There were a few sounds of approval from the guests, and we followed them into the saloon.

Adair was ready with servings of the New Grog. Between Adair, Helen and Marianna, I felt my billionaires were in good hands, and I headed downstairs to check in on other business.

Kang was in a rare sulk, as he still didn't have the main ingredient: human flesh. For someone with little reaction, his sulks were hard to detect, but I knew him well enough by now to be able to tell.

I'd asked him to see what he could do with the kidneys. I didn't want to be caught on a causeway with a Tupperware full of suspect organs. It was better and easier for Kang to import them onto the ship along with his other material. But he had done better than that, I now learned. 'I make tartlets,' he said, pointing to six little delectables, innocuous looking on the outside, which were stuffed with minced human kidneys. I trusted him to know how to make that delicious, and didn't question him about the recipe. We'd still have time to learn before service time.

'Fantastic,' I said. We had a fallback of some sort.

But Kang was implacable. 'Kidney is not meat,' he said grumblingly.

I could not disagree. I could not be charging what I was charging Viktor to fob off kidney as the only form of human flesh. He would expect there to be real flesh from major muscle parts.

'You trust me, right?'

Kang met my eyes. He was not ready to commit to this point.

'I said I'd get us human flesh, right?'

Kang kept staring at me.

'You shall have it by tonight,' I said.

I looked at my watch: it was 4:55 p.m. I knew that the kind of preparation he had discussed with me wouldn't take long. Everything else was ready. If I delivered him a hunk of human meat by 6 p.m., he could make it in ample time. The dinner was set for 9 p.m.

It was early evening, and our guests were occupied in their luxurious apartments. The Frenchman had gone to his room. I followed him there to make sure he found it alright. He was on the phone as he walked there and grew only louder once inside. The guttural outbursts that could be heard from outside his door indicated problems with a deal. I knew he was on the verge of acquiring some quartz rights in Inner Mongolia.

The other billionaires were on the top deck, mostly inside the closed lounge. The Englishman sat in the sun, with a fat cigar held at one corner of his mouth, and the *Financial Times* held open like a shield. No race on earth took more pleasure from the printed news than the English. The Motswana and the Mexican were engaged in a game of backgammon. The Mexican was issuing a torrent of teasing comments, to which the Motswana responded only with a placid smile and redoubled concentration. And Viktor had retired to one corner with the Chinese man in consultations of some kind. For all I knew, they were plotting how to fuck up the Frenchman's deal.

Satisfied with our VVIPs' apparent contentment (the Frenchman's personal inferno aside), I went down to our room for a breather. Things were finally in place and I needed to gather myself before launching into the final production – and presentation. I stretched out on the narrow bed, still fully clothed and with my shoes on. I wanted to close my eyes for just ten or fifteen minutes, and then freshen up. But five minutes didn't pass before there was a knock on the door.

'Fuck!' I said to myself, under my breath.

I dragged myself out of bed to go open the door. It was Marianna and she looked absolutely startled.

'What's up?'

'There's a man,' she said, in a horror-struck whisper.

'What man?'

'Slumped in the corridor,' she said. 'He's not one of us. Not one of the guests. And not one of your crew that I have met.'

Fuck! How did Boris get out? He was supposed to be not only sedated but even tied down.

I hurried out to where he was. He hadn't made it very far from his room.

'Boris, mate,' I said, pretending friendship, for Marianna's sake.

'He's a friend,' I said to Marianna. 'Sorry, I didn't know if Viktor would approve. But I owed him big time, and a sail on a luxury yacht was a good way to pay him off.'

Marianna looked at me quizzically. Too many questions batted about inside her head. She didn't know what to believe.

'Boris, buddy, I'll take you back to your room.'

Luckily, he was too groggy to speak. But he was also too disabled to move on his own. And too heavy for me to lift alone.

'Is he okay? Should we call someone?'

'Oh no, no,' I said quickly. 'We have a doctor, you know. If you can just tell him to come. And also tell Samad. We will take him back to the room, and the doc will check him out.'

'Are you sure, he's going to be okay?'

'I think he had too much of the grog,' I said. 'And maybe it interacted with some meds he's taking. The doc will know what to do.'

Marianna seemed satisfied with this explanation, but still looked at me warily.

'Go, go quickly,' I said.

She turned on her heels, but before she could tear away, I said, 'And hey, can you please just keep this between us? I mean, if you could not tell Viktor or the captain.'

She didn't say 'yes'. But she also didn't say 'no'. She just looked at me, as if calculating if this was a secret that was harmless enough for her to keep, out of innate niceness – or if her sense of duty to her employer should override any other concerns.

I was at her mercy, and I hated it. Oh well, there is only so much one can control. My real concern wasn't Viktor; he knew *le nouveau morceau* had to be sourced somehow. What I had really wanted was for the ships' crew not to know. No plan goes exactly according to plan. I sat down next to Boris, as Marianna trotted away, and I waited for the help to arrive.

Dr Hazari was in charge of the sedation. And Samad the restraining. There was no time for reproaches, though. And Boris's uncommon physical resilience was not entirely surprising. But there was no time for any more delays now. When we got Boris back to the room. Dr Hazari, Samad, and Hagi too were gathered in the makeshift operating theater. We had shorn it of all removable items and wrapped every inch of the room in clear plastic sheeting.

Dr Hazari sedated Boris again. And we strapped him more firmly to the bed where he lay. His mouth was taped shut, of course. It startled me for a second to see Boris in this condition. It is not easy, for most of us civilians, to be placed in total control of another body – and even its fate. I collected myself quickly. Having wrought this situation into being, I could not now hesitate. Too much depended on carrying through my plans. And we had come too far already to turn anything back.

Dr Hazari alone was unflappable. Any man who has worked as a field doctor in a war, especially in the wretchedly ill-equipped arena of a ragtag Third World guerrilla force, was the right man for our situation.

To everyone's shock, Boris's eyes fluttered and presently he opened them. It took him a second to register his situation, and he struggled against the restraints. Realizing that he was neither able to move his limbs nor his body, and not even open his mouth, he cast about with panicked incomprehension to see where he was.

'Oh dear,' Dr Hazari said. 'He needed a horse tranquilizer.'

As his startled mind settled into coherence, Boris looked at me.

Dr Hazari had quickly prepared an injection, but before he could administer it, I raised a hand to signal that he should pause. If Boris was awake, and even coherent, I wanted to have a say.

I don't know if you have ever had the privilege of looking into the eyes of a man in a state of pure terror. And, to know that you are the cause of that terror. Some would say that to enjoy such a moment of supreme control over one's enemy was revenge enough. But I wasn't here for half-measures.

'I could have taken a finger for a finger,' I said to Boris, as I approached his makeshift surgical table. 'But you have taken much more from me. You robbed me of my peace. You insulted and threatened my girl. You broke my business with your exorbitant penalties. You have driven me to extremes such that I may have to give up living in America. You have in a sense robbed me of my life. Thus, a mere finger will not do. I'll need a little more than that. I shall take a full pound of flesh.'

The room stayed silent as I passed my judgment.

'That's how we did it with Pakistani soldiers,' said Dr Hazari. 'We always read them their offenses, before passing and carrying out the sentence.'

I turned to look at Dr Hazari. Beneath his avuncular demeanor, the doctor was a more disturbed individual than we gave him credit for.

The doctor had assured me that Boris would definitely survive the operation, and thus our protocols would not be violated: no one was being killed for their flesh. Just harvested.

Lesson: Living well might be the best revenge, but don't ignore other options.

As per prior agreement, Hagi would act as Dr Hazari's assistant for what I was told would be a quick job. The doctor administered a fresh dose of narcotic once I indicated that my verdict was closed. They'd need Samad, too, to restore the room to its normal state afterwards.

Meantime, as the doctor proceeded with his surgery, I stepped to the side of the room, where Boris's personal effects were arranged on a table. I plucked out from the pile my TAG Heuer.

CHAPTER 23

The ship's dining room was a fitting setting for a high-end cannibalistic meal. Its walls were wrapped in dark wood and the floor was covered in rich red hand-tufted carpet. The room was lit up by a Hapsburg chandelier, meaning not a modern candelabrum created in that form, but an actual antique lifted from Hofburg. But what gave the room its character and an indication of its owner's twisted temper were the paintings. On one wall hung Francis Bacon's tortured, transfixing triplet, *Three Studies for a Crucifixion*. And the opposing wall was adorned by Salvador Dalí's soothing yet sumptuously unsettling classic, *Soft Construction with Boiled Beans*. Bacon's red-rage brushstrokes seemed to be set in a conversation with the luminosity of Dalí's yolk-yellow surface – and presaged, perhaps, the exchanges to commence among our guests – or victims.

The men were seated around the table, with Viktor at the head and the Englishman at the opposite end. All were dressed smartly for the occasion. Viktor, in a break from his usual subdued demeanor, wore a dark purple velvet suit, but left the collar of his handmade Loro Piana white shirt open. The Chinese man was cloaked in a burgundy-colored Mao

Tse-Tung-styled suit. He was young – and handsome – enough to pull off the retro, dictator-chic look. The Englishman alone came in a white dinner jacket and a black bowtie. The Frenchman flashed a cravat that seemed to be woven out of pure silver. The Motswana came predictably muted in a dark suit and a woolen tie. The Mexican came in a brown, Safari-styled suit and wide-lapeled mauve shirt.

Given how often they were all compelled to don tuxedos, no one could begrudge them the colorful sartorial departures for this cozy private gathering.

These men had tasted every exotic meal money could buy. And every experience that any man could ask for, from space travel to private tours of holy sites and palaces that were closed to the public. Their greatest privilege, Viktor had once told me, was that they could ask to meet almost anyone – the Pope, any royalty, any celebrity, every genius in any field – and usually get that audience.

Tonight, it was up to me, Kash Mirza from Dhaka, to give these luminaries an experience that would be utterly new to them, unforgettable, an experience to test their mettle, their morals, to shake – perhaps even shatter – their sense of the normal, of bonds and boundaries. For this moment of gravity, I was of course trussed up in my trusty Kiton.

When we first conceived of this Evening of Danger, my concern was about impressing the gathered cognoscenti. Through the journey of bringing such a meal together, however, my mood had changed. I no longer sought merely to impress; I wanted to shock and subdue these masters of the earth's core. I wanted supremacy, however fleeting. And, with luck, leave a few of them with a permanent psychological scar. The menu had thus been duly modified, with Viktor's approval. And it of course had undergone some changes from its original conception due to sourcing practicalities. But the spirit of the original mission to stun the guests, I felt, would now be more thoroughly fulfilled.

The billionaires were now all seated. My staff and I were at our respective positions.

'Gentlemen,' Viktor said, rising to his feet in a gesture of formality. 'Welcome!

'It's my great pleasure to invite you to this edition of the Miner's Club dinner. I thank you all for making the time. And really, foremost, for even letting me into this circle in the first place. I'm aware that my first effort,' Viktor said this, placing a penitent palm on his breast, 'was not quite to everyone's satisfaction. Since then, I vowed to myself that next time, which is today, what I'd serve would not be just good or even excellent. It will go beyond; it will be nothing short of unprecedented. I am confident you will not be disappointed.'

There was a murmer of approval around the table. The Frenchman produced a smile that felt more like a leer. The Motswana remained stolid as ever. The Chinese man, like his English friend, remained pleasantly impassive. The Mexican beamed heartily, as if fully onboard with the proposal, and eager to see it succeed.

'As you'll see,' Viktor continued, 'there is a reason why I have chosen international waters for this dinner. These open seas have always been the highways not only of trade and piracy, but also imagination. And what are we' – Viktor gestured at the circle of men around the table – 'if not creatures foremost of imagination? The world thinks we are all about acquisitiveness and calculation, turbocharged drive and bare-knuckle tactics. And that is true. But isn't it true of millions of toilers? So, what sets us apart? Why do we gain a level of success that is beyond all hope for most? They think it's luck. And sure, there's always an element of that. But what really sets us apart is that we actually have the gall – and the imagination – to reach for goals that others accept as unreachable. And that, my friends, is what we shall do tonight. Go beyond the limits, and that also always means courting danger.'

'*Salud!*' said the Mexican, and the others chimed in.

'Gentlemen,' I stepped up. 'Welcome to an Evening of Danger.'

The men turned to me.

'Each course tonight will present an element of danger. We want to challenge you to cross culinary boundaries, and to experience with each morsel the fundamental pact between man and nature: it is never only a source of shelter or nourishment. In its bosom lie myriad threats, countless pitfalls. We hope each course tonight will leave you with a fresh frisson of that realization, and that they will make for a dinner unlike any you've had before.'

Adair went around the table pouring champagne, making sure the label was clearly displayed. The two women, Helen and Julie – looking prim in their smart black dresses – stepped forward and set down plates before all the billionaires except Viktor and the Frenchman. Those two I served myself, for this first course. We three lifted the lids in precise synchrony to reveal the aperitif – and the first taste of danger.

Carnivore

Aperitif: Verrine de guacamole et ceviche
Champagne: Krug Clos D'Ambonnay 2000

For the opener, the danger came from the venomous scorpion fish. This *amuse bouche*-styled *petit divertissement* was presented in crystal shot glasses. It took bravado to serve it raw, and faith to ingest it. The white flesh of the scorpion fish was marinated in lime juice with vodka mixed with chopped avocado and a plethora of citrus and chili seasoning.

'Don't worry,' Viktor said, 'it won't kill you.'

The Frenchman snorted, half in derision. But the oohs and aahs that were emitted by the rest of the crowd as they ate sounded like clear notes of approval.

'I have had this before,' said the Frenchman.

'But have you had it in this particular manner?'

'No, but it's not so special, in my opinion.'

'Special or not, it was delicious, I must say,' said the Mexican. 'A lot of zest.'

'And a first for me,' said the Motswana.

The jousting had begun. We continued with the champagne and passed around tiny teaspoons of chilled raspberry-melon mousse as a palate cleanser.

I had to give credit to Kang. His specialty was Korean and pan-Asian cuisine, and of course, with The Hide, meats of diverse provenance. But he never balked when I told him we were going to 'go French' and needed to make it both danger-themed and as high-end as possible. I passed my serving role on to Marianna, and focused on keeping the kitchen and the dining room in perfect rhythm.

Kang never bothered to ask how the customers liked it. I figured that his indifference to his diners' approbation made

267

his devotion to his tasks that much purer and more perfect. Samad was there in the kitchen, along with Hagi, helping to rush dishes to the foot of the stairs.

Kang plated a risotto, the first main course. We had to fill their bellies at least a little before we steered them towards items that some might be less willing to swallow.

Entrée: Encornets farcis au risotto de langoustines à l'herbe royale
Wine: 1961 Château Haut-Brion Blanc

When we were setting the menu, Helen had joked, 'Is that French for "I'm going to charge you $10,000 for an ass-fucking"?' That was the general idea for the entire dinner, no doubt. This dish, however, consisted of a decent portion of squid stuffed with a basil langoustine risotto. And the cheese we used for the risotto was none other than the finest Pule, flown in from Serbia. As they bit through the succulent squid, they encountered a burst of rich and flavorful arborio rice. Kang had timed the risotto so expertly that you'd think he had spent thirty years in an Italian restaurant.

Of course, there had to be an element of danger. The squid ink was accompanied by a healthy portion of *Sannakji*, the South Korean baby octopus dismembered and served raw, the nerve endings in its tentacles causing them to writhe on the plate. As Helen had reminded me, their suction pods can latch onto the insides of the throat and choke the diner to death.

As I explained this feature of the dish, the Motswana put his spoon down. Everyone else paused but resumed eating.

The Frenchman consumed the dish in silence. The Mexican declared it the best risotto he had tasted in a long time.

'Haven't had this before, have you?' Viktor challenged the Frenchman.

'It's finely balanced. Hearty but mixed with delicacy,' the Frenchman said finally; the tone was bordering on admiration.

'And danger!' Viktor added, making sure the theme did not go ignored.

'It's a good meal, so far,' said the Motswana. 'I am curious to see, though, what will tip us over into the territory of the "unprecedented".'

'Open sea is a nice touch,' the Englishman opined.

'But hardly unprecedented for anyone in this room,' said the Frenchman.

'The evening is young, my friends,' Viktor said. 'Don't work so hard. You're not food critics. Enjoy the meal.'

'Hear, hear,' said the Mexican. 'Let's not forget to enjoy ourselves.'

The tension in the air seemed to lessen. The Motswana began to speak about his first experience of Pule – during a foray into the war-torn Balkans in search of mining rights. This prompted the others to share their memories of fine food in unexpected places. Throughout the day, and now during dinner, I was struck by how little of their conversation involved money. They also weren't prone, unlike many celebrities, especially from the worlds of music and movies, to common vices, such as women, gambling, booze or drugs. Such attenuating diversions involved losing control, and these men were all about retaining control. If they had affairs, as the Frenchman and the Mexican were both known to do, even that happened with a tight regime of logistics and PR that kept them off the front pages of tabloids.

The Chinese man regaled everyone with his experience of freshly killed seals in the Arctic freeze. For the Frenchman it was monkey brains with African head-hunters, so called. Also, snake rings in Papua New Guinea. The mining business, they opined, unlike many other trades, took one to places others were unlikely to visit. And this filled them with a pinch of pride and satisfaction.

Entrée: Gâteau de foie gras aux morilles fraîches et asperges blanches
Wine: 1945 Château d'Yquem Sauternes

None of them would be tasting foie gras for the first time. But our preparation, veinless and enriched with eggs and whipped cream, cooked over a bain-marie, was done to perfection. The morels were cooked with Mouton Rothschild and hints of nutmeg. The dish was served on a bed of sliced *hákarl*, the Greenlandian shark with no urinary tracts. With all toxins stored in its body, the entire thing was poisonous and took six months to clean out. We had paid handsomely to procure this fermented rarity. Even these connoisseurs had to confess it was their first time navigating this menace.

The foie gras – and *hákarl* – was our signal to switch wines. While we had planned an Ice Beer for this round originally, in the end we chose to stick to the classier and proven route of crisp and coveted wines. Adair took immense pleasure in describing the type of grape and the minerals in the earth and scarcity of rain and other tropes and legends that justified the $18,000 price-tag. In reality, it was $3,500 – but where's the profit if not in the padding? And that's where Yusep, in charge of monitoring us and the expenses, proved himself to be an ally, albeit at a hefty cut for himself. I wasn't sure that the oenophilic details were registering with our diners, who were chewing the *hákarl* with the attention that any potentially life-threatening mouthful demands.

'Bravo! Bravo! This is an absolute winner,' the Motswana gushed, in a rare burst of effusion.

Viktor gave me a beaming look. Kang had toasted the *hákarl* expertly to leave its edges finely crisp. The crunchy, smoky rind counteracted the smothering sweetness of the liver. There was nothing like contrasts of texture and flavor, and each rich in its distinct way, to tickle not only our taste buds but the corresponding nodes in our brains. The group by now felt properly primed to segue into meat.

Entrée II: Steak du Randall Lineback
Wine: Château Le Pin, Pomerol 1982

There was no way I was going to go through the night without a touch of America. I had chosen a steak from a rare and recently revived breed of American cattle. The first of its kind may have arrived from across the Atlantic, but by now it was as American as the tawny melodies of Bluegrass ringing in the twilight of a half-shuttered deep country mill town. There was no point trying to impress this crowd with wagyu. They were sure to have tasted cuts that were reserved for the Emperor of Japan. Besides, it so happens – and I know this is anathema among steak lovers – I was not sold on the theory of more marbling and more tenderness are always better. I liked a certain 'toothiness' to my meat. The bite should face a little resistance before it gave way to a juicy surrender of the vanquished flesh. And the Randall Lineback did that better than other meat I had come across. Our cuts for tonight – each plate featured a piece of tenderloin, short loin and medallions of rump – came from a farm in Tennessee. And allowed the diners to taste this particular steak meat in its varying aspects. Kang made the steaks with slow heat and little fussing, leaving each center with a nickel-sized pinkness of perfection.

This course came with *Casu martzu*, the cheese with live maggots. Let them travel to your belly intact and they will tear your intestines apart. The diners were advised to chew the cheese and the wiggly worms embedded in it together with the meat, as thoroughly as they could. The cheese offered a salty, creamy, counterpoint to the sweetness of the meat that would only heighten the experience.

This serving, the amplest of the entire dinner, formed a secret tribute to our temple of meat-eating: The Hide.

The men consumed their meat in almost reverential silence. After all, they were connoisseurs, and knew what they were eating. Their concentration was no doubt encouraged by the life-threatening cheese.

No one had balked at anything so far. They were going for every dish. The danger would have been easy to circumvent, but they took the challenge head on.

'Yes!' the Motswana said. And that's all he said.

'Yes, yes,' said the Mexican.

'Yes, very good.' China.

'Perfect. Absolutely perfect.' England.

And the Frenchman, 'Okay, this is new. For me, this is new. And this is good. Very good.'

An encomium at last from the Frenchman! The guests were by now suitably soaked in wine. The mood was starting to feel convivial. I felt that the beef had not only lived up to its billing but had also prepared the guests for what was to come next: the rarest cut of all.

I headed downstairs to supervise the final plating.

Finale: Le Nouveau Morceau
Wine: 1945 Château Mouton Rothschild

There is nothing extraordinary about human flesh on sight. Slices of pale, pink-colored meat sat on the cutting board like a strange new sea animal waiting to be named. Kang had marinated it simply in S&P sauce for a couple of hours. The meat was seared first in a Périgord Bordelaise sauce – not made of human bone marrow. I'm not Hannibal Lecter, for fuck's sake!

The prized flesh was cooked until tender in a red wine reduction – a Mouton Rothschild. The dressing was simple – dabs of sauce, in three little circles of red, a garnish of a single mint leaf planted in a tiny dab of chili-marmalade chutney, and a finishing touch of shaved truffle.

Once the plating was completed, I gave a signal to Viktor and he rose again.

'My friends, I want to thank all of you for taking the time on this Labor Day for my dinner. You could have been with your families – but I saved you from that.'

Laughter.

'Now, it's time for our finale – our *pièce de résistance*. It is, I guarantee you, unprecedented. It alone is unprecedented enough to earn that appellation for the whole meal.'

This was our signal for the customary simultaneous lifting of the silver lids.

Helen and Marianna went around the table shaving the truffles onto each man's dish, taking care not to cover the centerpiece, but to sprinkle around it.

'What you have before you, my friends, is the rarest of meats. Almost no man has tasted it. It is not exactly forbidden, in strict legal terms – and certainly not on these uncharted waters – yet it is rarer than the most endangered wild game. It is far more prevalent, yet harder to acquire – at least, within some ethical bounds that we set upon ourselves – and even harder to consume.'

You could feel the suspense rising like a climactic element in the room. The Frenchman put his glass down, but no one dared lift a fork yet.

'Gentlemen,' Viktor said, '*Le nouveau morceau.*'

I could tell that our guests were perched keenly between curiosity and wariness. The Chinese man was the first to fork a bite, but before he could lift it to his mouth, Viktor spoke again, 'Take a bite, and see if your refined palates can identify the species.'

Everyone cut small morsels and a tiny piece of Boris was dangling from the gleaming tines of their forks. The meat disappeared into the open maws of insatiable appetite, mouths that wanted to consume the world, tongues eager to taste everything, gullets keen to swallow not only all wealth but mountains and rivers, cities and histories.

The chewing proceeded with deliberation. I could detect

the collective keenness from the popping of temples and jaw muscles.

'Any guesses?'

There was a silence around the table.

'Crocodile?' guessed the Motswana.

'No, it's a mammal of some kind,' opined the Mexican. 'Impala?'

Viktor moved his head sideways in silent but smiling negation.

'It's a land animal,' added the Chinese man. 'I have had panda – it's not that.'

'No other guesses?' Viktor was playing a little coy.

'Is it a monotreme of some kind?' The Englishman was geeking out.

'Mammal, yes. Monotreme, no.' Viktor was thoroughly enjoying holding the secret.

'Why don't you just tell us?' said the Frenchman.

'Thanks for playing,' Viktor said. 'It is the rarest of all meats. Endangered, depending on your viewpoint. And unprecedented. It is the wildest of all games, gentlemen. I present to you, the *Homo sapiens*!'

The Mexican jumped up and pushed himself back from the table with a shriek. The leap from the Frenchman was more violent, and he tipped his chair onto its back. The rest of the diners froze, and the Motswana lurched back, tilting his chair on its back legs. Only the Englishman and the Chinese man held their place, and their calm.

The Chinese man broke into laughter, which he tried to restrain out of respect for his offended peers. Or maybe it was an involuntary titter of nervousness.

'*Horreur! Quelle horreur!*' The French lapsed into his

native tongue. A clump of his brushed-back hair came loose, dislodged by the violence of his reaction, and covered his left eye.

'This is an affront,' he said. 'This is an abomination!'

The Mexican crossed himself and began to mumble what I presumed were Catholic prayers in Latin. The Motswana and Englishman were impassive so far. Perhaps taking time to process the magnitude of what was transpiring.

'Oh Viktor!' the Motswana said. 'You've really gone off the tarmac.' But he seemed more amused than exasperated.

I had not heard that expression before. But it seemed befitting for people – and a non-native speaker at that – who were accustomed to private jets.

The Chinese man had a fresh morsel hanging off his fork. It was no longer a mouthful of forbidden flesh, but a question for which none of these men had an answer. We had given them a chance to examine themselves in a way that any man with moral curiosity would find fascinating. Two of them had failed to register the philosophical conundrum. But there was still hope for the ones who remained at the table.

'What is the meaning of this? What kind of joke is this?' The Frenchman led the charge, fixing his now disheveled hair as he turned to Viktor.

'This is a joke, right? This is not . . . not . . . what you say,' the Mexican stammered.

I could almost hear his secret prayer – *Dios Mio* . . . please, please, please . . . let it be turkey . . . let it be pork . . . let it be anything but a culinary incarnation of the original sin.

Viktor was calm. He was enjoying the affray.

'Calm down,' he said. 'It is exactly what I said it is.'

'It is most unusual and challenging,' the Motswana said;

even he had loosened his tie by now to cope with the stress of the unexpected fare.

'How dare you? This is preposterous!' The Frenchman.

'You are sure no laws were broken?' The Englishman.

The Chinese man was the first to have taken and swallowed a second bite. And that's why his race was going to rule the world one day – or rather *again* – I thought to myself.

Viktor forked another piece. The beauty of having fuck-you amounts of money is that you can afford to say fuck-you to others in so many ways.

'You asked for unprecedented. And that is what I have given you.'

'That is ridiculous. This is not unprecedented. This is madness!' the Mexican finally said. His hair was too thickly gelled and clothes too tightly tucked for any of that to be disturbed. But his perplexity expressed itself in the reddening of his otherwise congenial face and in the flaring of his large nostrils.

'This will not be allowed to stand,' said the Frenchman.

'What are you going to do? Report me to the authorities?' Viktor laughed, as he calmly and, let's face it, insolently, proceeded to finish his plate.

He knew, as they all did, that none of them could afford to have word of this go out to the public. Billionaires eating human flesh? There were some things you could not survive. Not because the act was ghastlier than many others that occur daily, but humans can't handle any violation of what they have decided is 'normal'.

'You've all taken a bite,' Viktor said. 'There's a piece inside each one of you.'

'Who's the victim?' the Englishman asked.

'Never you mind. We followed some strict protocols. Kash!'

I had a printed set of the protocols ready. I circulated them among the guests, who paused to take in the terms and clauses.

'My young friend and I had drawn bets,' Viktor said, pointing in my direction. 'About who would be willing to take a bite and who would pussy out. And I have to say the young man had it right. The Catholics will go into hysterics, he said.'

The Frenchman shot me an angry glance. I gave him the sweetest smiling fuck-you any underling could muster. Viktor had momentarily conferred on me a near-peer status. And I could not help but feel a swell of pride in my bosom.

'I'm calling my chopper,' said the Frenchman. 'I want no part of this.'

'I'm going with you,' said the Mexican.

'It'll take at least an hour to get here,' said Viktor. 'Relax. If you don't want *le nouveau*, have some dessert. Have some wine.'

'Fuck you,' said the French. 'What do you take us for?'

'For what you are,' Viktor said, his tone hardening. 'Cowards! You think you are all so bold, so brave. You think you're different from other men. But look at you, running for cover in the face of a provocation. No stomach – literally – for any real departure from convention.'

The Frenchman hadn't anticipated this line of attack. He tried to hold his own. 'This is not provocation,' he said. 'It's . . . it is . . . barbaric!'

'No, my friend,' retorted Viktor. 'It is just what it is. Face it, the world is what it is. When your ancestors colonized entire chunks of earth and dragged men into slavery, you thought your people were the "civilized" ones. You still think it's for you to define what's proper and what's barbaric. You don't get to set those rules anymore. Your time to unilaterally make such calls is over.'

There was one more course on offer. We had meant to serve the kidney tartlets as a curtain call to the mains, before moving to dessert. But the diners were no longer in the mood. Viktor didn't press it. He signaled for the course to be returned. Samad, who was at the top of the stairs with a large tray, took the cue and turned back.

'There's more for anyone who has the guts,' Viktor said. 'Once the faint-of-heart have departed, we can enjoy more of this meal.'

'We should have been told before we took a bite,' the Mexican said, with more sulk than anger.

'You asked for unprecedented,' Viktor said. 'Think, why you are really upset? The breaking of the taboo is often harder to accept than actual crimes. Gang rape of women in public, genocidal killing of ethnic minorities, kiddie porn; all that's happening every day. Where's the outrage? There isn't enough, because we lack the power to stop it, and through large-scale commissions all that grotesquery has become normalized. But take what still lies beyond the pale, and you get thunderous denunciation!

'Trust me,' Viktor continued with a wan smile, 'more crimes are prevented every day, not by any compendium of laws or customs, let alone any innate sense of morality, but by the sheer, terrifying force of stigma.'

'This is all bullshit rationalization, Viktor,' said the Frenchman. 'You chose to cross a line and you're now rationalizing' With that verdict, the Frenchman headed for the door. The Mexican followed him. I eyed Adair who followed the billionaires to the saloon. It was better that he go with the disgruntled, and hopefully use his charms to soothe them a bit.

'Fuck them, too,' Viktor said, turning to his other guests.

'I'll humor you,' said the Englishman. 'Let's judge the fare on its merits.'

The Englishman forked another bite and placed the morsel into his mouth. Every movement of his jaw, every popping of a vein in his temple was under scrutiny. From the corner of my eye, I caught Marianna looking pale, and I signaled for her to remove herself to the nearest toilet. I didn't want her to accidentally hurl on priceless Bacons.

Viktor's handsome face was beaming with the satisfaction of a mischief executed to perfection.

'All these rules and conventions,' Viktor said. 'Actually nothing happens when they're broken. See, I'm still here! Intact. And when I wake up tomorrow, I'll still be the same man. But I'll have the pleasure of extra knowledge that few humans can ever hope – or dare – to gain.'

'I won't say nothing happens,' said the Englishman. 'Something happened.'

'And I'm not sure if we stay exactly the same after certain experiences,' said the Motswana.

'This is definitely one of those experiences,' added the Chinese man, but not necessarily with disapproval.

'How did you come by this?' asked the Englishman. 'If it was from a dead body, how long after the event was the culling?'

Trust the unflappable Englishman to zero in on the

practical aspects. He alone was imperturbable; not a hair nor any article of clothing out of place through all the commotion of their shocks and their debates. The Chinese man was not perturbed, but he was excited.

'No one was killed,' Viktor informed his guests. 'There's a black market for human parts. It trades mainly in kidneys, and in case of dead bodies also in other organs, and there are body farms that'll sell whole bodies, so it's not hard to acquire, if you are willing to pay.'

'Body farms?' the Motswana asked.

Viktor explained the concept. It was one of our findings that I had shared with him. I'd told him that I had already tasted a sample, to be sure that it was fit for serving. That had impressed him.

'Better than wagyu.' That was the Chinese man's verdict.

'In the spirit of scientific enquiry then,' the Motswana said, forking another bite.

'Thinner than beef in flavor. More rubbery than pork. But not like anything else I've ever had.' That was his verdict.

It is customary in the world of wagyu, and increasingly too in other styles of cattle-rearing, to give the cows names. Customers took pleasure in being told that they're taking a bite of 'Yukio' or 'Junichiro' or 'Haruki'. Maybe they'd like to know the name of the human sample from which these mysterious medallions had been taken? The meat was certainly marbled like prime wagyu – Boris being a well-marbled chunky specimen.

To my surprise, the Frenchman came back into the room. He stood at the door, hands on his hips and legs planted apart.

'There can be no Miner's Club after tonight.'

He looked pale with rage, but his ears were flushed with redness.

'Really?' Viktor was not flummoxed. 'Who are we six to decide that? There are other members.'

'They won't want to be part of this . . . once they hear . . .' the Frenchman drifted off. He had not thought through the complexities of his own proposition.

'So, you want to call them up one by one and say you were at a cannibalistic dinner? You want word to get out?'

'No, but we didn't participate knowingly,' said the Mexican, who had joined his French pal at the door. The look in his eyes was no longer one of haughtiness but of perplexity – and seething resentment.

'Tell that to the world. See if it makes a difference. The papers will name everyone who was present. Like it or not, we are now bound up by an unspeakable secret, forever.'

'You cannot get an "unprecedented" badge with this stunt.' The Frenchman. 'And India would never consent.'

It seemed the Frenchman was unsure of support for his position in the room and thus invoked an absentee voter. And with pretentious decorum perhaps to add weight to his assertion.

'It's a five-person vote. Only those present get to vote. Rules are rules.'

'It is unprecedented,' the Chinese man said. 'The logic cannot be denied.'

'Indeed, I agree that the logic can't be denied,' opined the ever-unflappable Motswana.

All eyes fell on the Englishman; the original architect of the rules for his loosely formed club. He had pushed himself away from the table and was seated with one leg crossed over the other. From this position of relaxed authority, he spoke.

'Look, it occurs to me that we may have made a mistake when we created "unprecedented" as a category. There is a structural problem there that can't be easily resolved. What exactly is unprecedented? What have we not tasted? As long as we stay within the confines of what is permissible, in some human culture, can we make it new? Can the mere style of preparation or setting of service ever be that new? Are we not chasing a standard that can in a true sense never be obtained? By going beyond all known and acceptable forms of food, Viktor has indeed – literally – caused an unprecedented event to occur. But do we really recognize it as "food"?'

'It is obviously not food! Not for humans, for heaven's sake!' The Mexican sounded aghast.

Here was a man who came from a country where tens of thousands had been killed in drug wars in recent years, and often with brutal decapitations, filmed and aired, and bodies left hanging off bridges for weeks, to send a message to the public. Yet he was more scandalized by our little service.

'Nothing is ever obvious,' replied the Englishman. 'As long as the item served is edible and digestible, and indeed of organic nature, I don't see how we disqualify it as food – just because it's not within any accepted format, yet.'

'I will not be a party to this sick charade anymore,' announced the Frenchman.

'I won't be part of anything that he's part of,' said the Mexican, pointing to Viktor.

'So, no rare earth minerals in your future?' Viktor laughed.

'You are both free to make that choice,' said the Motswana with a professorial gravity. 'But my vote is for unprecedented.'

'I agree,' said the Chinese man, reaffirming his position. He seemed to be enjoying his role as an arbiter; and relaxed into it by unbuttoning his coat collar.

'If those two are out, then I have two of three votes in my favor,' said Viktor with a smile.

'You have my vote too,' said the Englishman.

I was glad to see he was no fence-sitter. The Frenchman and the Mexican retreated again to the front lounge to wait for their rescue to arrive.

The guests left by midnight. The Frenchman and the Mexican took flight in the Frenchman's black helicopter, nursing their wounded sensibilities with words of outrage and dismissal. The other three men took a separate flight, in an equally large white helicopter. Once we waved goodbye, we entered the main saloon. Viktor was beaming. By his standards, it had been a triumph – as it was for me. He issued words of praise for members of the team who were at hand – Helen, Adair and Marianna – and asked them to convey the same to the rest of the team, especially Kang. As Adair and the ladies left to finish cleaning, Viktor signaled for me to hang back.

'Let's have a toast, shall we?'

'Indeed, sir. What's your pleasure at this hour?'

'Your choice,' Viktor said, magnanimously.

Aprés-dîner: Vanquished Enemies
Toast: Calvados

I was in the mood for a strong drink and went behind the bar in search of something – and why not? – French. I found a beautiful bottle of Calvados and poured out generous portions for the two of us.

'*Salud!*' I intoned. I don't know why we always said '*salud*' instead of plain old 'cheers' or some other exotic form of salute – *Santé*? *Prost*? *Skol*? – but that Latinate tribute had become our standard.

'*Salud!*' Viktor said as we chinked our glasses.

We were standing by the bay windows looking out to the front deck, which was illuminated from the inside by subtle lighting that ran beneath the railings. The moon was partial, and frequently obscured by passing clouds. Beyond the shape of our boat, the ocean spread out, as smooth as a dolphin's back. Closer to us, the spritzing bow caused tiny phosphorescent crests on the waves breaking in our wake.

'We did it,' I said.

'Yes, we did. Fuck them. Fuck Miner's Club.'

'How about the kidneys?' I asked.

'Indeed, how about them. Let's have a taste.'

I beckoned Samad and whispered instructions to him.

'So, what are your plans now, Kash?'

'A fresh start,' I said. I'd hinted at my plans before, but I was more resolved than ever. 'Another continent.'

'Wise,' Viktor said. 'You don't want to be around after so much . . . commotion.'

'I think we have made enough noise for things to get a bit risky.'

Viktor was looking at me with an avuncular smile. 'Let me tell you something else. Your guy, Boris, he's not part of the actual Russian mafia. He's a thug, for sure. But not as connected as he makes himself out to be.'

'How do you know?'

Viktor laughed, as if to say it didn't matter how he came to know. Clearly, he had background-checked me thoroughly.

'You want to know something funny?'

I didn't say anything but stared at him with surprised obedience.

'He's not Russian! He pretends to be, as it's good for business in his line of work.'

'He's not?'

'No! He's from a small town on the border of Poland and Russia. That place has been shunted so many times between the two countries, I guess the residents are a bit confused as to who they are.'

Viktor laughed at his own joke.

'Boris is Polish?'

'His parents were Russian speakers. But he was born in a town that is now part of Poland.'

I sat there in a state of numbness. Unsure why this twist in Boris's presumed identity felt unsettling to me.

'Listen,' Viktor said. 'It doesn't matter what you pretend to be. What matters is how much you believe your own act.'

We had barely finished our drinks when Julie appeared with a tray and two plates carrying a pair of kidney tartlets. She set them down on the circular table between us, with napkins and utensils. When she lifted the lids, the dishes released an aroma that was as richly organic as a good carnivore dish always should be.

Viktor flapped the napkin open on his lap and picked up the knife and fork. I followed him and we cut into the round, lightly crusted, cupcake-sized delicacy in front of us.

'What will you do about The Hide?' Viktor said as he forked a mouthful.

I had given it plenty of thought and discussed it with Helen. I was going to write over my shares to Kang and Patti, and work in some ghost shares for Julie as well. Julie's shares would vest over a few more years of service. Adair would still own a plurality of shares by far. He could go on being an absentee proprietor – Patti and Kang were capable of keeping things humming along.

'Good idea, very generous,' Viktor said approvingly of my plans.

'How do you like this?' I asked, pointing at our plates. I had feared that it might give off a faintly rancid odor or a vaguely chemical flavor. None of that was true. Thanks to Kang's deft handling, the little tarts turned out to be creamy with a hint of capers, and speckled with tiny bits that possessed the texture of exotic mushrooms.

'Delicious!' Viktor said, as he dabbed the corner of his mouth.

I concurred. It was surreal that the partaking of human organs could feel as ordinary as a late-night snack.

'So, you're done with them?' I asked Viktor. He knew I meant the Miner's Club.

'Yes, and I think I've ruined gourmandizing for all of them,' Viktor said with a chuckle. His delight gave him a youthful aura.

'To rob that French asshole of that great pleasure forever, I'd say that's a win.' I felt I could speak freely about the French.

'Indeed, and worth the ridiculous prices you're charging,' said Viktor.

I didn't see that coming. I could not resist blurting out a defense. 'Oh c'mon, Viktor, you know the expenses. The wines alone were almost a hundred grand. And *le nouveau*! I've itemized everything for Yusep.'

'Don't worry,' he said. 'You think I'd pay if I didn't accept the charges?'

'No,' I replied. 'Some things are hard to put a price on.'

'Damn right. This experiment was worth every penny, though. It has clarified a lot for me.'

Viktor sounded serious. His brows furrowed.

'Experiment?'

'Yes, but what else?'

'To see if anyone would actually have a taste? To see how far your friends would go?'

'No, that part I had a sense of already – and my estimation wasn't too different from yours.'

Our glasses were empty. We had cleaned our plates. As I took Viktor's glass, along with mine, for a refill, he walked with me to the bar counter. The room's lighting changed by some preset algorithm to give it a soft moon-glow. And with our glasses refreshed, we went to a pair of white sofas.

'So, what was the experiment?' My curiosity was piqued.

'You still don't see?' Viktor looked amused.

I had no idea what he was getting at. It made me nervous. I took a sip of the Calvados and enjoyed its fiery ride down my throat. I sat at the edge of my seat, waiting for Viktor to spell it out.

'You! You were the experiment for me, my young friend.'

I heard the words but didn't register their meaning. The Calvados seemed to be spreading its fire-hot truculence to the remote reaches of my limbs and my brain.

'I wanted to see how far you would go. If you'd actually find a way to acquire human flesh. You see, I have this theory: men will go to any lengths given sufficient motive. They'll find the justification, too, for all the lines they cross, all the conventions they break. The deepest moral reservations will be cast aside, the oldest principles of decency or humanity discarded – if the price is right. I had a strong hunch, but I wanted a confirmation.'

I felt a hotness behind my ears, but I could not refute what he said. I had not only gone to extraordinary lengths, found the means and the justifications, but I had managed to bring my people along. But here and now, in a moment of apparent triumph for both of us, I needed to swallow the mild humiliation of being told that I was never the master of the script but an actor who wasn't even privy to the full plot.

'Oh come, don't be glum. It's not like I have harmed you. Unless you see some harm in the lines you've crossed. But you're not alone, are you? I took full part in it. And so did some of my friends.'

Viktor didn't know about what I had done to Boris, who lay mutilated and drugged below us, somewhere in the depths of the yacht. Would he think that was a step too far? Would he think the experiment had gone awry? There was no point telling him now. I needed to go through with what I had planned. Given that all the principal parts of this 'experiment' – those known and unknown to him – had occurred on his yacht, he'd have no choice but to make sure I didn't face any legal repercussions.

I didn't say that to him. It was better to let him enjoy his sense of superiority.

On the way to my cabin, I peeked in at the kitchen again. Kang was alone, cleaning up. 'The tarts were terrific,' I said.

Kang never responded to compliments – anymore than he did to criticism.

'Viktor loved it!'

'What I do with the rest?'

'See if anyone wants to try them, or chuck them before we deboard.'

As I mounted the stairs one flight up to the lower deck, I suddenly felt my head swim, and then a surge of nausea. I grabbed the rails to stop me from falling down. The enormity of everything we had done – and were still about to do – hit me. How was this my life? How were these my choices? Could I really be the author of these deeds – not one, but a series of them? I sat on the bottom step for what felt like a while, but I could hear cheerful music coming out of the lower lounge and then, amid the hum of voices, Helen's crystalline laugh.

I felt a light tap on my shoulder. It brought me back to myself with a small start. It was Captain Lewiss.

'Everything alright, young man?'

I whispered an unconvincing 'yes'.

'The ocean is the best keeper of secrets,' the captain said with a twinkle in his eyes. 'If you go out far enough.'

'Have we?' I asked, hopefully.

'We have, my friend,' the captain said. 'Pull yourself up. You don't want to let Viktor down.'

I thought I was the only one with the full plot of our plans. But apparently, others knew more than I realized. Whatever the case, the captain's words were true: I did not wish to let Viktor down.

I pulled myself up. And began to trudge upstairs. Sometimes we have no choice but to go deeper into our errors.

CHAPTER 24

When I entered the lower lounge, I found the crew in a festive mood. At Yusep's suggestion they had opened a bottle of the remaining Rothschild and billed it for the dinner. Adair had made the New Grog with a dash of Mandarine Napoléon, and a touch of something he refused to reveal.

In the lounge, I found Helen dancing with Adair in the middle of the floor. The music had changed, a throwback to a euphoric swinging past with Louis Prima.

I didn't want to break up this mood of merriment, but there was work to be done. So, I said, 'Hagi, go give Kang a hand. Samad, go see if the doctor needs anything.'

At this point, Helen also disengaged herself from her dance partner and walked towards me. As she sidled up to me, I whispered, 'Let's go to the room.'

Helen smiled knowingly, and teased me by saying, 'Send everyone to work and slink off?'

'Oh, I have work, don't worry,' I replied. 'But my next task won't be until everything else is done and the ship totally quiet.'

Adair approached us and said to me, 'A word, mate.'

This time I knew what it was going to be about.

'You have money at The Hide?'

291

'Yes, it's safe with Patti and Dolores.'

'That's good. But how come you didn't tell me?'

'Too much going on. And what's there to tell? I've made the money secure for all of us.'

Adair didn't look convinced. 'I hope we are not starting to keep things from each other?'

Adair said this as a statement, but also with that interrogative upturn common to American speech.

'No, man,' I said, half-heartedly. 'Just keeping things tight.'

Helen heard the little exchange. 'It's all very high-stress, guys. Everyone's nerves are on edge. Everything will get smoothed out once this episode is over.'

She brushed Adair's forearm, as if soothing a beloved Labrador. And it seemed to work; Adair took a step back and said, 'Yeah, that's all I'm looking forward to now. Things being over and returning to normal.'

Once again, this felt naïve to me. And while I find simplicity irritating, in this instance it felt touching. Ever since I discovered how much of his past he'd made up, I felt we were perhaps never truly so intimate. And now I feared we would drift apart farther as things settled down.

'Come,' Helen said, clasping my hand.

Ours was a cabin with twin beds – and the night before we had slept apart knowing that we both needed a solid night before the big day. But that day had now come and gone. Helen was tucked into her bed, dressed in a silky blue slip, freshly combed hair falling with lustrous abandon on her thin yet strong shoulders.

'Babe,' I said as I lowered myself onto the narrow bed.

'Babe,' Helen said softly.

I nuzzled her neck. Her scent, so familiar and yet so fresh

every time I drew close to her. I was feeling impatient and fumbling with my belt. Helen stretched herself beneath me and flicked a switch to plunge the room into a mellow darkness breached only by a blue nightlight. My hands were on her thighs and sliding up, under the crumpled fall of her dress to find the warmth between her legs. And she was unbuttoning my shirt with practiced rapidness.

'Baby,' Helen whispered. Her enlarged pupils denoting disbelief at our situation: the subjugation of Boris, annihilation of our debt and now making love on a private yacht.

I caressed the pimpled, textured skin of her crotch and she whispered in my ears, 'We did it.'

'We did. And . . . it was Boris from whom we were getting *le nouveau morceau.*'

'It had to be Boris! There was no better candidate.'

She understood; she always did. On our own we were both mere vectors without rudders, but together we were as lethal as a guided missile.

I put my arms tightly around her, supporting her head with one hand and cupping one of her muscled buttocks with the other. I kissed her face and the faint freckles that dotted her cheeks. And when we finally kissed, she thrusted her warm meaty tongue into my mouth. I don't know why or how, but whenever she kissed me fully like that I felt as if I were lodged inside an unassailable hearth of safety. When I entered her, I did so slowly, with no sense of hurry, not a care in the world, as if I had nothing left to prove, but simply feeling secure in the knowledge of our permanence.

When we finished, she lay in my arms, and I waited for her to doze off. I too drifted off to a state between sleep and wakefulness that was enveloped in a miasma of tiredness. A knock on the door brought me back; it was 2 a.m.

It was Samad who knocked on our door with light taps. Helen slept soundly but I was awake. I found it impossible to sleep. I was still on a high from the evening's proceedings, but there was also the anticipation of the final episode. I slipped out of bed and put my pants and loafers on as silently as I could. When I opened the door and stepped out, Samad said, 'It's time.'

'It's time,' I repeated.

'The doc?'

'He's there. Waking Boris up.'

I had not been to visit Boris since the surgery. The doctor knew how to keep him both free of pain and safely unconscious. If he needed any handling, he could call on Hagi and Samad. But there was no need to turn him over; he wasn't going to get bed sores in a day.

'Is the boat ready?' I asked Samad, as we entered our makeshift operating room.

'All set,' said Samad.

This was something I had asked Yusep to arrange beforehand. We would make use of one of the lifeboats. That was all the captain needed to know. Why and when we would use it was up to us; the captain and the first mate would be amply compensated for staying clear of our paths. All such expenses being in Yusep's hand made it easier for me to pad the bills.

'And the ladder is in place, too,' added Hagi.

The room smelled of medicines that I could not name. They exuded a sweetly soporific scent. Boris was awake but unable to move or say anything. Hagi and Samad had proved to be real talents when it came to tying down a villain and taping up his mouth.

'He's ready,' said the doctor.

'Okay then, let's do it,' I said.

Boris, uncomprehending, cast us wild glances. The plan was as simple as it was meticulous.

'Walk or carry?' Samad asked.

'He's fit to walk,' the doctor said. 'With support.'

'Good,' I said.

If we could make Boris walk, it made our job easier. We had made provisions for a stretcher, but the fewer items we had to disturb, the better. I had posted Samad between decks; he would intercept and divert any accidental witnesses.

Hagi and I used a box-cutter to slice through the tape that secured Boris to the bedframe. We helped Boris to sit up before we wrapped him in a blanket.

'Listen buddy, this is your last chance. Walk and be quiet, very fucking quiet, if you want to live.'

I'm not sure how much Boris heard, but he followed our orders. His mouth was still taped. We went through the hatchway to the weather deck and were greeted by a rush of sea air that felt surprisingly balmy. The moon was obscured by clouds.

He was panting by now. Even with the heavy dosage of opioids, he was in pain, and hardly able to stand up straight on his own.

Once we reached the ladder, Hagi proved mechanically adept and managed to winch down the inflatable boat without much hassle.

Clambering into a boat hitched to a moving ship can be a

tricky task for a fit man. To ask Boris to do so, given that the little boat's pitching was more violent than the ship's.

'I am giving you a fair chance, Boris. More than you ever did with me.'

Boris's eyes were puffy and red with tears. Sweat beaded his brow and rolled down from his temples. He smelled like cat piss. I pulled Helen's Colt .32, which was still with me, and pointed it at Boris's head.

They say it's not easy to pull a trigger unless you are trained to do so, a professional criminal, or a sociopath. I knew I wasn't trained to kill, nor was I a professional criminal. So, it left only one option, but it didn't perturb me too much. Not in this moment, though this sanguinity could be further proof of my true nature – a new realization. Whatever the case, I knew I would have no problem pulling the trigger at this moment. And I suspect Boris sensed it too.

Hagi grabbed him and pushed him against the rails.

'You wanna start climbing down the ladder, motherfucker? Or shall we just tip you over?'

'Listen, Boris. We are close to the shore. I waited this long so you'd have a good shot at making it there on the lifeboat. If you're lucky, some fishing boat will pick you up. We're not that far now. We are giving you a compass – keep pointing west.'

'C'mon now,' Hagi said. 'On the count of three.'

Boris was shuddering. He was looking from me to Dr Hazari, and violently shaking his head from side to side.

Lesson: Don't go to sea with your enemies.

'One.' Hagi started to count.

'Do it, Boris, start climbing over.'

'Two.'

Boris grabbed the railing and put one leg over the edge onto a rung.

'Good man, keep going,' said Hagi, with a hint of encouragement.

'You'll make it, Boris. Don't worry, I have faith,' I said.

'The fucker might puke,' Hagi said. 'And choke on his own vomit.'

It was a veritable possibility given that Boris's mouth was still taped shut.

'Well, we freed his hands, didn't we?' I remarked.

I believed he had more than a fair shot. I could not take the risk and trouble of deboarding his bandaged figure in broad daylight. And I could not wait for nighttime. But having learned the co-ordinates of our journey from the first mate beforehand, I knew that – from this point – a sturdy boat could make it to land. There were paddles he could use. Even if a carved-out pectoral made rowing a tall order.

Once Boris was seated on his boat, we untied the tether and set the boat free. He turned his stare from our faces to the sky; his eyes fixed, as if in calculation of the distance from the azimuth to the heavenly bodies, who were soon to be his only companions.

'You think he might make it?'

Everyone looked at Samad, who had appeared by our side. The lifeboat, whose markers we had removed earlier in the day, kept gaining distance from us, and bobbed over the waves.

'It's the wake of the ship,' said the doctor.

'You sure this was a good idea?' Hagi asked.

I knew what he meant. And I said, I had to give him a fair

chance. I didn't want the burden of finishing him off on my conscience. If he failed to make it, it was on him.

'Yeah, but aren't you worried he'll come for you once he recovers?'

'I'll be a new man in a new place. He will never find me.'

All three of my companions turned to me, but that was all they needed to know at this time.

'Good job, everyone,' I said. 'Thank you. You'll have your dues, and big bonuses, within three days.'

I turned as Boris's lifeboat receded to a speck on dark and distant waves.

CODA

I'm at the County Airport in Westchester, lurking by a Falcon 2000 LX, waiting to take flight to Reykjavik. The stopover in Halifax has me worried; let's face it, the pretense of Canadian sovereignty, for all its charm, is not reassuring to someone in my straits. The arm of American law is long. I need to put some distance between myself and the authorities reportedly in my pursuit. At least, that's what Patti told me. A bunch of agents came into the shop earlier today, asking about my whereabouts and then brandishing a warrant to do a search of the premises. There were supposedly serious allegations against our business – of trading in endangered species. Good luck to them in their futile search for evidence.

As you can see, things have gone south in the forty-eight hours since we disembarked from the *Analise*.

I'm tense. But let's take in this set-up: Kash Mirza, born and raised in a distant and putrescent swamp of a country, author of magnificent fortunes, pioneer of new tastes and new philosophical contestations, victim of humorless minions of the law, vilified by the witless curators of public outrage, stands by a Falcon 2000 LX.

News of our cannibalistic dinner has broken out, and with surprising rapidity. Viktor thinks it's the French. It could have been one of the ship's crew. Marianna was certainly quite disconcerted. When we deboarded, she had asked me in a whisper, 'Where's your guest?'

'Oh, you won't believe what a crazy guy he is and what a crazy night we had,' I had told her. I told her that after a bitter quarrel, Boris had decided to leave the ship – on a lifeboat. We were so close to shore by then; and he didn't want to be with us one more minute.

However implausible this might have sounded to Marianna, she didn't press the issue. The fact that she had kept it secret until then told me that she would keep this bizarre finale to an inexplicable episode to herself too. It was better and simpler even for her not to know.

So, with her ruled out, I feared there was now only one person who'd go as far as to report us: Adair.

This is what happens when you allow a man of limited talents and contributions to start feeling they are entitled to the whole. This was his revenge. There was a lesson here, but it wasn't formed enough in my head yet to make an aphorism.

The tale of our adventure was reported first on an online site, the same one that had cried out about our alleged trade in forbidden meats. But this time, one of the city papers – fuck Murdoch, he'd make a terrible meal – scooped up the startling claims real fast.

If it were only the papers! Viktor's PR machine can subdue that nonsense without a problem. But my worst fears have come true. American law is not something I care to tangle with. I called Viktor as soon as I got off the phone with Patti.

'You'd better get the fuck out, Kash. I have a plane ready,' Viktor said when I called. So here I am – no time wasted.

But I have to wait for Helen. She was out, having a well-earned day off with her sister, having lunch. If we belonged to another class, we'd say 'doing lunch', I supposed. They were planning to spend some time at the spa. I could not get her on the phone.

'You go ahead, Kash,' Patti had told me. 'I'll get a hold of her.'

She had a point. Even if I picked Helen up from the spa, we'd have to come home again to get things and her passport. I was better off getting to the plane. Viktor knew this moment might come and the plane – his own, which happened to be onshore – was made available. With the FBI scouring The Hide, he was happy to swoop me away. It occurred to me that the nosy inspector, Boswell, who had decided to paint a target on us, could also have tipped off the authorities.

The sky is a blistering blue, a marvel of these upper latitudes, the northern world, which has not ceased to amaze me even after all these years. The jet is already revved up. A stewardess, blonde, svelte, strikingly like Helen, in a Pan-Am-blue suit, waits smiling by the door, ready to draw up the stairs as soon as we board. A 2000 LX is not the fanciest of private jets, as its owner will be quick to tell you. Indeed, he can't wait to upgrade to something better, as prices of rare earth minerals go into a new boom cycle. A midsize Falcon is the equivalent of an E-series Mercedes of the skies, I'm told.

It's just past three o'clock in the afternoon and I expect Helen, coming up Hutchinson Parkway, won't be too long. Meanwhile, let me state for the record that I don't accept any of the allegations against me.

'There is no crime if there's no proof,' Viktor had told me.

It saddens me to say so, but America has turned out to be a disappointment. When Kang offered the remaining kidney tarts to my crew, predictably all the foreigners – Hagi, Samad, Dr Hazari and Kang himself – partook of the forbidden flesh. But the Americans – Adair, Marianna, Julie – all refrained. That should tell you all you need to know about the State of the Union.

Of course, Helen was the exception, and that was all you had to know about her.

I am aware that my hasty getaway weakens my case in the eyes of justice. But I don't care to be judged by a jury of my peers! That's one thing the Founding Fathers screwed up. One should be judged only by people who are superior to oneself, and that elevation should also be reflected in their garbs and props, rituals and exhortations. The bench should harness the wisdom of the ages in the form of vast libraries of references, an army of gnomes to comb through them, and wizened lords – and ladies – peering over their pince-nez.

If I am hauled before a bench that will judge me, it should be so exalted and irreproachable in its mien and in its acumen that, even if I'm not required to, I should feel inspired to shout out: *M'lord!*

It is 3.15. We are running out of time. The blue angel at the door is casting me polite glances laced with impatience.

A moment like this makes you look back. I knew my father had debt troubles. And that's what got him killed. But it wasn't just the failure to pay. I know now that they had felt insulted, too. No one does what they did to him without feeling an affront to their dignity. But I still don't see my vicissitudes as some playing out of that old and obscure tragedy.

It's 3.43 and I see a black limousine aiming for the runway. A Crown Victoria that makes me jump out of my skin for a second. Agents are known to be partial to this make. I felt a sick slacking of my intestines, a dampness in the back of my shirt. The car kept heading straight towards me, or my plane. There is no great fanfare as it approaches me – no lights, no sirens. And then slowly the panic eases. It is just one car! Surely, agents of the FBI would not be making a dash for a man-eating criminal with a solitary vehicle. Still, when the car stops, for a second I feel a swoon, as if the world is finally slipping out of my grip. Then I see the liveried driver step out. And he opens the passenger door. Helen steps out.

'Baby! You made it!'

She looks radiant in an emerald-green dress. The chauffeur unloads two blue leather suitcases. Fuck me! She took time to pack? Never mind; she made it here safely, that's all that counts. I cast a glance at the hostess, and she looks as pleased to see Helen as I am. The thing about private planes is that they can simultaneously pull up their stairs and close the door, then turn around to taxi in minutes. It doesn't take long for us to take off.

I have always loved looking at the earth from the height of a soaring plane. To see ourselves from any altitude can be an ennobling experience. But it is this bird's-eye view that's the real privilege. As I look out the window, I feel renewed in my faith that this earth of ours will not end in a shower of asteroids or a sweeping plague, massive droughts or battering storms.

That's all juvenile fantasy; B-grade sci-fi.

We will not go extinct as a race because the conditions

will be too hostile for our needs. We have been adapting to changing conditions forever, from ice caves to blazing deserts and deep forests, we have always known how to survive. We can cope with the conditions. What we can't cope with is ourselves. We will die out because we are running out of the desire to live.

The last of the species will not be ragged mobs begging for scraps at the foot of water-hoarding, technology-studded citadels. They will be tall, slender figures; genetically too refined to be recognized as a continuation of humans as we know them today, but devoid of memory and ardor, grief or longing. I imagine their skulls will be diaphanous; and, like the ticks and whirrs of the finest open-faced watches, the synaptic firestorm in the various lobes of their brains will be visible to all, a marvel of evolution. They will have worked out the final mysteries of the universe and decided that there is no point going on.

I turn to Helen. Her face is still flushed from the rush and the tension. Her hair is ruffled. Her eyes glisten with excitement.

I smile at her. It's all I can muster as the magnitude of what she has done suddenly creeps up on me. It's one thing for me to leave America. I'm not leaving home; I did that many years ago. People like me are leaving their ravaged nations all the time. But for an American to leave America! My only thought is that for Helen, it may not need to be a permanent departure. She's not technically an owner of The Hide. Her name is neither on our restaurant nor on the apartment lease. We have no joint accounts. There is nothing they can pin on her.

The plane has straightened out. Our first time on a private

jet feels more entertaining than sumptuous. It has a toy-like quality in its smallness compared to commercial jets. The hostess brings us glasses of champagne.

'Were you worried?' Helen asks me.

'Yeah, of course, it was taking so long! And you took time to pack?'

'Well, I had to get some stuff. Who knows how long we'll be gone.'

I look at Helen's face, not knowing what to make of her – or the look. Her face beams with a smile. I decide it is brimming with love.

'I knew you'd come,' I say.

'Oh, did you Mr Cocky?'

I look at her again, and I don't need to utter any words for her to know that she's right: all my anxieties, my hopes, are surrendered to her and her rare courage, her inexplicable affections. I touch her arm and raise my glass in a silent toast.

'*Salud!*' says Helen.

'No, to you!' I respond.

Viktor has hinted that he has plans for me in Dubai. I'm not sure what he would want me to do, or how I can be of aid to him. He can afford to hire the best talent in the world. I know nothing of his line of business. Perhaps it's some personal project. Surely, not in food. I am done with that. But given my enterprising nature, I suspect he may want me for something that requires extra inventiveness and deftness. Not the kind that your minted MBAs can deliver. I've heard him speak of branching out from rare earth minerals to what he says is becoming the most precious of commodities: water. He has talked of acquiring islands with untapped aquifers.

Of plants that can convert pure hydrogen and oxygen into water. And of desalination plants on desert coasts.

I have my own kitty now to invest. Even after donating a whopping $25k to the fund-drive for Mrs Zaman, I was left with a solid six-figures sum, since I no longer needed – or intended – to pay Boris anything. With Viktor's guidance, Helen and I would embark on a new adventure, in a new world.

America for me was never just a country. It was an idea and the highest form of desire – one that called on me to leverage my talents and abilities to reach for some unattainable feat. Even as the country appears to have lost that spirit, as it blunders into the end of its era, its real gift is intact in the world, in the form of people who know never to yield, never to balk, never to surrender.

ACKNOWLEDGEMENTS

The writing of this novel was made possible by friends who helped me with the generosity of their souls, precious time and sage insights: Michelle Alumkal, Richard Beard, Ed Cumming, Luke Neima, Alex Preston and Olivia Smith. Special thanks is owed to Chris Heiser for rescuing the tale from foundering in creative cul-de-sacs.

I am most thankful to my agent and friend Charlie Campbell and my editor Morgan Springett for betting on a story that wasn't the right dish for all palates. I am indebted to Juditha Ohlmacher, who has always extended unquestioning support for my writing and provided crucial edits in the early stages of this work.

I can never thank my family enough, especially my mother and my brothers, Nabil and Inam, for their unflagging enthusiasm for all my literary endeavors. My wife, Shareen Rahman, the most indomitable spirit I know, has been a cheerleader par excellence. She also supplied me with expert guidance on menus and recipes. Gregory Tuttle was sommelier supreme to this novel. Lastly, I am grateful for my children, Alex and Aida, who fill my days with light, laughter and faith in the future.